AF374312

SISTER EARTH

SISTER EARTH

DANI FANKHAUSER

READTHISNEXT PUBLISHING

ReadThisNext Publishing

Cover design by Kelly Lipovich - kellylipovich.com

ISBN 979-8-9882915-2-7

To my Grandma Elsie ... thanks for the help 😉

"The future belongs to those who believe in the beauty of their dreams."
- Eleanor Roosevelt

"You never change things by fighting the existing reality. To change something, build a new model that makes the existing model obsolete."
- Buckminster Fuller

ONE

I'm not a mother yet. My mom says I'll know when I'm ready. I've watched my childhood friends leave Earth on the two-month voyage to lay their eggs on our sister planet, and return to their celebrated artistic debuts. Each spring, when the wild-flower hills blush lavender, I know it's still not my year.

I knot my sundress to climb the rope ladder hanging from the sycamore tree. A marine layer is thick in the air, diminishing the sun's light as it sets over the Pacific. As I climb, the floor-boards of the treehouse creak and whine, and the rope ladder trembles as if it might tear loose.

I poke my head through the trap door to see my friends already inside.

"Good goddess, is this treehouse made of twigs?" I say.

"Deer, our favorite poet!" Lava's gravelly timbre welcomes me in. She's lounging on a poof, glass of red wine in hand. "My aunt built it. It's only as unstable as her mind."

Sequoia, all sharp edges to Lava's curves, sits cross legged on the rug. "I didn't know you had an aunt who's an architect," Sequoia says. She's the youngest of the three of us, though she and Lava knew each other as kids. I only met Lava last year.

"Not a very good one," I say, pressing my toes onto each floorboard as I tiptoe towards the bucket hammock. I'd feel safer if it was hung from the sycamore tree itself, but the hammock is only roped to the treehouse beams. I tug at it a few times before trusting it with my full weight.

Lava pours another glass of inky red wine and crawls over the fuchsia handwoven rug to hand it to me. "Try my mom's latest vintage of Petit Sirah. It's a year 3100. Already winning awards."

I nod and swirl, taking in the aroma.

Lava turns back to Sequoia. "And my aunt, she was good. But she transitioned early."

The wind picks up from the north and a tree branch rattles against the side wall. One of the sconce candles blows out.

"Eww," Sequoia shakes her head. She stands up to relight the sconce with a taper candle. "A talented artist would not transition early. What happened, she built something that spooked the Sages?"

I've been to this treehouse with Lava before, and she's never shared so much about the aunt who built it. I wonder if I just never thought to ask.

"It wasn't like that," Lava says. "She knew something the Sages didn't want her to know."

"Like what exactly?" Sequoia says. I can tell by her squint that she's already coming up with pushback.

Lava sighs. "Never mind, forget I said anything." She looks at me intensely. I can read her, and she wants me to change the subject. Luckily, I don't need to look far for a redirection.

"Sequoia, what on our foremothers' green Earth is that monstrosity on your head?" I say.

I lean over her in the dim candlelight. She's wearing what looks like a winter solstice wreath, strobili and all. "Is this a performance piece? Are we playing crucifixion? That looks like it hurts," I say.

The wind picks up again, blowing ocean spray through the open window. The treehouse leans.

"This is a pine crown. At my last annual scan the Sages said the flower tinctures weren't working fast enough. I have to wear this 'til my next emergency scan."

"Pine?" Lava says. "My dad takes that tincture after he pisses off my mom. It's for guilt."

"Mine is for my kidneys," Sequoia says. "The Sages say they're out of balance."

I gulp my wine and grin. "Just thinking about intuitive scans is going to give me the squirts," I say. I lean in to whisper. "I haven't gone in years."

Lava gasps. "They'll know if you skip one."

"They'll know more if I go! My poetry isn't exactly Caleafean ballads. I don't need someone reading my thoughts before I have something polished enough to share."

Lava switches the cross of her legs. The deep slit in her cherry red sundress exposes her magnificent thighs. "You know, you're insane, but I respect it."

I nod. We each play a role in the friendship. Lava is the sexy one, Sequoia is the smart one, and I'm the clown. I don't mind. It gives me a place to belong.

"So the real reason I invited you both here, other than to try my mom's incredible wine," Lava says with a smirk.

"It's good," I say, raising my glass as if to toast. I've nearly finished it. Sequoia hands me the bottle.

Lava continues. "I wanted you, my best friends, to know that ..." She pauses for dramatic effect.

"I'm going out for mating season!"

"Whaaaaa!" Sequoia squeals in a tone far above my own vocal range.

"Congrats, babe." I nod with a smile.

Lava leans in. "And that's not even all of it. I'm already up to three!"

"No," Sequoia says. "I mean, yes, but no! How did you get them so fast?"

Lava takes a luxurious sip of wine, soaking up the attention. The flickering light glints off her coiled hair like a halo.

"My mom sent me and my sister Isla up to the vineyard, to help manage the workmen. And Isla thought one of the guys was cute. She bet she could get him first, and you know how competitive I am with my sisters ..."

The rest of us know how futile it would be to compete with a Primrose sister. Lava is one of four, all dancers. They look identical until you get to know them. I first met Lava at an amateur dance party, when she saw me sulking. I'd barely introduced myself when she pulled me onto the floor, mesmerizing me with her rhythm.

"How were the men?" Sequoia asks.

"You know what surprised me is, for being so big and strong, men are gentle," Lava says. "They ask permission before everything."

"Do you feel different?" I ask. After my childhood friends went out for mating season and became mothers, we drifted apart.

"I feel ... more me," Lava says. "Each of them was so different but it always brought out a different side of me. Yeah. Now I feel more fully myself."

"Look who's speaking poetry now," I tease.

"Ha! But seriously, now I understand why they tell you to get as many mates as you can. It makes your art better," Lava says with a wink.

I can see how mating with men might enhance her dancing,

but I'm not sure the same would be true for my poetry. Love stanzas are not exactly my specialty.

"To mating season?" I hold up my glass.

"To the foremothers, and their advanced birthing technologies!" Lava drains her wine. "Sequoia! You haven't touched your wine, what's the matter?" Lava says.

Sequoia takes a tiny sip, as if to comply.

"I'm—I'm taking the Motherhood Voyage this year, too," she says quietly.

Lava claps her hands above her head. "Hooray!"

I know I should join in with the celebration. It's what a good friend would do. I did it for Jacara. And Lolanda. But now?

Maybe this is why I can't hang on to friends. The words are halfway out of my mouth before I process what I'm saying.

"Sequoia, you're only 20," I say. "You're fresh off your Homecoming Voyage, you've barely been in Caleaf a year, don't you want more time to settle—maybe work on your art—before you go back to Sister Earth?"

Go when you're ready. That's what my mom told me. But she never would have let me go my first year.

Sequoia frowns. "Every woman who hasn't taken the voyage yet, is permitted to go. Age doesn't matter."

She's mistaking her photographic memory of the Code of Caleaf for knowledge. Me, I've been around a little longer.

"Ok, sure," I say. "Your reproduction is activated the first time you mate with a man, so scientifically speaking, you could do the Motherhood Voyage at any age—"

Lava lifts her wine glass. "To the foremothers..."

"But most women wait. Like Lava did, she's 22."

I look at Lava for support. She shrugs.

A good friend would offer advice. I try. "You've got to develop your art. Whatever style you debut at the Amateur Art Show is what you'll be known for. "

"I'm a classically trained oil painter," Sequoia says.

"Different artistic timeline than a renegade poet," Lava says, lifting her glass again.

I roll my eyes.

Sequoia sucks in a slow breath. "But what really matters is that Edgar and I already decided," she says.

"Whoa." Lava's voice jolted us both. I tense up, expecting her to reprimand me for being hard on Sequoia.

"What does Edgar have to do with it?" Lava says, emphasizing the name of Sequoia's boyfriend.

From my perch in the hammock, Sequoia looks small. She chews a clump of her long black ponytails.

"You know we've been in love since we were kids on Sister Earth," Sequoia says.

But they couldn't mate on Sister Earth, because no one knows who your siblings are until the Sages do the blood test on the Homecoming Voyage.

I tilt my head. "Ok wait. When you say decided, are you saying you and Edgar, like—"

"We mated." Sequoia looks down.

So she has to go on this year's voyage. Her reproductive system is activated. Eggs could already be developing. And when her body births the fully developed eggs this summer, it'll release all her eggs, fertilized or not.

You only get one chance at motherhood.

"And when I get back from the Motherhood Voyage, he'll be my husband," Sequoia says.

"That all sounds romantic, babe," Lava says. "But Edgar can't be your only mate. You need lots of mates. You want as many of your eggs to be fertilized as possible. Too few eggs, the other women will doubt your creative potential. And what if Edgar's sperm is no good?"

"The Sages check your fertilized egg count before you

board." Sequoia readjusts her pine crown. The pine needles poke dangerously close to her eyelids.

"By that point it's too late!" Lava's voice cracks in fervor. "Deer, convince her." Lava says.

"What? Do you mean because I'm an only child?"

Lava coughs. "No, I would never—I mean because you're a poet. Good with words."

"Oh."

The wind blows, rattling branches against the treehouse again. My hammock rocks as the tree sways. I glance up to see the rope is fraying where it is tied to the ceiling beam.

"I've had friends go," I say. I struggle for the right words. "You do what you can in mating season. But then, it's going to be 20 years before you meet your kids. Before they show up on their Homecoming Voyage, like you just did in the fall. Before you see if they have Edgar's coarse red hair, or resembles the mates you've long since forgotten. Until then—well, they're just eggs."

I let the words sit.

Then I worry I've made motherhood sound too sterile. That's the kind of thing I'm terrified I'll accidentally slip into a poem. I adjust. "Motherhood is celebrated in Caleaf because it's an act of creation," I say. "Anything you do to limit that would be—" I look to Lava.

"Not very Calefean," Lava says. "It's a numbers game. More mates means more fertilized eggs. That's how the foremothers designed it. It's the only way."

Sequoia is shrinking under her pine crown. I decide to change the subject. "How was Edgar, anyway?"

Sequoia shrugs. "He was shy at first, but I think he had fun by the end. Yeah."

"Oh!" Lava claps with amusement. "He couldn't sustain himself."

"You know how men are! They don't have the same mind-body connection as women," Sequoia says.

"Was he at least as good as being with another woman?" Lava asks.

"I would say he needs practice." Sequoia giggles.

"Practice is good," Lava says. "Frequency will help your numbers."

Lava turns toward me. "So, Deer. Poet, daughter of Rain the watercolorist, granddaughter of El, the famous ceramicist whose dishes the Queen herself dines upon." She quotes my maternal lineage as I would in a formal introduction. "Your turn. Come with us?"

I should have known this was coming. Should have known when I saw the wildflower hills changing color again. This is how it happened with my childhood friends. Jacara, the cheesemaker, went when we were 22, and the dressmaker Lolanda went when we were 23. Now they're established artists, selling their work at the craft market and entering juried art shows.

But my poetry still isn't ready.

"Oh no, I'm going to be the leading poet of my time, " I say. "I can't possibly debut this early."

"Early?" Sequoia says. "You're the oldest woman who hasn't gone."

"Am I?" I look to Lava. "I mean, I might be among the oldest, but—" Sequoia's conveniently forgotten what she just said about the Code of Caleaf. Age doesn't matter. With the wine sitting heavy in my belly, I can't be bothered to argue details.

"My poetry needs more work," I say.

"But really, are you nervous about mating season?" Lava says. "Because it really is fun."

"Oh." My face heats up. "No, nothing like that."

As if on cue, Lava and Sequoia slowly say together, "Omar?"

My younger male friend.

"Oooh, that's not happening," I say. He'd grown at least a foot when he showed up on the Homecoming Voyage with Lava's class, but I still see him as the stuttering child Omar I first met on Sister Earth.

"It has nothing to do with intimacy," I say. My friends don't look convinced.

"Is it about men? Sequoia's mom never took a husband," Lava says.

"But she does have a female partner," Sequoia says. "My mom says mating and lovemaking are not the same, you can find men who are gentle and quick. Even women who only like other women can get through it."

The wind has died down enough that I hear waves crashing on the beach.

"With the foremothers' advanced technologies, you'd think they could have come up with a way for us to fertilize eggs without men," I say.

"That's not the Calefean way," Sequoia says.

"But your mother's partner isn't a mother. She never did mating season," Lava says.

"See, I'm not actually the oldest woman who's not a mother," I say. Though it is true that all the women in my class have gone. And the year below me.

"That's why she's an assistant calligrapher. She can't sell her own art," Sequoia says.

If my poetry mentor Adollo hadn't transitioned two years ago, I wonder if she'd have let me continue being her assistant. The years passing. My friends all debuting. My poetry, still not ready.

"There's no motherhood stipend if you're not a mother. So if she hadn't found a mother who'd take her on as an assistant, she'd have to do manual labor—like a man," Sequoia says.

"The Calefean way?" Lava shrugs.

"What I'm saying is, just get through mating season—" Sequoia says.

"It's not that," I say. "I like men. Just not Omar—not like that, anyway.

I reach for the neck of the wine bottle and drain it to refill my glass. This conversation is tiptoeing around every sinkhole known to women.

"Anyway, have you ever wondered why, when we're the only surviving civilization on this planet, we stay on this L-shaped island?" I say.

"The climate on Caleaf is ideal for agriculture—" Sequoia says.

"She's changing the subject again! Nice try," Lava says.

Lava turns to Sequoia. "I bet she's afraid of laying eggs. Sequoia, remind us with your photographic memory, what does the Code of Caleaf say about the eggs?"

I'm being cut from the conversation. I lean out of the hammock, only to hear the rope groan as the hammock jolts an inch closer to the planked floor.

Sequoia gazes to the far wall as she tunes in. "In their pursuit of collective peace, the foremothers have innovated away every unpleasant aspect of motherhood. They struggled so we could expand and prosper. Women no longer give birth to live infants. And childhood innocence is no longer distorted by adult needs—"

"See? Laying eggs is basically painless. Nothing to worry about," Lava says.

"—so the children remain free to roam their imagination until they come of age and come home to Earth, fueling their lifelong creativity," Sequoia says, completing the Code retrieval.

I rub the soft callous on my bare foot, thickened from my jogs along the coastal cliffs. Here I am at 27, not ready for motherhood. My friends, ages 20 and 22, as confident as ever.

All these years my fear was that I'd rush into it and fail.

But if I'm not ready now—maybe I never will be.

"Maybe I don't need to be a mother," I say. "I wouldn't mind a man's job—residence construction, or farming. I like being outside."

I lift my wine to my mouth, but I feel dizzy. I've had too much.

Sequoia clears her throat like she's getting ready for a speech.

"The Code of Caleaf doesn't require women to be mothers," I add. To be honest, I had never really considered not going—ever—until Sequoia mentioned her mom's partner. This was an option? I could feel my curiosity opening up.

"You can't waste your intuitive capacity on manual labor," Lava says.

I nod my nose to Sequoia. "But it's not fair—that your mom's partner can't sell her art, I bet she has some good stuff—"

"Fair?" Sequoia says. "It's science. Motherhood creates life. Creativity is self-fueled. You stop being creative, you lose power. A creative block means bad art. Your cells stop regenerating. Your health fails. And, you start to drain the power of everyone around you, because we're all connected." Sequoia tightens her ponytail.

The more my friends pushed back, the more urgent I felt the need to defend this idea I had only just conjured up moments ago.

"What if I don't want to?" I say.

"Would you withhold your capacity for making beauty from the collective?" Lava says. "That would be ... selfish."

I nearly drop my wine glass. With both hands, I take a big

gulp and carefully place the stemless glass on the edge of the rug. My closest friend just accused me of the worst offence in all of Caleaf. You show up for an intuitive scan and a Sage finds selfishness—that's an immediate red flag.

But, I'm no poet if I can't extract myself with words.

"No, of course not. I want to make art. I want to make good art. I just—"

"So what is it?" Lava says.

My friends have told their mating excursions. Now it's my turn to share. I sense that our friendship depends on me being honest.

I gaze up at the rope, where it gnaws at the ceiling beam. I wonder if the hammock was part of the architect's original design—or something Lava added later. Imagine if my weight were to break the beam in two, and the ceiling comes crumbling down.

"I could have been a glassblower," I say. "I'm physically strong enough. Even a ceramicist, like my grandma El. But I chose poetry, because—" I think of my close friends and their art —making dresses, cheese, oil paintings, dancing. All so tangible.

"It's like there's something inside me that can only be expressed in a poem. And I want to have it ready when I do the Amateur Art Show."

"So this is about your artistic debut," Lava says.

Only one person has ever heard my poetry.

"My mentor, Adollo, before she transitioned—she said I have potential," I say. "Potential to be the best poet Caleaf has ever seen."

"So what's the problem?" Lava says.

"Look, the Craft Arts, like Lolanda's dresses and Jacara's cheese, you can sell those at markets. Even dancing, Lava, you can get hired for parties."

I curl my legs into the hammock so I'm almost upside down.

"The motherhood stipend only covers the basics," I say. "For the Fine Arts like mine and Sequoia's, we need to make money from juried art shows."

"Oh!" Lava says. "This is about your mom."

My mom's paintings don't win prizes at art shows. Her watercolored ocean sunsets are, in a word, repetitive. But I would never criticize my own mother's art, not even to my closest friends.

"Babe. I've got a theory, and you're going to like it," Lava says. "Get this. Talent skips a generation."

I consider it. Grandma El's ceramics. At this very moment, the workmen at the Queen's residence will be laying El's handi-work out on the long oak dining table. The iconic swirled color of her latest design earned so many awards that no one else could afford to purchase it.

I don't want to tell Lava, but this comparison is almost worse. I have a fighting chance of outperforming my mom, but I know I'll never live up to Grandma El's success.

"You have four weeks 'til the Amateur Art Show. Plenty of time to write a poem," Lava says.

She knows nothing of my creative process.

"Come to the Lunar Party, bag your first mate, and you'll have loads of inspiration!" Lava says.

I consider. "But—I couldn't. I don't have a dress," I say.

The spring Lunar Party is the official start to mating season, and the only day of the year the Queen's gardens are open to all Calefeans. Well, mothers and mothers-to-be. And any men who are age-appropriate mates. I've never been to one.

"I can't tell my mom with two weeks notice that I need a new dress for the Lunar Party!"

Beauty, fertility, and artistic potential—these are all up for criticism the minute a woman joins the Lunar Party parade to publicly announce her entrance into mating season.

The Lunar Party dress is an art form of its own.

I know from Lolanda that custom dress orders are typically made at least six months in advance. And Lunar Party dresses—sometimes a full year.

"I bet your mom's been saving something for you," Lava says with a wink. "She'll be thrilled."

I shake my head. My mom's watercolors haven't won an award this year. Or last year. Or the previous? It seems like the years before I arrived on my Homecoming Voyage were her best.

Maybe she has been holding onto a dress—for when I'm ready.

"Fine, I'll come," I say.

Sequoia jumps up. "We're all going together!"

Lava twirls Sequoia with one arm, and grabs my hand with the other. The treehouse creaks from our movements. I can't tell if I'm dizzy from the wine or if the treehouse has actually tilted on its side. When an empty wine glass rolls all the way across the small space, I decide on the latter.

The candlelight throws our spinning shadows onto the walls. Lava's expert timing keeps us in sync with our silent beat, swaying, twisting, squatting, and leaping.

We all hold hands in a circle and spin, faster and faster, until we tumble to the soft rug.

As I gaze at the ceiling beam, I could swear I see a crack forming near where the hammock is tied. At least the treehouse has held us this long.

I'm sweaty and drunk, but the night isn't over yet. I promised my mom I would swing by her art show, a small curation of artists in our neighborhood. It's probably already started.

"You babes want to take a swim?" I say.

My friends follow me down the rope ladder and we drop our dresses in a heap.

The cold water tingles against my hot skin. Being nude with my friends reminds me of of Sister Earth. Back then, we knew with each other's developing shapes, the uniqueness of each person. I've seen women with round bellies and breasts like Lava's. Short and slim like Sequoia. I've seen full bellies with flat chests, and generous breasts on narrow shoulders. I've seen tiny breasts on short girls and tall girls. There were men with thighs like tree trunks, men with forearms like twigs. We're made of the same parts, but each of us is wholly unique.

On Sister Earth, we moved together like a swarm of bees. I can still picture the boulder at the highest point of the landmass. I would sit and stare at the ocean horizon, eating a handful of purple berries. It wouldn't be so bad to go back, to see the cozy little planet one last time.

It's just that it's two full months of being cramped in a spaceship with hundreds of fellow bloated women. What's worse—according to my mom—they feed you the same bland porridge for every meal. If I have to do it, it would be better to go with friends.

Lava dives under a wave and shakes the water off her hair. I tiptoe over the sharp underwater rocks to catch up with her. We dog paddle past the break, the dividing line the Sages negotiated that separates sea and land creatures.

"Want to hear an original? I just made this up," I say.

Caleaf, Pacific island of plenty

Foremothers who curated entry

Peace on Earth finally ready

"I bet the Queen would hire you to rewrite the Calefean anthem if you keep that up," Lava says.

"That was a joke!" I say. "That wasn't even a real poem."

Sequoia floats on her back. "Remember when Deer made us paddle south to find the Monterey Ruins and we got stranded on a tangle of seaweed?"

The others aren't as fast as me on a surfboard. It was a mistake to invite them along.

"Ha!" Lava says. "Oh, yeah. We thought there'd be a search party sent for us, if we all missed dinner."

"There's still time to be the first Calefean woman to discover the Ruins," I say. Old maps indicate they are only a mile down the coast, on a wide bay, but inaccessible by land ever since the Great Earthquake. "There could be some old relic there that inspires your next art piece—"

"Heck no! Right here is plenty of ocean for me," Sequoia says.

"I wonder what mischief Deer is going to pull us into on voyage." Lava splashes me with both hands.

The bioluminescent waves dazzle in the night. These waves are lit up by algae, emitting a soft glow as they crash onto the sand.

"It's a shame we couldn't swim in the ocean on Sister Earth," I say. We used to bathe in streams and lakes. Every kid knows the ocean on Sister Earth burns your skin because of the acid content. But at night, there were light shows of glowing algae like nothing I've seen here on Earth.

Back on shore, we pull our dresses onto wet bodies to walk the few miles back to town. The residences glow under starlight. Cedar beam, white limestone, classic red brick—each home is a unique expression of its matriarch's architectural whims. Once we are within the residential roads, it is safe to split up.

After I turn from my friends, I question my decision, once again. Will my mom have something for me to wear to the Lunar Party? Can I get a poem ready in time for the Amateur

Art Show? Or, will I reveal myself to be lacking in beauty and talent, destined for a struggling career.

If I don't lay a healthy number of eggs, I might wind up having an only child. The biggest problem with that is, it'll make me just like my mom.

TWO

I dread going to mom's art show only because I know art shows put her in her worst possible mood.

The show is at a stylish residence a few blocks from my mom's. I follow the narrow walkway past yellow rose bushes and step onto the raised front patio. A harp tingles through open windows.

The host is a textile designer. She produces patterned fabrics for each season, to be used for apparel and home furnishings alike, which is why you might find your new dress matches your neighbor's curtains, if you don't order something custom.

Now I know how Lava felt, bursting with her news about mating season. Even though I'm still wearing my air-dried sundress, crispy with salt, my skin feels aglow like a firefly. Yes, I should have stopped home to switch to a clean outfit, but I feel free and light.

The work of the show's participants is arranged in a sweeping horseshoe shape that extends the full length of the ground floor. I see paintings, sculptures, blown glass, jewelry, and upholstery.

This is where Sequoia is wrong. It's not just creative acts

that fuel creative energy. It's also observing the art of others. There's that line from the foremothers:

Beauty begets beauty.

I weave my way through a huddle of women wearing sheer knit dresses, long strings of pearls, with hair piled high. The women are gesturing widely. I overhear a charged exchange about the ice shortage. Just past the table of the glassblower's storage jars, the host's husband refills champagne flutes.

I grab one and nearly spit out my first sip. It's room temperature.

No wonder the women are mad about the ice shortage. What's the point in cultivating the soil to produce grapes identical to those grown on the other side of the planet, if the sparkling wine cannot be served at the optimal temperature?

The ice expedition accident has some winners—specifically, Lava's mom. She switched her production to reds, which have grown in popularity, still tasting as the winemaker intended without needing to be chilled.

I exchange the champagne for a handful of baguette slices.

Past a pastry chef's celebration cake display, there's a quilter's summer patterns and a woodworker's wall hangings. These Craft Artists will be able to raise their prices if they win an award tonight.

By the time I reach the center of the U, I know the pastry chef's husband was caught kissing her neighbor's oldest son in the bushes, the woodworker's amateur mentee team blames the unpleasant noises from the wine bottling plant for why their commissions are three seasons behind, and the Sages have still not reached the necessary unanimous decision on the future of the ice expedition.

There are no secrets in Caleaf.

Except for mine.

I want to whisper to every woman I pass.

This is my year. I've chosen to go. I'll be with the women at all the mating season parties, and on voyage, laying our eggs together on the planet of our childhood.

But the first woman I must tell is my mother.

I see her. Three easels. The same ocean sunset watercolor style I've harshly judged so many times. She's mine—my mom. I'm her daughter. The news I'm guarding will make her proud. It's what every Calefean mother wants for her daughter. To bring peace, love, and prosperity to Caleaf through motherhood and through art.

I gulp down a chunk of bread.

"Mom!"

She's with my dad. She yawns as he speaks, then turns to share a laugh with a taller woman in a leather crop top. July is a furniture maker and has a red loveseat sample in the show.

They're talking about the failed ice expedition, too. My dad is saying something about how many workmen die every winter collecting ice from the mountain lakes.

"We don't need to risk mens' lives to get ice," my dad says. "There was a woman, years ago, a home lighting designer. She created a cooling machine, fueled by the sun's energy. It turned water into ice—"

"Oh, Paul," my mom says, looking at me and then to July, with a smirk. "Didn't you see how ugly those things were, or was this before your time?"

My mom is several years older than my dad. She reminds him whenever it will help her win an argument.

"My parents had one," my mom continues. "We kept it at the far edge of El's backyard garden and I still felt nauseous anytime I went within 50 yards of it."

"I'm not surprised—form always outweighs function," July says. "I heard the dairy farmers dismantled theirs and had the parts turned into tree ornaments. It was giving the cows some disease the Sages were unable to cure."

"Imagine access to ice, all year long—" My dad lifts a hand as if to emphasize his point.

He's making a losing argument.

"Piezoelectric," I say.

They turn to me.

"Deer." Mom's lips spread wide into what must be a polite smile. "Did you just remember a word?"

It's one of my intuitive talents. Recalling words from civilizations past.

I feel the syllables in my mouth, licking my lips, to sense the meaning. "It's how we power the spacecraft. The sound waves from the women's voices apply mechanical pressure to the crystals, producing electrical polarity. And thus, fuel."

I never know when a word is going to come through and sometimes I can't help but blurt it out.

"Energy is never created or destroyed, only changed in form," my dad says. "Who said that? A poet?"

It's an eloquent quote, but lacks the rhythm that would make it work in verse. "Albert Einstein was more of an orator," I say. "He did some rudimentary science."

Mom turns back to my dad. "Anyway, Paul, I hope you won't bring up the ice machine again," she says. "Why risk an eyesore to make something nature creates for us freely?"

She looks at July and they both laugh. But July is looking across the room like she'd rather be in another conversation cluster.

"You're right, as always," my dad says. He's endlessly sweet to her. Sometimes I wish he'd win an argument, just for the fun of it, but he's got to pick better topics.

Like me. Like the good news I'm about to drop.

"Mom, I'm going out for mating season," I say. "This year."

July coughs, and backs away from the group.

"Deer, not so loud," my mom says.

I didn't think I spoke loudly. But when I turn, I catch a few gaping mouths in my direction. I thought she would be excited, but I realize my mistake. I should have waited until we were alone.

Mom turns to straighten her easels, abandoning me with my dad.

He puts a soft hand on my shoulder. "We're proud of you, Deer."

I chew a mouthful of bread. I've blown it.

Dad leans in. "You missed the judges."

"What do the judges have to do with my Motherhood Voyage," I say.

I look back to the center of the U, two couches facing each other by the hearth. The blue capes are neatly folded. The ribbons are already distributed. I see one pinned to July's furniture sample.

"Your mom got 10th place," my dad says.

I count the displays. Tables for smaller pieces, bigger pieces stacked on crates. "There were 10 entries?"

Warmth rises up from my belly. I get the urge to hurl a tray of warm champagne glasses onto July's furniture display, marked with a bright yellow ribbon for second place. It's only a show. The purpose is to fuel creativity through celebrating individual expression. Why do I care so much if my mom wins? A woman at peace with herself would not feel this anger.

"The judges complimented her use of light and dark," Dad says.

The three pieces Mom chose for this show are her usual watercolored ocean sunsets. Most artists have a specialty. Hers is an obsession.

"Again?" I say to Dad.

Despite his loyalty, I can see him squirming to say something positive.

"You know how it is. She hasn't sold a print in six months ... when you're not selling, you don't get selected to be one of the judges—"

"You can't pay for the honor," I correct.

"—and when you're not regularly on juries, your own scores suffer."

"Yeah," I say. "I do know."

Mom knows too. She's the one who has the power to interrupt her sad cycle.

"Well, I'm sorry my good news dampened her already failed show." I speak with just enough poise that anyone overhearing can't accuse me of being sassy. It's exhausting.

"Anyway, my friends are going, and I—" My voice gets small. "Do you think she'll be mad we don't have more time to order a dress?"

"I think you look great in what you're wearing now—"

My throat tightens like I'm choking. I swallow hard.

"Oh, Dad, no, this is one of the three sundresses I rotate, the ones Mom got for me seven years ago. They'll assume my poetry is uninspired if I don't wear something that reflects my personality."

Women always judge. Even when you're not in a show.

He leans in close enough for me to smell sourdough in his warm breath. "Your mom would be happy to offer her watercolors in a trade with a dressmaker, but she hasn't managed a winner."

I turn to her.

So it's not my tangled hair or loud voice that embarrassed her. She's avoiding attention because of her own shame.

I speak barely above a whisper. "You can't sell a painting,

and you're mad at me for—for doing the one thing every Cale-fean woman should do?"

Like a wave moving through the space, the chatter of the crowd diminishes, ears waiting on what would be said next.

"Deer, my only daughter, I'm happy—delighted for your next stage of development."

She's saying the words I most wanted to hear from her, but only because people are listening.

"But I cannot have you question my work," she says, firmly enough to be sure her words carry. "An artist must make what she is inspired to make."

An epiphany falls in. When she told me to wait until I was ready, I blamed myself. I blamed my poetry. But maybe I've never been waiting on me. Maybe, I've been waiting for my mom to elevate her art so I could enter motherhood with full support. So I could go to the Amateur Art Show and the Lunar Party in the best dresses, to contribute to a maternal legacy, not resurrect one.

It's never going to happen.

"You've had decades to come up with a style that is prof-itable—" I say.

"Deer, not so loud." Mom's fake smile is gone.

My dad stares down at his lukewarm champagne. I wonder if he feels vindicated now, both of us challenging her on the same night. If we were home, he would cut the tension by making a cheesy joke. Once, he dropped a crystal vase of flowers during a dinner party to stop her from yelling at me. But even he can't help me out of this one.

So I tell her exactly what I think.

"You ruined my life."

My vision blurs. The colors in candlelight, blues and blacks and purples and reds, all blend into a foggy rainbow. I walk the reverse route around the horseshoe, this time the crowd parting for me as if I'm the art show's late-night act.

The women at Mom's art show are not my peers, but they have daughters and nieces who are young mothers, who will be judges at this year's Amateur Art Show. I avoid eye contact so I don't find out what they think of my mother, or of me, or of us both.

I want to run to Lava's treehouse in the cool dark. I could run the path at night. I could do it with my eyes closed.

Even if I went back, my friends aren't there anymore. That moment is gone.

I can't reverse the decision I made back at the treehouse. I can only move forward into the bleakest mating season since the beginning of time.

EVERY TIME I approach the door of my mom's limestone four-story residence, I feel like a wobbly-legged 20-year-old just off the Homecoming Voyage.

I had wanted a sister. Jacara and I had our fingers crossed that we'd have the same mom, even though she's half a foot shorter than me. When the Sage took our blood sample, she pointed us in opposite directions on the map of Caleaf.

As a child, I often daydreamed about what it would be like to meet my mom for the first time. I imagined her in a dress the color of mint leaves, so long even her toes were covered. I wondered if she would sing to me in the mornings before break-fast. And when we hugged, would our bodies clamp together like a seashell, our shapes a perfect reflection?

It was nothing like that.

Mom opened the door with a wide smile. That's what I

noticed right away. How her lips dropped into a pout as she looked at me, clothed only in the terrycloth robe they give you on board. Then she looked past me. That was before I had ever seen myself in a mirror, before I knew the full lips of her smile mirrored my own.

Tonight, the kitchen looks the same as it did on that first day. There's a dinner plate Dad left for me on the counter. It's roast beef from the market, sliced tomatoes from the garden, and steamed stinging nettle Dad foraged in the hills. I rub my hands together to generate energy and hold them over the dish to clear toxins. As a nice side effect to the creative energy transfer, the food is heated to a tepid warmth. For good measure, I hold my right hand to my liver until I feel the wine from earlier fully metabolize.

Through the dark living room I see the moonlit hills to the east, where the L-shaped patio wraps to the backyard. From the hallway, I climb the stairs past my parents' second-floor loft and up to the third, which belongs to me. There's another floor above mine, but we don't use it.

In the washroom, I rinse the salt from my hair with the fresh water Dad carried up for me. I rinse my dress and hang it by my other two sundresses. They're sturdy, made by Mom's favorite designer, and they've lasted me these seven years without much visible wear.

I don't know how my dad handle's Mom's moods with such patience, after their many years together. That alone is proof he's not my father by blood.

He couldn't be.

Dad was still a teenager on Sister Earth when Mom did mating season at 25. She came back, settled in this residence, and kicked off her career. They met five years later when he came on his Homecoming Voyage. So she's ten years older than him. And he's 15 years older than me.

Even though we're not linked by genetics, I feel a connection with my dad. At the very least, he doesn't laugh off my remembered words or fascination with ancient Monterey.

I'm about to slide into the silk sheets of my four-post cedar bed, a gift from Grandma El, when I hear a knock at my door.

Dad wouldn't bother me this late. I know who it is.

I'm feeling mischievous so I pull out that old voyage robe and wrap it over my pajamas. It's tight on the chest and butt. I'm long past the nuts-and-berries diet of Sister Earth.

"Deer?" Mom pokes her head in from the stairwell.

I step up to the doorway.

"You look ridiculous," she says.

Her thin mahogany hair is now loose from the bun, and she's taken off her gold necklaces.

"My art shows—not the best time for an intimate conversation," she says. "Now you know."

I don't know if it's a reprimand or an apology.

"But I am happy for you, about mating season. And who's that kid who follows you like a bird in formation? I bet he's excited."

I want to savor her words of affirmation. I want to forgive the lack of a decent dress. I do—but I need to correct her embarrassing assumption.

"Omar?" I say. "No, not for mating season. He's just a friend." Why am I explaining this for the second time today? "And only because I saved him from losing a cloud race one time on Sister Earth—"

"Ha!" Mom bursts into a genuine laugh.

I didn't mean to make a joke. I was just saying what happened. I was a teenager, and Omar was still a squeaky child who couldn't intuitively move a cloud to save his life. The ice crystals in cumulus clouds are the easiest to program with your mind. I made his opponent's cloud dissolve, just for fun. The younger boys were panicking like the sky was falling, until they noticed me, braiding dandelion stems and ruining their game with only half my mental capacity.

That's when Omar started trailing me, until it was my turn to come home to Caleaf. When his Homecoming Voyage landed, the same class as Lava's, he'd gotten taller, but not much else had changed.

"Even friends can boost your mating season," Mom says. Her voice sounds tired.

"Okay," I say. I'm not agreeing to anything. I still picture Omar as a helpless kid with a high-pitched stutter. I don't want him to be a man—not with me.

"The voyage isn't exactly pleasant, being stuck in a single room with hundreds of bloated mothers to be. Some women lose their minds, some get sick and never recover—I hope you're up to date on your scans?" Mom says.

"I—of course." I make a mental note to go for a scan. Soon.

"And you know they've lost ships before," Mom says.

"Mom! That was decades ago," I say.

Mating with Omar, flubbing my poetry at the amateur show, and now dying in space? This is supposed to be the best time of a woman's life. My version is a hall of horrors.

Mom turns to go. Her bare feet echo down the covered stairwell. I take in the silence.

Beyond the hills out my east-facing windows, there is an ocean that separates our island from the landmass it broke off from in the Great Earthquake. The larger landmass was home to many fallen civilizations, but currently stands empty.

The sun will rise again in a matter of hours. Thirteen days until the Lunar Party, when I'll announce my choice to the whole collective. I am about to enter a new phase of my life. One where I won't wake up in my moms's home, eating her choice of meals. I'm about to become my own woman.

If I want to do it right, to become the woman I want to be, my best move is to do the opposite of anything Mom advises.

I don't want to be anything like her.

THREE

The next morning, I wake to rays of sunlight peeking over the eastern hills into my loft. I decide I won't leave this room until I've written one good poem. Then, I pull the covers over my head.

When I wake a few hours later, a cup of sipping chocolate is sitting on my bedside table. It's cold.

My dad is the thoughtful one. Mom wouldn't come check on me in the morning. More out of her disinterest than respect for solitude. She drinks her chocolate on the patio, watching the butterflies on the eastern hills, before going to her watercolor studio to work.

As I press my face into the silk pillowcase, I am distinctly aware that Lava wants to go look at dresses at the downtown boutiques. This happens sometimes, with friends. When it starts, you show up at the same place at the same time. You question which of you had the idea first. Were you the receiver, or the broadcaster, of the electromagnetic signal? It's a telepathic connection.

I curl up under the covers and wait for the feeling to pass.

Sequoia will agree to it. I see their whole day. Lava's only looking at dresses because she wants to outshine her sisters, who will be in whatever their mom chose. By the third shop, one of them will say, hey, it's curious that Deer isn't here with us—and they'll exchange what they've heard, so far, about my blowup at Mom's art event. They won't make accusations yet, but they'll both be thinking about what I said at the treehouse. About not wanting to do mating season.

I wasn't serious.

I don't think I was serious.

As they walk along the sea glass-paved main streets of Caleaf, they'll hear amplified versions of what happened at the show.

She was screaming.

Her mom slapped her.

She broke the peace.

With my face under the covers, I sense Lava's presence again.

"Come!" She is imploring. A sensation on my scalp feels as if she's pulling my hair, even as my long dark waves are splayed out on the pillow.

My body refuses to doze. I come close to drifting off but wake myself by mumbling that word again.

"Piezoelectric."

I know what it means.

To convert energy.

But what does it mean, figuratively, for me?

Why did the word come for me at this point in time?

The night I remembered the word, I agreed to go on voyage. We swam in the ocean. We walked the three miles back to town together. Then, not long after I announced my decision to my mom: This new word.

It has relevance to how we power the spacecraft, so there's meaning related to voyages.

So my logical explanation would be that it was triggered. By my decision.

Pee ... Zo ... ELECTRIC!

My mom would say it implies some kind of danger, but I'm not listening to her advice anymore. She always thinks the worst of things.

I consider other options. The Amateur Art Show is just a week after the Lunar Party. This will be the first time I share my poetry with my peers.

Piezoelectric. Five syllables. Contrasting sounds. Could this word be the seed of a poem?

I sigh. I've written poetry in my head, swaying in a beach-side hammock, many times in years past, simply committing it to memory through repetition. Sometimes a poem drops into my mind, just as I'm shifting from dreams to awake, only to drift away just as quickly. I need to work in the waking world, on paper.

I roll out of bed.

My desk is on the opposite corner of the loft, past the stair-well, the windows facing a row of residences leading west, and indoor plants in a cozy semicircle.

I flip to a fresh page. I write the word.

Piezoelectric.

I wait. Nothing comes.

New page.

I close my eyes and let my hand move my pen, drawing letters and words without critique. After a few minutes, I open my eyes and read what I've written.

I want beauty

I want power

I want to see things as they really are

I want to look past the self-doubt and (something illegible)

I rip that page and crumple it.

I want to be someone else, I write. That part isn't a poem. It's just what I'm thinking. Why did I choose poetry, anyway? There are easier arts.

But somewhere I picked up the idea that I had something to say that could only be expressed through a poem. So what was it, exactly?

I'm beginning to worry it doesn't exist.

Typical Calefean poetry celebrates the miracle of nature, motherhood, and peace. My transitioned mentor, Adollo, was known for her poems that explored the inner workings of the mind. Right now, my poetry sounds too much like the work of my mentor. I haven't yet made the leap to my own style.

My talent must have receded since she worked with me. I'm no longer the high-potential poet she trained. It was a mistake to wait so long. I need more years to be ready.

Many more years!

FOUR

After one entire day in my loft and nothing written that resembles an actual poem, I decide to expand my self-imposed isolation to the extent of my mom's residence.

I venture out to our ice cave in the yard. No one survived last year's ice expedition, and the ice we got from the year before is long gone. So perhaps we could rename the underground pantry a cool cave. A cool-ish cave.

It's where we keep hard cheeses. I slice off a hunk of parmesan I got from Jacara. The only time I see her is when she comes to town for a weekly market. Her dairy is a day's walk north.

Inside the kitchen, Mom is eating heirloom bean salad with her fingers over the dish basin.

"Good day in the studio?" I say.

"As good—what are those bags under your eyes?" Mom says. "You don't need cheese, go back to the ice cave and get a chamomile mask."

"No one's seeing me, I'm just writing poetry today," I say. The woman can't look at me without finding a problem. And goddess forbid she has the kindness to ask me how my art is going.

"If you're really serious about taking the Motherhood Voyage, you need to start taking care of your appearance," she says.

"I need to work on my poetry," I say.

"Can you write good poetry if you don't feel your best?" Mom scoops the vinegar-dressed beans into her mouth, wiping the corners with her wrist.

Despite my irritation at her delivery, my mom has a point. Adollo was big on routine. She made me do a whole series of exercises before writing.

"Fine," I say, exiting through the patio door to go back to the yard.

I tear off a piece of cheese and place the rest back in the cloth. I dip a clean cloth into the chamomile, squeeze it, and fold it onto my forehead. When I reach my third floor bedroom, I set the chamomile cloth onto my eyes and count my slow breaths until I reach 120.

While I rest, I remember my first day training with Adollo.

ADOLLO'S POETRY won many awards. She was also sought out of commissions. A love poem for a romantic proposal. An admiration poem for a daughter's art. A celebration poem for a family.

She'd interview the client, and she had a way of capturing their emotions in words better than they could on their own. Her intuition was strong.

Adollo's studio was a wide-windowed sunroom attached to her residence with a small desk and lots of floor area for exercises. She was a stout woman with gray hair who didn't look especially nimble, but she told me her best poetry was not written at the desk, but on the floor.

"Always write with a clear signal," she told me. "Moving your body is like shaking the kink out of the hose, so the electrical signal can travel from your gut to your brain."

She drew a series of physical postures for me on a lined sheet of paper.

I laid a woven mat on the floor. From flat on my back, I dropped both knees to one side and turned my face the opposite way to twist my spine. After ten breaths, I switched sides.

"Do you feel the fluid moving through your spine?" Adollo asked.

So that's what that sensation was. "Yeah, I do," I said.

"Good. Now do the squats," Adollo said.

I tilted my hips so my tailbone pointed forward and down. Then, I arched my low spin so my tailbone pointed back, to the wall behind me—as far as it would go. I oscillated with slow intensity, at least 20 times, expanding my range of motion with each movement.

Then there was a core series. Balancing on one leg. Shaking of the limbs.

Finally, the jumps. My bare feet thundered as they landed on the hardwood floor each time I jumped, high as humanly possible.

By the time I completed the series, an hour had passed. All the tension in my body was gone, and my skin was buzzing like static on a blanket.

If I'd thought Adollo would have me write poetry that first day, I was wrong. Because the next part of my initiation was to train on the Records, the collective knowledge base of humanity.

"When you were on Sister Earth, you practiced with the

Records, right?" Adollo asked. "Tell me what that was like for you."

I didn't want to tell her, at first, because my first query of the Records produced a death scene, and I still don't understand why.

THERE ARE no classrooms on Sister Earth. No textbooks. Just the Records, an intuitive storehouse of every memory of every person who has ever lived. The information in the Records is vast, but information alone does not have value.

Kids start playing in the Records before they start speaking in full sentences. It is human to ask questions. When kids are old enough, they join the lesson circles, an experiential learning experience. We would sit cross-legged on the great meadow, knee to knee, and take turns querying the Records.

A girl in my class named Copal had her turn right before me. She asked the Records, "What was the greatest innovation of the foremothers?"

It was a good query with lots of roles. Everyone in the circle got to be one of the foremothers, back in the lab, before they ever traveled to Sister Earth. I thought for sure the innovation was going to be the womb upgrade that took us from birthing infants to laying eggs.

But the Records presented a higher innovation that went back further. It was the discovery that everything could be healed with plants. Not hallucinogenic mushrooms. Not nauseating teas.

The foremothers learned that the most potent part of a plant is its bud, and the most powerful flower of them all is the rose. This became the foundation of our plant remedies: flower tinctures.

"More beauty, more power," Copal said at the end of her query. "That's the lesson. That's how you can identify the right flower remedy. And that's why Caleaf's economy is art."

It's no surprise that Copal went on to become a Sage. On our Homecoming Voyage, she declined the blood test that would identify her mother, choosing instead to further train her secondary senses for three years in a pitch-black cave to do the work of a wise woman.

I wanted my first query to be as good as Copal's.

"What is true love?" I asked.

They say the Records work fast but I was still surprised how quickly the circle of cross-legged kids disappeared. The sunny day on the meadow was superimposed with a visual of my Record Keeper, a stooped man with white hair and wire-rimmed glasses.

Everyone's Record Keeper looks different. It's a projection of a part of yourself. Lava says hers is a cat.

My Record Keeper stood with me on a cloud. He motioned for me to follow him through a door into a library, with filled bookcases floor to ceiling. He pulled one off the shelf. Its cover was a rough red fabric. As I opened it, the library scene faded.

I could still feel the warm sun on my face and the knees of the kids beside me. I also felt a chill as I looked around a dark room.

This is the part where I would tell the group if we were going into fact or fiction. There's less density when you're in a classic work of literature or film. This felt heavy.

"True story," I said.

What had I been expecting—a lush wedding? An Audrey Hepburn film? I comforted myself. At least it's not a genocide. It was often the most disturbing Records retrievals that inspired our childhood games, like Protestant and Anabaptist hide-and-seek, or Nagasaki all fall down.

I wasn't alone in the dark for long. Two men wearing hand-kerchiefs over their faces demanded I give them my valuables. Robbers. I stood to take my role.

My sleeves were long and thick, suggesting a cold climate. I picked up a rock and it became a wallet in my hand, with paper currency poking out the side.

Tory, an older boy, stood and became one of the robbers. His normally smooth voice became gruff as he named the objects he wanted from me. I picked up more rocks. An electronic device with flashing lights. A set of earrings.

My character didn't seem to mind. She breathed easily. This will be over soon. Most of these objects, especially the electronics, are ugly, and perhaps she is aware her wellbeing will improve once they are gone.

"Now we'll take the dog."

Both the robbers are skinny. My character is well-fed. My heart pounded. In my arms there is a little terrier, itself skinny as a rat. But she knows they're desperate enough to take the tiny dog for food.

"I'd kill us both before I let her go with you," I said.

I cradled the shoulders of Violet, a younger girl.

The robbers stepped closer.

I squeezed, but the small dog squirmed from my arms.

"Run!" I said to Violet.

She's fast. Violet swung her arms but tripped over the branches at the edge of the clearing and the boys tackled her.

I fell to the ground crying.

The scene faded. The boys and Violet returned to their seats. We all shook off these emotions of people from long ago. I wiped my face. "Loss cracks open your capacity to love," I said. "That's the lesson."

It could have been worse. In all the roles I've ever taken, from my own queries or someone else's, I've never been a killer.

"THE RECORDS ARE VAST," Adollo had told me in her sun-warmed studio. "There is no safety from unpleasant material."

Adollo drew a diagram of the human body, a funnel overlaying the skull, connected to a library in the sky, which itself was connected to the Earth.

"Every human memory is uploaded to the Records when they die. Some memories, public events experienced by many people, are stored as one collective memory. And it's a two-way connection."

Adollo drew arrows going from the skull to the sky, and from the sky to the skull.

"Every human across time has had access to the Records. It is innate, remembered. Every culture has called them something different, and accesses them a different way," Adollo said. "Some use crystals, others use hallucinogenic plants. We use sound."

"But of all the results I could have gotten—why that one?" I asked.

"The Records have their own intelligence. Sometimes you get the answer you wanted. Sometimes you get what the Records think you need. Sometimes you get nothing at all. You get what you're ready to see, in that moment. Your job, when you work with the Records, is to put forth the best query."

She challenged me to experiment with query formats.

She taught me to use geographic coordinates with a date-time. Just to see what was there! No guarantee it would even be useful. I've walked through Monterey when it was a tiny shipping port and when it was a blissful tourist town. Once, I watched it burn from a small boat a mile from shore. All memories in Monterey cut off after the Great Earthquake.

For her poetry, Adollo liked to query with a single-word emotion, to collect literature and real-life experiences that match. The two of us could search the same word and get different results, depending on the nuances of our mood.

Each time I'd complete a difficult query, she would pat my shoulder and say, "You're safe. You're in Caleaf. Nothing bad can happen here."

I'm told the Fine Artists use the Records to learn techniques through tactile practice. They become the master herself, painting a famous piece in her studio. Nature Artists use the Records to identify plants and reproduce the ideal growing conditions. I've heard the architects gave up using the Records, finding it more efficient to direct the workmen

The only artists who scoff at the Records are the architects. Our intuitive skills makes the old extensive measurements redundant. When it's time to build a new residence, an architect just looks at the available materials and commands the workmen as the next step occurs to her. She can build a perfectly balanced home in a week or two.

After a few months, Adollo was satisfied with my Records queries. She challenged me to write a poem. A love poem. Which meant going back to my original query.

This time, I changed the query slightly. Instead of true love, I asked about powerful love. This is what I wrote:

The attraction is dying,
but I don't want to let go
of the yearning and the pining.
Not yet willing to admit
there could be an 'other side' to this.
It gives me a sense of control
to make it a yes or a no.
So I'll go.

It's not a happy love poem. It's not the kind of poem a

woman would commission for her lover, but Adollo liked it. When she liked something, Adollo used to say, "You're onto something, Deer. Keep down this path."

But never, when I showed her my work, never did she say, "This one is ready for the Amateur Art Show, should you choose this as your year."

If I had known she was getting ready to transition, I would have done mating season while she was still with us. I could choose another mentor, face full of wisdom and wrinkles, but the other poets in Caleaf wouldn't understand my work like Adollo did. They'd steer me to the boring stuff.

Nothing I wrote ever shocked Adollo. Part of the reason she guided me to use the Records, the way she did, was to get closer to capturing the great truths of humanity. She believed I could do it.

I STILL HAVE Adollo's exercise diagram in my desk drawer, fraying on the edges it's been folded. My body aches from months away from doing these particular movements.

All I need to do is check the Records, write a poem, and then I can see what kind of fun Lava's planning for the evening.

Once my body is ready, I take a deep breath and close my eyes.

As always, I start by humming the C tone that opens the Records. I imagine myself lifting out of my body and rising up to the clouds. In the cloud, there is a door. I open the door and enter the library. My usual Record Keeper is there. Still old, but never advanced in age. He waits for my request.

"Piezoelectric," I whisper.

I follow my Record Keeper down hallways, around corners, up stairs, and down an escalator. We walk up to a dim doorway.

He wiggles the handle to open the room. Messy shelves cling to the walls, floor to ceiling. Some books are in piles on the floor. This space isn't exactly organized.

My Record Keeper has no problem with it. He pulls a book with both hands, colored beige with white text, and an illustration of the human body on the cover. It is a science book.

I open it. The role immerses me.

"True story," I say.

I'm lying on a table covered only with a thin sheet. The room is candlelit. A woman looks down at me. I worry she's going to cut me open with a knife. The medical procedures of the past are unpleasant. On other Records journeys, I've experienced a gallbladder removal and a root canal, both procedures easily avoided with Caleaf's flower tinctures.

This woman has no sharp tools. She holds her hands near me and I realize she can see the electromagnetic energy running along my spine and around my body. This is also an archaic method, both time-consuming and completely unnecessary when every member of society has access to high voltages from childhood.

Still, I understand. This scene is showing me that the human body, through the fascia tissue, is piezoelectric.

Fascinating, but not exactly the emotionally compelling anecdote I need for a poem.

"Piezoelectric," I repeat firmly, as Adollo taught me. If this man is ever surprised, he does not show it. He pulls another book from the shelf.

The candlelit healing room vanishes and I'm thrust onto a beach. The wind blows around me. I'm not dressed for the cool dusk; in fact, I don't seem to be wearing any clothes.

I immerse myself back in the scene and scan the night sky for what I'm meant to learn. I climb down the rocks onto the sand—still warm, though the sun has gone down. Small waves sparkle, rolling in with fingers of friendly foam. There is no sign of life. No wildlife on the land, and no clumps of seaweed in the water.

I wonder if this is supposed to teach me something about piezoelectric, or if my Record Keeper has gone completely off script.

"There's nothing here," I say.

The beach disappears. I'm back in the library, and the Record Keeper and I float like ghosts through the floors until I'm back on the cloud, then back in my body, seated with crossed legs, in my loft at my mother's house.

While inside the Records I didn't notice time passing. Now I see the sun has already set.

I drink some water. My legs are numb from sitting cross-legged for so long. Perhaps I'm being too hard on myself. I could go have fun with Lava, and then write a poem when I get back.

I lay down to send a message to Lava, but before I can connect, I drop into a deep sleep.

WHEN I WAKE UP, I'm screaming. The sky is dark. My pillows are soaked in my own sweat.

I hold a hand to my hoarse throat. The memory flashes in.

If I move too suddenly I'll forget the images rattling through my mind.

I shuffle towards my desk. The length of the loft never felt so superfluous.

I flip to a fresh page. Instead of writing, I sketch long lines down the page. A scene comes into shape. It looks like the beach I saw in the Records.

But this time, I recognize it.

It's the beach on Sister Earth, where women lay their eggs.

The eggs are soft when they are buried in the sand, but over nine months, the outer membrane stretches and hardens into a gold shell, poking out of the sand like a mushroom pileus. I recognize the exact spot, between two dunes, and a few yards away from the rocks jutting into the water. It's where I hatched with my class 27 years ago, and my mom and grandma before me.

In my dream, there were no eggs.

There was just the vast beach, and the face of a girl young enough to be just hatched.

She looked like me.

She was a toddler with chubby limbs. Her face was filled with the delight of seeing the world for the first time. She'd made it. She'd broken out of her shell. All she needed to do is to stagger up the beach on her fledgling legs to the plateau, where she'd find an abundance of sorrel leaves and berries.

I flip to a new page. The part of the dream that jerked me awake was the rumbling coming from the ocean depths. A creature rose from the sea. Its face was a creamy white, and blended with the froth of the waves. With its long neck, it stretched closer to me until our noses almost touched.

With a loud crack, the snaky beast disappeared back into the water.

That was when I woke up.

I don't want to go anywhere near Sister Earth's ocean. Not the planet. Not the solar system.

I scribble a few more words on the page.

The details are fading. I read back what I've written.

My baby is dead.

My hands shake. I crumble the piece of paper and toss it in the corner.

FIVE

At sunrise, I'm dressed with my hair washed and braided. A few hours later, my dad taps on the door. He's not coming with sipping chocolate this time. That's okay. I've already decided pleasures won't resolve my new affliction.

"Your friend Lava is on the patio," he says.

I walk down the stairs and out the side door. This wood-planked yard could host a party of 50 people, but I've never seen it used by my gawky parents.

"Babe! I've been waiting for you to go dress shopping," Lava says. "What's holding you up?"

Lava pulls a big brown box from her woven purse, and I accept a chocolate chip scone.

My body sways with the breeze. The restless night hits me. I can't remember what I ate yesterday, if anything.

I keep my voice casual. "Didn't you go with Sequoia?"

"Sequoia? I haven't heard from her," Lava says.

My memory flashes back to the treehouse. Sequoia's pine crown. No wonder—Lava doesn't want to be seen with a friend who's so obviously marked by an internal imbalance. I'm aware of how quickly this friendship could dissolve if I don't keep my energy balanced. I resolve to be on my best behavior.

We follow the eucalyptus-scented path along trees drying from an overnight drizzle. Lava catches me up on her mom's recent awards for her red wines—and enough sales to purchase two new vineyards.

"Your mom must be glowing," I say.

Lava's heart is too pure for her subconscious to produce a weird dream. If she did, she could tell one of her sisters about it. You can trust a sister.

"People are wild for reds, with the ice shortage," she says.

"Hey! Maybe the ice shortage is for the greater good," I say.

Lava tilts her head. "You're perky today."

We reach the final residential row before crossing into the downtown blocks.

"Whoa!" I stop and grab Lava's arm. "Is that a new red flag?"

The coarse crimson fabric hangs limply to a pole perched above a pale blue craftsman-style house. I often pause by the gardenia bushes by the porch to take in their pleasant aroma.

"The Sages ruled in favor of her neighbor, the pizza chef," Lava says. "The blacksmith is the one who complained about that black oak tree throwing shade on her yard."

The blacksmith is an older mother. Her lovely porch is always vacant, even though there's a great pair of cushioned lounge chairs turned to face southwest towards the sunset. I would sit in those chairs every day, if they were mine. I feel a horrible sinking in my stomach, because I realize this house is only two red flags away from becoming available. Am I the sort of lunatic who fantasizes about another woman's demise?

"But she wouldn't get a red flag for requesting the tree be trimmed," I say. "If it was upsetting her, she had to speak up.

Otherwise, the resentment builds internally—harsh words spoken—emotions are contagious—"

"—harsh words were definitely spoken," Lava said. "On both sides. I bet the pizza chef gets a red flag of her own by next year. For something unrelated, sure, but it's because Queen Ande is in the twilight of her reign. She wants to keep up her spotless reputation."

"Well I hope she wants peace to outlast her reign, not suddenly disintegrate when she transitions," I say. "I'm joking," I add, before Lava can accuse me of seeding fearful superstitions.

Before I can stop it, I'm imagining myself lounging on the blacksmith's porch, sipping champagne, and glaring at the black oak tree's shadow. Would I be capable of a different outcome?

"Every decision is supposed to be a win-win-win," I say. "A trim would be healthy for the tree. Warm sunlight, good for the pizza chef. I wonder why she wouldn't agree to it?"

"I don't think they were really fighting about the tree," Lava says, slowing her pace and turning to me. "The only way to win a dispute is to avoid it."

I hold her gaze. For a second I think she's going to kiss me, right here on the dirt road that winds through the eucalyptus trees into the center of town.

"At least we can count on flawless pizza this summer." Lava winks with a grin.

The pizza chef, on invisible trial. My happy friend, always redirecting her thoughts to the greater good. Lava spins in the road and skips ahead.

OUR FIRST STOP is the recycled fabric boutique with designs by Lolanda's former mentor. She repurposes prints from former seasons and turns them into formal occasion dresses.

"Look at this green," Lava says, pulling out a mint suede strapless dress. "No offense to Lolanda, but these older fabrics are far more interesting than what she does now.

Since returning from voyage to start her own line, Lolanda split from her mentor's legacy of party dresses and chose to specialize in men's linen basics. I went to her Amateur Art Show. My favorite part was how the judges awarded the apparel designers with the most outrageous category titles.

"This one wins Best Seaweed Soup," I say.

Lava rolls her eyes. "What about this deep red color—feel how smooth this silk is, Deer!"

I follow Lava and run my fingers along the fabric.

"Overripe Tomato of the Week," I say.

She laughs.

The woman watching the shop is not the designer herself, but one of her current students. She's at the desk by the window, sketching.

Lava reaches for a black dress with silver embroidery.

"Spiderweb—"

"Deer, c'mon, don't make fun of them all." Lava slaps my shoulder. "I actually want to wear one of these."

I drag my fingers along a clothing rack. Any other day I'd be suffocated by such beauty, such craft, knowing I'm not able to take anything home. But today I'd take any distraction to get off the terror of my dream.

"Didn't your mom choose your dress for the Lunar Party already?" I say.

"Oh, but there's the day-after afterparty, the weekend picnic series ..." Lava grins. "Isla and Roxana are getting extra dresses to have on deck. Especially stretchy ones in case they go overboard at the pastry tables."

The chocolate chip scone is still in my front pocket. I break off a bite and it crumbles through my fingers.

"Speaking of, what does yours look like?" Lava asks.

Shadows pass on the opaque front wall from foot traffic outside.

"Did you hear what happened at my mom's art show?" I say. I'm surprised she hasn't specifically asked.

Lava heaves her armful of dresses onto the fitting room armchair.

"Can you imagine being that singer, and finding your dad in the bushes with your male neighbor?" Lava laughs loud enough that the woman at the desk looks up. I close the curtain to the changing area.

"Oh—Ivy," I say. "She reported her own dad to the Sages?"

The pastry chef's daughter. She's a year below me. There's someone who will never get a red flag. She's always poised, always smiling. The ideal Calefean woman. Maybe more so than Lava, even with her boisterous cheer. Ivy would simply forget troublesome dreams upon waking up. She wouldn't let it ruin her day, her week, her life.

Lava spins in front of the mirror in a peach taffeta skirt set. "The real question is, how can they get aroused without the softness of a woman?" Lava says.

I realize Lava's gossip has less to do with Code nuances, and more to do with the lovemaking preferences of men, something I've not given much though. Intimacy is her favorite topic.

"Anyway, the scone you're eating is a pity buy from the pastry shop," Lava continues. "Anna's had a line down the block all week."

There have been no extra callers looking to buy Mom's ocean sunsets after our public fight. I'm offended—even angry—that our gossip from Mom's show was overshadowed.

What makes one woman's misfortune the object of generous

pity, and another's quickly forgotten? I realize how little I know about how to succeed, not just as an artist, but as a woman. There are a million invisible rules. My Grandma El is a master of them all.

"I'm wearing this," I say.

"What?"

I look down at my sunflower-patterned dress, my favorite of the three. My second favorite is a solid pale blue. My third favorite is a warm brown, the color of fertile soil.

"To the Lunar Party," I say. "Even my dad says—"

"No," Lava says.

"You don't like it," I say. The remainder of my scone is too dense to break apart, so I gnaw on the edge and use my saliva to slough off a crumble.

"Can't you ask Lolanda for a dress? You two were tight once."

"I would never request a gift! And she really only does menswear now."

"Ooh, that's not how you do it. You admire her talents. You describe your ideal dress. You mention the need. Then you've given her the opportunity to make a marvelous gift. Win, win."

Lava peeks past the curtain at the shopkeeper, who is still sketching at the front desk. She's our age—well, one of our ages. She's likely the budding dressmaker who took Lolanda's spot under her old mentor.

"Wear one of mine," Lava says.

I laugh. "Babe, that's sweet, but our sizing is so off."

I'm long and she's wide. Her dresses would look silly on me.

Lava unzips and drops the green dress to the floor, and holds one up with an elastic waist and criss-crossed ties on the back. She pulls it over her head. The front opens into a deep V with stiff fabric that molds to her curves.

"Look at this." She spins. "All you have to do is tie the back tighter, and it will be perfect on you."

It's a mustard yellow, the color of my favorite flowers on the hills.

"It looks amazing—on you," I say.

The hems are lined with gold ribbon. It feels familiar.

"Grandma El's dinner set," I say. The plates and bowls come in yellow and white, and have gold rims.

"Wear gold jewelry and you'll have everyone talking about how you honor your matriarch," Lava says.

The blue curtain divider moves as another shopper walks by. I jump back in surprise.

A memory from last night flashes into my mind. The ocean foam.

"I had a dream," I say.

She slaps my butt as she walks past me. "Ooh la la, tell me everything!"

Lava plops three dresses on the shopkeeper's desk. "I'll use credits from my mom—Primrose Wines," Lava says to the shopkeeper, who folds each dress into a canvas bag.

"My mentor will be grateful to stock up on reds," the shopkeeper responds.

Lava pushes the door open. I follow her onto the meticulously crafted sea glass pavement. Each smooth piece is held in place with dried seaweed paste. A eucalyptus breeze envelops us. I could be crushed by the beauty of it all.

Once we're a few paces down the road, I groan. "Why do you think everything is about sex?" I say. "It's our eggs. They're at risk—"

"What was that?" Lava turns around. "Deer, you'll give us all nightmares."

I'm already having nightmares. My limbs feel weak. This is

how it starts. Inner conflict drains energy, siphoning off creative power, and health, until—

The government tower looms in front of us. It's the only downtown building taller than three floors.

"Omar," I say.

"You had a dream about Omar?" She hands me one of her bags. The one with the yellow dress.

Omar works in the government tower. I have an idea.

"Eww, no. I'm late to meet Omar at the cafe!" I kiss Lava on the cheek and walk off before she can respond.

SIX

By the time I reach the tower, I am triumphant. I am armed not just with a dress to make my Lunar Party debut, but a whole new perspective. What if I go through with mating season, with my friends, because let's be honest—it's too late to back out, now that I've told everyone close to me. And I become a mother and a professional poet. But without wasting my summer on the Motherhood Voyage?

It's a harebrained scheme, and the only person who can help me is my friend Omar.

Omar begins his workday at sunrise in the government tower. By midday, he takes a break at the cafe on the second level.

I drop in at least once a week because I like the way he admires me. He'll laugh at my animated retelling of my mom's petty gossip. It's a boost to my mood.

Today, I need more than that, because I have an idea for how I can get out of the Motherhood Voyage.

This is how it usually goes. I'll spot him, wearing the polo shirt with the embroidered Calefean rose on the front pocket, sitting on the balcony. I'll wave an arm and holler to him from the street. He'll look down and nod his soft curl-framed head. Once I've grabbed a mug from the counter, I'll approach the table. His eyes will trace my body top to bottom, then back up, landing around my left ear because he's self-conscious about staring at my chest, something we've never discussed aloud and yet I'm certain we both know.

Is the sunflower dress also his favorite? I think yes.

Today is only different because he notices the canvas bag. It distracts him from my dress. I sit down and place a hand on his arm before he can speak.

"What's happening, Omar? Tell me the latest, the most invigorating news from the government."

I hope he talks through his updates fast. Mine are always more entertaining.

And today, I have a favor to ask. It's a long shot, but his access to government data might help me.

"I got a promotion, actually." His warm brown eyes light up. His polo shirt is snug on his chest more than I remember. His growth spurt may have happened on Sister Earth, but it's his time in Caleaf that's filled out his frame.

I sip my drinking chocolate and lick the foam off my upper lip. "So what does that mean, more work? You already work so much. You're stuck indoors during the best part of the day."

I never understood why Omar didn't choose a more interesting role. Something outdoors, at least, with a more pleasant view. But then, I remember his cloud race fails. Omar's intuition is lacking.

"I'm an analyst for International Relations now," Omar said.

"Inter-national? So all theoretical, then." He must really be failing at work if they've assigned him to work with civilizations that no longer exist.

His wide eyes seem sad, so I try to sound interested.

"So it's like, making plans for how to respond, if we were to see signs of human life approaching the island? How to say, 'no contact' in a variety of old languages?"

"Right," he said. "We work with the Records—and the Sages, obviously—to study languages of various cultures. Another surviving civilization may not have our intuitive technologies. Which would make them prone to conflict. "

"What can be done for them?"

"Well, we can't send them back to a childhood on Sister Earth so their right brain can fully develop. But perhaps they could gain their intuitive abilities like the foremothers did. With silent meditation."

"Oh, like Sage training? Just three years in a pitch dark cave and then we'll let you infiltrate our society?" I smile, but Omar doesn't seem amused.

"And Deer, we don't know everything." Omar looks across the balcony to a bearded man seated by the railing. He's wearing the burgundy polo shirt of a fellow government worker.

"What if I told you the Queen regularly sends messages to other civilizations—and receives responses?"

"Whooo," I whistle. I lean back in my chair, onto its hind legs, kicking one of my legs up onto the balcony railing. "That sounds like an elaborate training exercise."

Omar leans forward. "I've seen the space maps—"

"Space maps?" I say. My chair lands with a thud as my elbow hits the table, sending sharp pain to my shoulder.

Omar's face freezes. The man on the balcony is still drumming his fingers on the railing, as if he hadn't heard. Laughter erupts indoors from a large group of women.

"Shh, Deer. Top secret," he says. "What I just told you, is top secret."

"We're the only ones left." I pull my hair loose from the

braid. "Aside from Calefeans, no one has added to the Records in 500 years. There was the famine, the wars, and by the Great Earthquake, it all cuts off." I stretch my arms out to the sides. "And not just from Earth—the sky, the solar system, the universe. We're alone here."

Omar looks up at the green awning.

I sigh. "The impossibility of such emptiness. The improbability of our survival, against all odds."

This is why motherhood is the highest honor. It's a chance to add to the inconceivable story of life. It's the least I can do. The canvas bag by my feet reminds me to tell Omar I'm doing mating season this year.

Omar switches the cross of his legs. "Also. I can use the Terminal. To send and receive messages. With anyone who has access to one."

I blink, letting his words settle. The Terminal.

The sipping chocolate hits my belly. When that happens I get a surge of exhilaration. For a moment, all of life is perfect. The sun angles down, offering its warm glow. Downtown Caleaf smells familiar and exotic, with a mix of sea salt, sawdust, strawberries, and just a hint of fresh compost. There are the sounds of constant construction. Materials are being repurposed to make more beauty. Plants are re-homed to new environments. Without knowing it, Omar had set me up.

Ever since I made my decision in Lava's treehouse, I worried about how I would tell Omar that I'm doing mating season. I know he's going to think I'll mate with him, and I don't want to hurt his feelings. I need to say this casually.

"Oh yeah, the Mothership has a Terminal," I said. "I suppose I'll see it. When I'm on voyage this year."

Omar claps. "That's incredible news. Why didn't you say something earlier? Cheers, babe." He holds up his drink. I clink his mug and gulp my chocolate.

I want to move away from the topic of mating season as quickly as possible. I'm running out of time to ask him the favor. He'll have to go back to work soon.

"Do you know what? I also had this weird dream," I say.

"A dream? Tell me more." His eyes focus on my ear.

"Oh, not that kind of dream, Omar." I knew he would get the wrong idea and think it was some kind of innuendo. People only hear what they want.

"You mentioned once that you analyze the sensor data from Sister Earth—the chemical levels, the power coefficients. I'm just wondering. How much phosphorus does an egg need, for the shell to develop?"

It's such a nerdy question. Right up his alley, though.

"I suppose it could be calculated. There's no shortage of phosphorus on Sister Earth, though, if that's what you're thinking?"

"It's for a poem." I smile. "Something new for the Amateur Art Show. A celebration of the foremothers! Isn't it such a coincidence that there was an abundance of the mineral they needed on the first habitable planet they discovered?"

I rub my forehead. "Did they lay the first eggs here, then find the planet, or find the planet and then create the reproductive plant technologies for egg laying? Which came first?"

"Sometimes I think you're not listening to me," Omar says. His voice cracks.

I rewind to trace back to where I hurt his feelings. I've barely said anything.

"I just need to know if it's possible for a woman to lay eggs here on Earth."

"Fine." He throws up his hands. "I'm sure you have a perfectly good purpose. But if I start making calculations that aren't part of my job, that's going to look like some self-initiated project, so I need to know."

"I told you. It's for a poem!"

"But then—why don't you make a formal request to the Sages?"

I cringe.

I go to the Sages for my annual scan just like everyone else. Okay, most years. I've been sent off with holly essence, to resolve resentment, or mustard essence, to boost joy. Roses, with their superior beauty, can resolve almost any imbalance, no tincture needed. Just stand in a rose garden. The Sages hand them out as a boost on the equinoxes and solstices.

I wouldn't want to run into a Sage on the street. There's no lying to a Sage.

Their training requires living in a cave because it blocks their primary sense so their secondary senses can develop. From there, each Sage develops a few intersectional senses. Seeing with your fingertips. Touch from a distance—with your ears.

Afterwards, a Sage wears a hood that covers her face. For the dark, yes, but also to merge identities. Each Sage is every Sage. With eyes closed, they can read your mind with just a glance.

If a Sage saw the contents of my dream, she wouldn't just send me away with a few plant remedies. A healthy person doesn't imagine up such a troubling scene. A peaceful person doesn't dream about killing her own daughter. I'd get a red flag.

"Ok, it's not for a poem." I wipe my hands on my dress. "We have to stop voyage."

"What—" Omar laughs. "Deer, is this a joke?" When I don't respond, he speaks again. "What did you dream?"

"It was ... graphic," I say. "Someone died." I can't tell him any more than that. This is how it always starts. Troubling emotions, leading to knee-jerk reactions, multiplying through the population, then all-out war. This is what the Queen wants us to avoid.

"Oh." Omar looks over his shoulder, at his workplace. The tower.

"Even if I find the information on phosphorus, you can't lay your eggs here," Omar says. "It takes isolation for the right brain to fully develop. That's why we do voyage. That's why we grow up on Sister Earth. It's not just the phosphorus for the shell."

"Maybe I haven't thought this through," I say.

He nods.

I hunch my shoulders, searching my mind for options. I just need to convince him to help. I can solve the other problems—later. "But Omar, we don't know everything. You said so yourself." I push my chair onto its back legs and cross my ankles on the balcony. "And you say I don't listen."

"You think you can improve on the childbirth process of the foremothers?" For the first time, he looks me straight on. "I'll lose my job if I get caught."

"Do you like your job?" I say. "If I were a man—I would work in a garden. I'd sign up for the ice expedition. I'd—"

"And get killed?" Omar says.

"At least I'd be outside. At least I'd have some excitement. Don't you want excitement?" I say.

He pulls at the floppy hair above his temples. "I can look, but I don't know that I'll find anything."

"Thanks, Omar," I say. The idea might be absurd, but for a moment I dare to imagine a future when I—and maybe other women, too—could become mothers without the long voyage.

Omar looks down the barrel of his empty mug. "Speaking of jobs. Would you still write poetry, if you didn't have to?"

I tilt my head. "Huh. No one's asked me that before!

He smiles.

"I guess I don't know," I say. I stand to leave. "You're going to the Lunar Party?"

He's even more of a rule-follower than Sequoia, and he's

pushing his limits to help me. I want him to feel there will be a reward for all this.

"I thought you hated parties," he says.

"Well, this year, they're throwing it in my honor."

His eyes light up. "Oh, yeah. I'll watch for you."

I pick up Lava's dress bag and let him watch me as I leave.

SEVEN

"If you want to keep your hair long, braid it or comb it," Mom says to me when I come down for dinner that night. Her hair is thick and wavy like mine, and she's no hypocrite. She keeps it in a braid.

I compliment Dad's scalloped potatoes. Mom dips her dinner roll in vegetable broth. We sit on opposite ends of the long oak dining table, and Dad's place is between us on the wide edge facing the fireplace.

My dad tells a story about his failed efforts to revive our avocado tree, and for once, Mom doesn't interrupt. I wait for them to ask about my day, but I suppose no one noticed me come in with the canvas bag containing Lava's dress.

After I finish my asparagus, I bite into my cheesecake square. The crust crumbles beautifully into the mildly tart custard. I'm lucky to have a dad who's such a good cook. I'll miss that when I have my own residence—when I'm a mother.

I stand to leave.

"Deer," Mom says. "I hope you don't have plans tomorrow. Your grandmother is transitioning."

She dips another bite of bread. I grip the back of my chair.

"But—now? Why?"

Mom drops the bread onto her plate and her elbow knocks a knife clattering onto the floor.

"Oh, honey, she's been saying for years that she's ready to go." Mom sips her wine. "Then she says, oh, I'll do one more season, I have an idea for one more design."

Mom sets down her wine glass. "Now she's truly done her best work. She's reached her peak. It's time."

She leaves her plate of bread and half-full glass of wine on the table and ducks into the kitchen. I hear her pour a beverage, then her feet on the stairs.

I look at Dad.

"The party will be at her residence tomorrow night. The invitations were sent out today," he says. "She has a lot of fans who want to admire her ceramics one last time. You'd better get there early if you want to speak to her."

My empty plate belongs to a set from El's early work, before she evolved the style that made her famous. Still, it was crafted by her hands. I graze it with my finger.

"I never had a chance to buy a set—what about that vase that she refuses to sell, the one with the lilies painted on?"

"Ground to powder, anything she hasn't gifted or sold. I imagine her lot will be desirable for some of the new mothers, or someone looking to upgrade their residence."

I've seen beautiful homes demolished so someone else can build in her style. Knowing our system preserves the market for up-and-coming artists and equitable wealth distribution does not make it easy to say goodbye.

To be honest, I still haven't gotten over the loss of my mentor. I still have those exercise diagrams she drew for me. But all her notebooks were burned. Sometimes I try to recall a poem of hers, and can't—and maybe never will again.

"Why does she think she can drop news like that and just

walk away?" I say. "I've never lost a grandmother before. She has. She could—offer some guidance."

"You have to be gentle with your mother," Dad says, more softly. "It's her own mom she's saying goodbye to."

I hate to admit that he's right. "Fine, I get it," I say.

My grandmother is prolific. Popular. I can't say I am close to her or even know her well. I should feel lucky that El stayed as long as she has. I assumed she would be here for my Amateur Art Show. It would be my chance to impress her. I wish I could tell her it would be worth the wait.

But I know better than to overpromise.

THE NEXT DAY, I arrive at El's residence in the late afternoon. Workmen move her furniture one last time to make way for a standing room-only crowd. Florists bring long-stemmed roses from her garden to display in her iconic vases. The walls are plastered with first-place ribbons and framed awards from her long illustrious career.

What was it like for my mom to live here in the years before her own voyage? El spends half her time in her desert studio. During the years in between her husbands, the home would have been empty.

I hear her voice a few rooms away, calling out directions to the chefs.

El's third husband offers me lemonade. "There's a porch swing on the second floor balcony where you won't be in the way," he says.

I've been alone with my Grandma El twice in my life. The first was in the lobby of a stage performance when my mom went to the restroom. She repeated, "Wasn't it a nice show?"

maybe five or six times while she watched the crowds pour out of the theater and waved to her friends.

The second was last summer when I delivered a custom glaze to her desert studio. I knocked twice and waited. I could hear ceramics shattering as if she was slamming them against a wall. When I knocked louder, she cracked the door just enough for me to hand her the jug. Her smiles are reserved for shows and sales. She specializes in orders, not small talk.

That's what she's doing now. I can hear her shrill voice correcting workmen on how to rearrange the furniture.

I set the ceramic tumbler of lemonade onto a side table. It's chilled with ice—a full year after the last successful ice expedition. With the delay on the Sages' decision, the only way she could have gotten ice is a gift from the Queen herself.

My last words to my maternal grandmother are important. I want to appear both grateful and confident.

She's hours away from consuming her final plant medicine and drifting into the next dimension. What can I tell her that will add to her bliss? What can I say to a woman who's already reached the highest level of success in Caleaf?

With all her accomplishments, I wonder: What would Grandma El do, if she had a troubling dream like mine?

She approaches me holding a potted peace lily, its pearly bloom matching her tight curls.

"My favorite granddaughter," she says.

"I'm your only granddaughter," I say.

"Ha! Always with a sense of humor." She sits close to me on the swinging bench. "You know that will come in handy. When you're a mother," she says.

So she's heard my news. "I'm looking forward to mating season," I say.

All my words collect in my throat like a rubber ball. Instead of saying something meaningful, I'm repeating generic pleas-antries.

"We all must rise to our roles. When the time is right. Myself, I couldn't hold out much longer." She pulls the shoulder of her puffed-sleeve peach dress down to reveal a sore on her upper back. I lean away as if it might be contagious. Any wound at transition continues with you in the next dimension.

"Your mom—" She sighs. "If she fails, she fails. I can't go back and fix what I've done."

I've never heard her praise my mom. She only gives kind words when she wants something from someone. Still, this is the closest she's come to outright criticism.

I follow her gaze out on her spiral rose garden, with towering eucalyptus trees along the edges of the property.

She pats my hand. "I remember what it was like to be your age and think I knew better than anyone else. This is my advice: Pour it into your art. Or you'll destroy yourself from the inside."

I study her face and see that her dark brown eyes are like my own. The outer edges tilt down with wrinkles flaring out like webs. She has the smile lines and thought creases of a life well-expressed.

"Is that the same advice you gave my mother?" I ask.

"You're not your mom," she says. "And I mean it as a compliment."

I ponder her advice. Is my dream something I can put into my art? Not without giving the whole island nightmares.

But it is bursting from within me, and I'm not sure anyone will like what I have to say. I don't even like it.

She reaches over and runs her fingers through my long hair. I spent an hour combing out the knots this morning, and now I freeze, thinking of the shame I'd feel in this moment if I hadn't done that.

"And you really are beautiful," El says.

I feel numb. It's the first compliment I've received from El. I touch my hair after she moves her hand away.

We sit side-by-side, staring out at her gardens.

"El, if you knew something bad was going to happen—you'd tell people, right?" I say. "Even if they didn't want to know?"

When she doesn't answer right away, I look over. She's halfway down the porch steps, directing the workmen on the display of one of her larger pieces, a decorative garden urn.

It's back to orders. Her final orders.

IN HER FRONT ROOM, a dance floor has been laid over the rugs. The fireplace mantel is cleared off. The vase normally kept there, the one with the lilies that she had always refused to sell—gone. I wonder if she's gifted it to someone after all. She has many friends. Important ones.

Sequoia arrives with Edgar. A guitarist plays ballads. Women in colorful dresses twirl through the big open room.

"She could have been queen," I say.

Sequoia nods. She tilts her head. "Technically not. Because Queen Ande was chosen by the Sages the year Queen Tentee transitioned and your grandma El was still in her 19th year on Sister Earth."

I press my lips together. "That's what I'm saying. If the timing was different, she could have—"

"But it wasn't!" Sequoia laughs. "This is a celebration of the amazing life she had! Do you want to go look at her pink dessert bowls upstairs?"

"I've already seen them."

Sequoia gives up trying to engage me in conversation and takes Edgar out to the gardens. Women, young and old, weave through the rooms on three floors, admiring the displays of El's lifelong work in ceramics. The gold series that earned a commission from the Queen. The mint green churns, a staple at all the dairy farms.

I'm moping on the dance floor when Lava arrives.

"I barely said a word to her," I say.

Lava holds my shoulders as we sway to a flute solo from the quartet on the back patio.

El is on the second floor in a guest room. A long line of friends and collaborators stretches down the center staircase, all waiting to pay respects and receive one last impression of her wrinkles and wisdom.

"I was going to tell her I'm nervous about the voyage," I say. "It was my last chance."

"What? No, Deer," Lava says. "Be glad you didn't do that."

"Why?" I say.

"She'd take your anxiety with her, you fool! Anything you're experiencing at the moment of transition travels like baggage into the next dimension."

I pull my hair over my shoulder to get it off my neck.

"She's done her best work. She's surrounded by beautiful music and friends. She's—"

"You know they're going to grind all this to a powder," I say. Trays of mugs, vases, and pitchers decorate every windowsill. "Anything she hasn't already gifted or sold."

I motion to the built-in bookcases. "They'll demolish the entire residence so some new mother can custom-build her own."

"Let it go, Deer," Lava says. "Her work delighted the collective for many years. It's honorable to redistribute her wealth upon transition."

Her face, her pottery, her kind words, however minimal—my memory of her would fade. Unless I can find that vase—her favorite one. Perhaps they just moved it.

Lava lets go of my shoulders to spin, and I halfheartedly do my own turn. We face each other and link fingers. I look into Lava's soft brown eyes. They are lighter than El's. With Lava, I feel seen and safe.

"You'll be okay," Lava says. She pulls me into a tight hug.

Another hand grips my shoulder. I look up. It's a Sage. Her hood shadows her face. "Your grandmother is ready," she says.

The Sage takes my hand and pulls me out of Lava's arms, across the dance floor, to the stairs. Some of these people waiting won't get a chance to see El. My dad was right—it's a good thing I came early.

El has moved from the guest room on the second floor up to her master bedroom on the third floor. My mom and El's current husband are inside. El is seated on her bed, surrounded by pillows, and covered with a bright floral patchwork quilt.

The sun is setting, and the room is dim. I stand next to my mother.

"Once she inhales the plant medicine, she'll lean back and drift into a deep sleep. She will feel no pain. Her spirit will remain in her body for a few minutes longer. El, my dear, are you ready?"

El nods. Her eyes are wide, almost childlike. Already, she looks like a different woman than the one I've known.

The Sage lights the pipe.

No one told me we smoke the plant medicine to transition. I'd always imagined it being more of a tincture.

El purses her lips around the pipe and inhales slowly. Her eyes grow wide. Fearful, even. Then she falls back onto the pillows.

The Sage reaches over and pats El's eyes closed.

El's third husband places a hand on his heart. I'm not sure she chose him for lovemaking. I think theirs was more of a domestic support kind of union.

He steps out the door, and as my gaze follows him, I see it. El's favorite vase is on the oak dresser. The Sage leaves, and only me and my mother remain.

"Is she still breathing?" I say. I lean over El.

My mom sighs. "When I'd tell her I finally found my style, she'd say, don't stagnate, and when I'd tell her I was in exploration mode, she'd say, don't risk it." Mom throws up her hands. "She was never happy. Eventually I quit telling her anything and that's how we lived. Some mom, huh?"

She's barely talking to me. I realize she's saying her peace to her own mother. What she doesn't realize is how much her own mothering mirrors what she got from El. She doesn't even know she's doing it.

I know my mom will object to me taking that vase. The party downstairs could continue for another hour into the night. If I can get the vase under my dress, and grip it through the fabric, I may be able to exit through the gardens without being seen. So, as soon as my mom leaves—

El's body violently jerks. Her arms land with her elbows splayed out to the sides and one knee pointed up, her mouth gaping open.

My mom grabs my hand. For a moment, she holds me.

When my mom turns to leave, I reach for the vase. I don't want to be alone with the body. The tall vase is between my palms when the Sage appears in the doorway. I gasp and the vase tumbles onto the hardwood, breaking in two.

"It's okay, we're going to grind that anyway," the Sage says.

I shield my face and keep walking, chasing my mom down the stairs, not wanting to invite any suspicion.

El is gone. Her art—gone. The last I have of her are her final words: "Pour it into your art," she told me. Deer, beautiful. Deer, funny. Deer—not like her mom. The least I can do is live out her better impression of me.

Actually, that's not true. What I'll always have from El is my body.

Through my eggs, I can keep El's memory alive.

If El got through the Motherhood Voyage, and so did my mom—why can't I? I've got to forget my wild idea of laying eggs on Earth and stick to the task at hand: getting ready for the Lunar Party.

I'm going to need some mates.

EIGHT

The daily downtown market is not my favorite. It's crowded. My mom goes early, when the vendors are barely set up, to beat the crowds. I used to go with her, until I realized we were missing out on the best gossip. It's a market of knowledge, not just goods.

Today's market is the final exchange before they shut the downtown blocks to set up for the Lunar Party this weekend. I want all the intel I can get. I scan the tables for Jacara's dairy, but then I remember she switched days. She only makes the trip down once a week now. I missed her—she might not even know I'm doing mating season this year, unless she heard it from someone else. I should have told her myself. It's my fault for not keeping track of the days.

I head for the baked goods. I can get some poppyseed muffins on my mom's account—they're her favorite, so she won't complain. The smell of olive pecorino pizza wafts my way. I pause, letting the flow of foot traffic swirl around me on the sea glass stone walkway.

The pizza chef, a boisterous woman, is belting her conversation to someone across the aisle.

"It's the biggest Motherhood Voyage yet!" she says. "Linden's painted her murals on half my indoor walls, just wait 'til you see my daughter's work, her style is—" The chef kisses her fingertips with pride.

I feel my body sway. The heat from the morning sun bakes my forehead. Of course a mother would brag about her daughter's art. It's just that I can't even fathom my mom announcing her confidence in me to a crowded market. Who is Linden, anyway? A younger woman. With that kind of positive appraisal from her mother, of course she'd develop her style quickly.

I turn deeper into the market. The crowd is shoulder to shoulder. I question how badly I want, or need, those muffins.

If Adollo had just—I stop myself. I got praise from my mentor. But there are some things only a mother can give.

On the empty-handed walk home, I make up a poem in my head.

The ocean is gray
The sky is blue
The tortoise walks
The rabbit flew
Some women rise
Some women fall
Some women don't
Want to be mothers at all
At the end of the day
The end of the life
The end of civilization
No more recorded time
It won't be your seed
That outlasts your memory
Nothing then remains
Only final peace.

NINE

On the night of the Lunar Party, when the moon is at its most full, it will be perfectly framed in the ceiling of the gazebo in the Queen's gardens. The assigned watcher will strike the gong.

When you hear the gong, the man you lock eyes with is your mate. The gong will play until no one is left standing.

By the end of tonight, I will join my friends in ascending from amateur to mater—one step closer to becoming a mother. The Amateur Art Show is only a week away now, but I promised myself I won't worry about my poetry until I've gracefully—gracefully!—completed tonight's initiation.

I gaze at myself in Sequoia's bronze mirror to practice. Her mom's residence is the closest to the beginning of the Lunar Party parade. Her five brothers will be doing their own preparations in the loft below us. It will be their first time attending the Lunar Party, too—but for them, as mates.

"Deer, you look like a scared squirrel," Lava says. She shines like she's made of obsidian. "Don't gawk at me. It's just lavender oil. It's a pleasant scent."

I take the hand-blown glass pitcher and pour a pool in my palm.

"It deflects mosquitos, too. They get wild near the gardens at sunset," Sequoia says.

She's been to the Queen's gardens before. Her mentor took her for plein air training with the other visual artists.

"With all the cross-species peace pacts our Sages have negotiated, mosquitos seem like an oversight," I say.

"They tried," Sequoia says. "The mosquitos refuse to expand their palate beyond human blood. I suppose there must be some benefit to us, according to the law of mutualism."

Sequoia's silver bracelets rattle as she combs her silky black hair. "There is something different about your face, Deer. What is it? An herbal tea from the Sages to improve complexion?"

I look to the mirror again to admire my oval face and long hair, parted in the center. My lips are stained red with berry coconut oil. The usual tension in my brow is relaxed.

It's because of what Grandma El said at her transition party. *Pour it into your art.* I've been writing poetry. My intuitive skills are slowly coming back.

"No, let me guess. Mint tea?" Lava says. "My mom drinks it. Wait! Yellow roses? A dozen perfect buds in each corner of your loft can do wonders—"

"Oh, I hardly need extra plant remedies from the Sages," I say. "My morning run on the cliffs keeps me in perfect bliss. I'll never stop swooning at the blue horizon."

"You've been doing that forever," Lava says. "It's not new."

I pat oil onto my belly and hips for good measure, then pull the borrowed yellow dress over my head. Lava ties the back for me and fastens the extra bunch of fabric over the butt with a hair clip.

The top fits perfectly. My breasts are as large as Lava's, just on a smaller frame. Through the deep V in front, they hang together like grapes. The thick fabric on the bodice molds to my shape. I raise my arms and spin.

"I'm free!" I say. The draft of air against my bare back feels thrilling compared to my usual princess-bodiced sundresses.

Lava adjusts the tulle full skirt of her strapless green dress. She chose well. The composition allows plenty of space for movement. She practices a twirl and leap in front of the mirror.

"It needs something," she says.

Sequoia plucks a sunflower from her vase and clips it to Lava's curly hair.

"Now, perfect," she says.

Sequoia clasps a cascade of silver necklaces around her delicate neck, adding to the sparkle of her sequined crop top and mini skirt.

She goes back to her jewelry box and holds another necklace up like a pendulum. My spine tingles with the charge of nearby laughter.

"Clockwise," she says. "That means yes—the women from South Caleaf are here. We better get in line."

THE SPRINGTIME LUNAR PARTY, held on the full moon halfway between the spring equinox and summer solstice, is the only time of year the people of Central Caleaf and South Caleaf mix together socially.

The 600-mile path between the two is well-worn from southbound wine deliveries, and on the reverse trip, avocado shipments, all carried in self-fueling carts.

The women maters from South Caleaf travel up to kick off mating season with us, and many of their men come along for the festivities. They sleep in temporary canvas housing on the fields north of downtown. That's also where the line will start. In a majestic parade, the maters—mothers-to-be—will weave through downtown, past the government building and the

Queen's residence, out to her massive gardens for the overnight party. There, the mates are waiting.

Along with the South Calefeans, the daughters of farm and forest bosses have traveled into town for the party week, too. Though it's been many years since I was with them on Sister Earth, I recognize some faces. All the maters are in their best dresses to make an impression.

"That woman in pink silk—your class, Lava?" I say.

The rural South Calefean women stand out because they braid their hair into intricate styles versus wearing it in loose tangled curls like mine. I've heard there's more wind on the lower end of the island.

"Look!" Sequoia says. "The tall woman walking with a cane. She's blind, and I heard she paints the most magical abstract pieces with her fingers. She was born able to sense pigment with her skin, like a Sage."

"In pink, that's Fern with the chestnut hair. She's a singer," Lava says to me. "Not mine, one year older."

"Oh. That's why she's with Ivy," I say. The pastry chef's daughter, who reported her father to the Sages. Ivy's thick brown curls are combed to a fluff so she appears three inches taller.

Ivy's dress is simple, but stunning. It's a navy A-line with sheer cutouts in the center of the back. She turns around and I see the bodice is made of fresh flowers.

"What happens when those petals start falling?" I say.

"She's clever. All the men are thinking the same thing," Lava says. "It's a sure way to catch eyes, despite her flat chest."

I smile. The art of a Lunar Party dress is visual magnetism. That way, when the gong rings, you have choices. You decide whose gaze you meet. The delicious appeal of different body shapes doesn't matter as much here. All women optimize for attention-grabbing accessories around the chest and face.

But it's not the other maters I'm most eager to check out. It's the mates—the men. They'll be gathered on sidewalks and side streets when we walk through town.

I'm looking for someone I don't know. Someone Lava hasn't already slept with. Someone mysterious enough to be exciting, and distant enough I won't have to see him at daily markets if my first mating experience disappoints.

I'm looking for a South Calefean.

A harmonium plays in the distance. Musicians climb onto raised platforms backed up to the buildings so they won't block the view of the women as we walk down the sea glass-paved street.

My parents might be somewhere in the two block-deep crowd. They might not. Mom hates large gatherings. And, how convenient: The recent transition of her own mother gives my mom an excuse to skip the Lunar Party of her only daughter.

The line begins moving. We walk in twos and threes so each of us can be admired by both sides of the road. A cool breeze tickles my chest and I spin again, feeling the fabric flutter around me.

The walk is slow and steady. By the time we pass the fields and residential area, and enter the business district, beads of sweat are gliding through the lavender oil on my neck and arms. Spectators lining the sidewalks toss flowers to the women and call their names.

"Hey! It's a Primrose sister!" I hear. I step back so Lava can wave. Some men whistle. She steps out of the line to shimmy and spin. She's a natural at soaking up attention.

"Spot us all and you win a prize," she jokes when she steps back into the line. "One out of four sisters, three to go."

"If I had one fewer brother I'd set you all up," Sequoia says.

"Deer, want to sub in as the extra Primrose sister?" Lava says.

Normally I'd recoil at the thought of being the odd one out among beautiful women. But today, I'm wearing one of Lava's dresses. It makes me feel like some of her confidence has rubbed off on me. I don't have sisters of my own. I imagine the scene.

We're in a wildflower field with Lava and her three gorgeous lookalikes, with Sequoia's skinny brothers crawling over them like lost ants.

"I would do it." I laugh. "But not tonight. I want someone special for tonight."

I kick a pebble loose from my toes. Ahead of us, men are throwing blueberries for the women maters to catch in their mouths.

"Omar?" Sequoia says.

"What? Where?" I bring a hand to my exposed chest. We're getting closer to the government tower, his workplace, the section of town I've avoided so I wouldn't run into my male friend. I shouldn't have told him about my dream. It was a moment of weakness.

"No!" Sequoia says. "I mean, are you having a rendezvous with your best friend?"

That's right. Omar said he would come. I'd been so swept up in looking at the South Calefean faces that I forgot.

I groan. "If Omar follows me around tonight, I'll never meet someone special."

"Omar understands," Lava says. "You can have him anytime. Tonight you need numbers."

"I don't know if he does," I say. He said he'd look for me, and he's a man of his word. There's no way I'll avoid him.

The wrought iron gates to the government building are uncharacteristically wide open. The line splits in two. Sequoia to the left. Lava to the right. Me to the left. We'll reunite at the back of the building. With the Queen's residence in our left peripheral, we'll follow the brick path down to her expansive rose gardens.

THERE ARE shrubs twice as tall as a woman. Adjacent to them, protected by their height, are blossoms that prefer shade. Some gardens are arranged in spirals, others in grids. For the party, 12-hour tapered candles are lit on fences. They'll burn until sunrise.

Once we're inside the gardens, the women split off, exploring the gazebos and plazas for the perfect perch. Nature Artists climb on top of awnings and Craft Artists put their feet in the fountains. The swings hanging from the majestic oak trees fill up first.

Beyond these ancient trees are the eastern hills, where the Sages harvest their plant remedies along the freshwater stream.

We choose on a brick retaining wall where we can sit elevated and watch the musicians come in, mothers who have already done their mating season and Motherhood Voyage, all donned in white so they won't be mistaken for maters when the gong rings. The chefs put final touches on trays of cheese, custard, and cakes. Barrels of wine are stacked in the gazebos.

The first note of a violin plays, tuning the other instruments.

I lean back-to-back with Lava. Sequoia reclines against my knees.

"Do you think I'll find someone?" I say. "I mean, someone I really want."

"You'll have hundreds of choices," Sequoia says. "See? Here they come."

"Even you still have choices." Lava leans to the side and flips Sequoia's hair onto her face. "Come full moon."

"Oh, Edgar and I already chose a spot on the hills. You won't be able to find us if you try!"

Lava laughs. "I'll be too busy breaking records. I bet I can get at least three, just tonight."

The men wear loose linen pants, the kind my childhood friend Lolanda makes. Their shirts are stretchy, snug, and black, to hide perspiration. They stand out against the greens and pinks and purples of the gardens.

"Strong ones make good husbands," Lava says. "For gardening and foraging, cooking and cleaning." She points to some men I recognize as workmen who rotate farms to support harvests.

"For lovers, someone who makes you laugh."

I think of Omar. He amuses me when I recall his childhood foibles, but I don't think that's the sort of laughter she means.

"And for tonight? A good mater is not at his first Lunar Party, no offense, Sequoia." Lava glances back. "But also not too old. You want a dude who's curious, see that one, hanging back, taking it all in?" She points to a short man with dark freckles and a buzz cut. "I'd grab him, and two others for variety, and next thing you know we'll be seeing our dawns."

The musicians start with an upbeat song. Trumpets and percussion play from the biggest gazebo, and guitars follow along, harmonizing from the center of each garden. Vocalists hum along. The vibrations of sound ripple through the outdoor space. Even the flowers perk up in anticipation.

"I just want one," I say. There's no use in even trying to match Lava's stamina. "I want—"

A man pauses by a bush of red roses. His braids, the South Calefean style, are nearly as long as my own hair. The definition of his chest is visible through his tight shirt. He drains a glass of red wine, and as if he can feel my stare, he looks straight at me.

"That one," I say.

Lava stands up, removing her counterweight from both Sequoia and me. "There will be a time for that," she says. "But look, my sister Isla is getting the dancing started."

Like a model Calefean, Lava's sister exudes devotion to her art. She's dancing alone along the brick promenade leading to the big plaza. She sways, flips her hair in a backbend, and spins to the middle of the plaza, finally landing in the splits. A crowd of maters circles up. Another woman, a dancer from South Caleaf with gold hoop earrings and fringes decorating her dress, steps into the circle to pick up where Isla left off. Isla stands and the two mirror each other. No one can tell who's leading the dance, until the other woman misses a beat. They both laugh. The crowd cheers.

It's freestyle. More women step into the circle. Lava leads us through the crowd, my hand on her shoulder and my other arm reaching back so Sequoia can grip my wrist. The freestyle interlude morphs again, into harmonious movement. We join the circle and fall in step with the choreography. It's led by no one and everyone. Now all four Primrose sisters are here, and Lava joins her sisters in the center. Each footfall is so perfectly matched that a tempo rings into my ears. I can keep up with my eyes closed, even though I'm not usually much of a dancer. Our mind-body coordination is amplified with so many of us moving in sync.

The line dance is easy enough that some men join in. The edges of the circle become porous. Everyone on the plaza and promenade is dancing along.

Back on the brick retaining wall, a group of women have taken our place. They're dancing, too, elevated six feet off the ground. The skip and twirl at the edges, never missing a beat. Men gather to watch. The women are wearing full skirts and low-cut tops like mine. On the spins, the take turns flashing the men. A boob. A butt. A full chest shimmy.

The musicians respond to the energy of the dance and pick up the beat. As crowded as this plaza is, it can't hold everyone. Women are dispersing deeper and deeper into the rows of flowers. For most of us, this is the only time in our lives we'll have the honor of seeing the Queen's gardens firsthand.

It's only an hour into the party and some wine barrels are already empty. Men lift them over their heads, handing them off until there's a triad at the center of the plaza. It's the beginning of a tower. Lava hoists Sequoia to the top, where she strikes a pose. The men whistle and holler. She rattles her bracelets, and strikes another pose, this time balancing on one leg, the other hooked into her outstretched arms. Next, a backbend, to more whistles. Her jewelry flashes the candlelight. Day is turning to dusk.

I hold hands with other women to make a circle. We face the center and spin one direction, until the group spontaneously lurches and pulls to the reverse. Another circle forms behind us, and then another, each on its own timing.

Our hands slip from the sweat. My chest hurts from laughing. We get sloppy, crashing into each other and tumbling in a pile before getting back up to swing the other way. Men are joining in and their strength pulls us faster and faster. I look at my hand and up the arm attached. I recognize the braids that hang past the shoulders. It's the man I saw across the grass.

In the pandemonium of laughter and music, feet stomping and drums, I don't hear a thing, but I watch his lips and read a word.

"Hi," he says.

My hand relaxes and falls from his. I let go of the person on my other side. My gaze is blurry. I grab his shoulder. I lean towards his ear and shout as loud as I can.

"Do you know where there's some water?"

It's not so easy. We're trapped in the circle. There are at

least eight rows of linked hands holding us hostage. We walk clockwise, looking for a way through. Everyone is too drunk and too ecstatic to let us break out.

Finally, he lifts a pair of hands so I can duck underneath. He crouches and follows, tripping a few people in the process, who giggle as they tumble into a pile. We dodge our way through like this, one line at a time.

Next to a barrel of wine is a barrel of water. He lifts the lid for me and I dip the shared mug in, and pour water into my mouth. Now that we're a few yards away from the crowd, my ears are ringing from the sound. Smaller dance circles and laughing conversations radiate out from the quieter sections of the garden. A pile of women share a hammock, passing around a mug of wine.

Some men perch on fences, content to watch and admire. They know not to join the Nature Artists up on the patio covers. A man fell to his death a few years ago, landing on the edge of the brick flower bed. The limited mind-body connection of men is most poignantly illustrated when they cross their limits. No plant remedy can stop that much bleeding. Not even tuning forks heal crushed bones fast enough.

We're on the promenade that leads back to the garden gates. Above a row of jasmine, I see a familiar fluff of soft hair.

Omar. Before he turns the corner, coming into full view, I duck behind the water barrel. I need to tell Omar to call off his research, and I need to tell him that privately. Also, I'm not letting this gorgeous South Calefean man out of my sight until that gong rings. And thirdly, I'm a little drunk.

"Get down here!" I say to the man with the braids. I've nicknamed him FM, for First Mate, in hopes my intention is amplified by putting words to it. Plus, I haven't bothered to ask his name yet.

He grins and crouches next to me.

"We have to hide," I whisper. "I have a ..." I consider how to best explain Omar. "I have an admirer."

"Of course you do," he says.

I bite my lip. I remember how I gazed at my reflection in Sequoia's mirror. He's right. I look amazing tonight.

I point down a row of thick bushes. "This way!"

We crawl onto the grass. I pull my long skirt into a knot. Lava will want to know how I got wet dirt on her dress. I chuckle at the thought of me retelling this story. I'd call it, "The great escape from Omar." She'll be amused.

At the end of the row, I peek over a yellow rose bush. Omar stands by the water, where we just were. But this row is a dead end. It turns in a U and takes us right back. We can't get to the next section of the garden without climbing through thorns.

"That guy?" FM points.

"If you stand next to me and block my face, we can walk by and he won't see me," I say.

We stand and brush off our knees. Omar's drinking water from the same mug I just used, and is scanning the landscape. He's never been to a Lunar Party before, as far as I know. It's not for everyone. I put my hand around FM's waist and lean my face into his shoulder, keeping my nose down. We walk casually, until we pass Omar and then we drop arms and run for the crowded gazebo. There's an a cappella group gathering. From behind, I look like any woman. In this dress, I don't look like myself.

"Deer!" I hear him yell.

We sprint past the singers and around a potted palm tree, almost tripping on a kissing couple huddled in a shadow. A second man taps her arm as if to join in. She glances up and the flicks him away. He moves on.

Ahead of us is the sweet odor of freshly replanted shrubs, a thick wall of them.

"The maze!" I say.

TEN

The Queen's maze has the tallest hedges. The Queen is said to walk in it with her cats to make all her important decisions. Her gardeners uproot bushes and rearrange the rows at random intervals so she never knows if she's entering a new maze. It stretches 100 yards square. A person could finish in as little as 20 minutes, or be lost for days. The inherent challenge of the maze is a function for how the Queen tunes her intuitive abilities. If she's stuck amongst the floral pathways, she knows she's headed in the wrong direction mentally, too.

I've always wanted to try the maze.

The first row forks into three options, divided by hedges of honeysuckle. Our first choice.

"Middle," I say.

"You sure about this?" FM says.

"What, you don't trust me?" I slap his shoulder the way Lava always does to me.

We hold hands. Our feet brush together as we find a rhythm in our pace. A marine layer blows in from the west, bringing a moist chill over the plants. From an epicenter in my palm, where it meets his palm, heat rises through my body.

At the end of a row of green giant trees, we turn right to face a long, narrow path. I start to run.

FM pulls my hand back

"What's the hurry?" he says.

I flip around to face him and laugh. "I want to win!"

He walks closer until our noses touch. "Speed doesn't matter for that." He puts a palm on each of my cheeks. "At least that's what the tortoise told the hare."

He knows my favorite children's book. I always think of it when I see rabbits on the ocean cliffs. "So you're a literary type," I say.

Behind him, a brown rabbit jumps across the path.

"Ahh!" I yelp, jumping backwards.

He laughs.

"I think you planned that, somehow," I say. The small animal disappears under the hedges.

"Communicating with animals? Ha, if only I had the skills of a Sage, that would be...." His voice drifts off. "But, I'll race you to that next bend."

He runs ahead. I try, but I can't catch up. Even after years of morning jogs, there's no way I can match his long, graceful strides.

He stops short at the next corner. I collide with his back. It's a small clearing encircled with trellised white rose vines. Three women and two men are intersecting on the grass.

A hand holds a cake to a mouth. A tongue licks a breast. My eyes follow the white flowers up to the starry sky and rising moon. We have at least another hour.

"Cake?" The hand holds out a square of fluffy yellow pound cake with pink frosting.

I'm tempted. The maze will only become harder to navigate in the dark. I inhale body aroma from FM's shoulder. I don't want to share him.

I pull FM past the clearing.

"Have a good night," he says to the group as we exit, as if he regrets leaving so quickly.

The route splits again. A long hall in the reverse direction, or a curving path lined with poplar seedlings.

"It's tricky, but I bet that one dead-ends," I say, pointing to the curved path.

We turn down the long hall, and this time we walk slowly.

"Are the stars the same in South Caleaf?" I ask. I know they are, but I want to hear his voice again.

"They're never as bright as they were—on Sister Earth," he says.

"We were closer then," I say. "To the center of the galaxy."

"I could feel it when we stepped off the Homecoming Voyage," he says. "The atmosphere here is less charged. Less alive."

I laugh. "We had no responsibilities on Sister Earth. Eat when you're hungry, sleep when you're tired."

"Sometimes I want to go back." His bare foot brushes mine. "Living at one with nature. Not adjacent to it. You get a little of it back, on nights like this."

His voice is smooth in my ear, like a cup of warm cacao. I want to ask him every question in the universe. I can't decide where to start.

"How many years ago was it for you?"

"More than you," he says.

So he's older.

"I didn't know you on Sister Earth," I say.

"I remember you," he says.

I look down at my dress. It's wrinkled from our crawl and damp with sweat. I've never exposed my breasts so boldly. I'm tempted to gawk at them myself. Usually, they're comfortably tucked in my sundresses—well, ever since Sister Earth.

If he knew me on Sister Earth, he's already seen everything.

I look up at his face, rough with facial hair. I see a few speckles of white. He might be close to 40, when men age out of mating season to avoid mating with a genetic relative. Older, they can still become husbands or lovers—with Sage permission. I wonder if that's his goal—to be chosen as a husband.

"Do men do this together?" I ask. "I mean, without a woman present?"

"Make love?" he says.

"Because women do," I say.

On Sister Earth, it's like we're all siblings, all naked, our hands all over each other but never in an intimate way. The initial years in Caleaf, before Lolanda or Jacara went out for mating season, we experimented.

"I prefer women," he says.

We turn a corner. We're facing the hedge of honeysuckle back at the beginning of the maze. We went in a circle.

I made a mistake. We're running out of time. If Omar followed us into the maze, he's in here, too.

"Are you giving up?" FM says.

"Your choice." I point to the remaining two options.

FM CHOOSES the entrance on the far left. I'm relieved. I was going to pick the opposite side. It would be just like me to accidentally choose the route Omar is on and run right into him at the worst possible moment: when the gong is played.

We pass the honeysuckle and walk along a horizontal row of juniper bushes, then a switchback. If this is a series of switchbacks that stretches the whole length of the maze, each one two yards wide, well, that would mean we had 50 rows to get through. At least we'd be getting closer.

The switchbacks get shorter on every turn by the length of one bush of juniper. Like Sequoia predicted, there's a flurry of mosquitoes around the plants, increasingly drawn to our warm bodies.

"I'm getting eaten alive," I say.

I stop to stretch my legs. My thigh muscles are sore from the earlier dancing.

"We don't have to finish," he says.

"No, I want to."

We step into a large clearing. There's a stone fountain and a carved wood bench. To my surprise, it is vacant. Fewer revelers have wandered this way.

My sense of direction is twisted from the switchback turns. On the other side of the fountain, the path continues. An ivy-clad boundary wall marks the eastern end of the maze. To the right, we're free of the tall trees and shrubs. Rows of thorny rose-bushes are lit by the moon and stars, their scents filling the open air.

The rosebushes are pruned to the height of my chest. The colors don't seem to be in a particular order. I tilt my head.

"I think it's a square spiral," I say. "Let me climb on your back."

FM kneels and I press my foot to his hip. He stands and I get a better view. Our path along the boundary wall doesn't connect with the square spiral. It must have an entrance further along—or be connected to the path we didn't take. At a far corner, I see a figure moving. It's not a bunny this time. It's a man, and he's getting closer.

I slide off FM's back.

"Deer!"

It's Omar. He's halfway to us, still a few rows away, jogging, and I half expect him to attempt a high jump over the rose hedge. He sees the turn, and keeps going—he thinks there will be an opening down the line. But the spiral bushes will keep taking him back into the center. He can't get to us.

I know he promised to look for me, but you'd think me disappearing into a maze with another man would send a message. I remind myself that Omar doesn't always pick up on nuance.

Our path may not deliver us to victory. It could still take a twist that dumps us into the exact dead end Omar is in. Or, if my theory is right, Omar took a different route completely, and we won't cross each other.

We enter another section of green giant trees, more switchbacks, more juniper bushes. A fork breaks off. I jog down one direction and a turn opens into a clearing with a wooden swing hanging from a mature oak tree.

A couple sits in the swing, hip-to-hip, facing opposite ways, gaze locked. Sequoia and Edgar look at each other like that. Even those who have started mating before tonight, like Lava and Sequoia, are waiting for the gong. It heightens pleasure when we all do it at the same time.

More pleasure means more mating. More mating means more eggs. More healing. More art. We all come together at the spring Lunar Party, united with a common goal.

Abundance.

Prosperity.

Delight.

When Jacara was a mater a few years ago, she told me mating is not so different than lovemaking. It's just a particular arrangement of body parts. She was glad her first time was at a Lunar Party.

"You have options in a crowd," she told me a few years ago, in those final days before she took voyage. "The men show up, thinking they're ready. But you always ask first, and sometimes they're too shy to go through with it. Sometimes your first choice can't complete the mating, so you move on, and you know, all the men cry after."

I must have looked worried, even then. She added, "Babe, you can't do it wrong or right. Your body takes over. You're along for the ride."

I look at the moon. We have 30 minutes to go.

The next clearing, however beautiful, is occupied—and a dead end. I turn back to FM.

The party music is growing faint. The musicians will trail off a few minutes before the gong as an early warning. The gong will be impossible to miss. Even from my mother's residence, a mile outside of town, I hear it every year. Even fast asleep, the deep vibrations ring through my heart and wake me up.

"Is this your first mating season?" I ask.

He might remember me from Sister Earth, but I don't even remember seeing him pass through town in previous years.

"I've lost count," he says.

I nod, but I doubt that is true. There are only two kinds of men. The ones who come to the Lunar Party once for the novelty and then never again. Or, the ones who come every single year until they turn 40. It's a thick energy, seeing people doing things they wouldn't dare talk about the rest of the year. A person would love or hate it.

I want to ask about other women he's been with. Did she have Ivy's flower bodice? Or, Lava's flowing skirt? I've seen a medley of shapes, splashing in the ocean with my friends.

Our pace slows to an easy stroll. Even with the switchbacks, we're getting closer to the far end of the maze. The southern brick wall comforts me with its anchor of direction. That doesn't mean we'll reach an exit. We could come all this way, only to collide with a late dead end.

I stop to sniff a hibiscus blossom. When I look up, FM has turned the next bend, and I'm face-to-face with Omar.

"I found you," he says.

There's only one way out. He must have gone back to the entrance, then ran along the hills on the outside of the maze, and entered through the exit.

"Hi, Omar," I say.

The night is quiet. Too quiet. Even the crickets have taken the cue to pause their song.

FM comes back around the bend. I look at him, then Omar, then the moon.

It's bright, as full as it can be to my naked eye.

"I need to tell you something," Omar says.

I know I'm drunk, but he looks crazed. This isn't just a return on his promise to look for me. I think he is really expecting us to mate.

I told Lava he wouldn't understand. Men always conflate mating with romance, especially younger men, like Sequoia's Edgar. They don't understand that it's just about fertilization.

My night is ruined. When I reject Omar, the beautiful man I've been calling FM is going to feel awkward, and leave me here alone.

Omar looks at FM and pauses.

"It will just be a minute," I say. FM steps away to give us privacy.

Omar leans his face up to my ear. His soft hair brushes my cheek.

"Deer, I don't want you to go."

"With him?"

"No, on voyage," he says. "I found something."

It takes me a moment to remember. That research that I asked him—that I need to tell him to not do. Whoops.

"Someone was missing from the last Homecoming Voyage."

I slap a hibiscus branch. "So, one of the kids forgot to board with her class. It's not like we keep track of our ages on Sister Earth."

"Kids always know. They know in their gut when it's their turn," Omar says.

"Well, what else could have happened?" I say.

"There might be a problem, some kind of problem on Sister Earth. They'll find out for sure on your voyage, and if it's bad, they might not let you come back."

I find his eyes. He's blinking fast. His gaze drops to my dress.

"Oh Omar, this is what women do. We can't stop now. It's up to us to advance the next generation."

I sound like my mom lecturing my dad about dinner party table arrangements.

FM comes back around the hedge. "Hey, uh, the moon is getting close," he says.

We're alone, the three of us, in this corner of the maze.

FM smiles at Omar. I hadn't considered that. He wants both of us. My heart pounds.

Omar clears his throat.

For once, I don't think of Jacara's advice, or what Lava would say, or what a respectable Calefean woman would do for the greater good. I think of myself. I don't want to share FM with anyone else. Not other women, and certainly not Omar.

I grab FM's hand. "Let's go to my loft," I say.

I pull him around the next bend of the maze. More switch-backs. A row of jasmine. A trellised arch.

This is the exit. We made it out.

The hills beyond the trees are the same ones that run along the south side of my mom's residence, but it will be difficult to navigate the uneven terrain in the dark. Going back through the gates of the government building and the roads in town will be faster.

We exit the government building and continue down the sea glass-paved main street. At the end of the business district, we turn left, the opposite direction of the South Calefean tents on the fields.

When the gong rings, we're on a tree-lined street of four-story residences.

I slow down and inhale a familiar scent—gardenia. I see the bushes in the corner of my eye, the white petals bright with moonlight. I avert my gaze from turning further. I know the house with the lounge chairs on the patio still has only one red flag. It still hurts me to think of the blacksmith. A single red flag is just a warning. It won't take away your motherhood stipend. But it's the women who shun you, who exclude you from shows and social events, not wanting to be associated with a woman worthy of the Sages' warning.

With the vibration of the gong still echoing through my chest, I look up at FM. This spot is as good as any. His rough palms frame my cheeks. I reach my fingers up to his braids, pulling his face down into a wet kiss.

"It's not that much further," I say.

We run faster.

I let the front door slam behind us and take two steps at a time up to my third floor loft.

It's dark. I consider lighting a candle. I remember what Jacara said about letting your body take over.

I feel his lips with my fingers and replay the day and evening. The dancing. The maze. Now Sequoia is somewhere on the hills. Lava is breaking her records. Even at a distance, I feel the sexual energy flowing from the gardens. It's creative power. It's in all of us.

I pull the strings of the dress loose and close my eyes. He runs his hands down my chest, my back, and my legs, then lifts me up and curls me on top of him.

"WHAT'S YOUR NAME?"

"Walt," he says.

I roll off the bed and walk through the dark to the washroom. In the mirror, I admire my naked shape, then my face. My hair's fallen out of the bun and braid.

Lava was right. You feel more yourself afterwards. Who the man is doesn't matter.

I lick my lips. They're raw from his rough cheeks.

Back on the bed, I climb on top of him.

"I want you again," I say.

He grabs his black T-shirt off the pillow, folds it into one long piece, and sits up. He wraps it over my eyes and ties it behind my hair.

I flinch. The dim star-lit room is gone. All I see is pitch black. I can feel his breath near my lips. My own breath warms my nostrils.

"Is this okay?" he asks.

He tickles my neck and squeezes my butt. I laugh and try to keep up with where his hands are going next. He's better than any woman I've been with. I'm breathing harder. I swing my arms around but can't find his body.

I am spinning in open space. The black in front of my eyes lightens, even though I still feel his shirt snug over my nose. It turns into a scene. There's movement—whitewater of a crashing wave. Then, another. My body is falling, rolling in whitewater on the way to Monterey, and I can't feel which way is up.

I relax into the surface beneath me. Is it my bed? Is it sand? I'm back on a beach, and a gentle wave rolls toward me. It's foam reaches my toes.

Here we go again.

I OPEN MY EYES. The T-shirt is gone. I'm in my bed with a sheet pulled over me. Walt is on the floor, fully dressed, leaning against the bedside table.

"Did I hurt you?" he says.

"Was I asleep?" I say.

"You were screaming."

The dream always starts with the empty beach I saw in the Records, and it always ends the same.

"Did I say—any words?"

"You said a few things. The last thing I heard was, *run*."

I sit up. There was more to the dream. Every time it plays out a little differently. This time, something happened between the empty beach and the whitewater. It's like something in my peripheral vision, in time or space. I can't quite grasp it. If I had turned my head—

"I need to write this down so I don't forget," I say. "You should go."

"Now?"

I pull a blanket off my bed and wrap myself with it. He's seen too much of me.

"I have to be alone to concentrate."

He stands up.

"When I have a bad dream," he says, pausing by the stairwell. "I just say to it, 'You aren't real.'"

"Thanks for the advice," I say.

"Can I see you again?" he asks from the stairwell. "I'll be at the art show."

The art show. My poetry debut. It's either the worst thing or the best thing for this gorgeous man to be there. "I—I would really like that," I say.

Whatever I said in my sleep, at least it wasn't weird enough to scare him away. The front door latches as he leaves.

At my desk, I write in big letters, filling the page.

Run.

The little girl said it.

No, I must have said it.

Wait. Who am I?

In the Records, we always see through a human memory. In the dream, I couldn't be myself. I wouldn't be standing on Sister Earth's beach, as a grown woman, watching my own child hatch.

That would mean I'm seeing through the eyes of someone else. Another child?

When we query the Records, we can tell right away if the role we've taken is male or female, young or old, from contrast in the body anatomy. In earlier versions of the dream, I felt more like I was viewing from some disembodied bubble. But in this version, the scene was solid. I felt real. I was there, with her, but I couldn't save her.

Again.

ELEVEN

A few years ago, when Lolanda was a few weeks into the festivities of mating season, she started skipping our early morning surf sessions.

I'd mostly given up on seeing her. She surprised me, waving like usual from the beach, her arm wrapped around her fuschia shortboard, acting as if she hadn't broken our rhythm.

There was a lull in the break, the ocean temporarily at ease. She paddled right up to me and rested her heel on my board to link us together.

"Promise you won't tell," she said, then continued her story, confident of my trustworthiness. "I had a dream," she said. "I saw my daughter."

I couldn't tell if she was crying, or if the saltwater was draining her nasal fluids.

"I get it now," Lolanda said. "Childbearing is the most profound of arts."

That was our moment. I was the one she wanted to tell. I'd kept her secret.

Now it haunts me.

If she hadn't told me she dreamed of her daughter, I might be able to consider my own dream to be cognitive dust. But it's as real as daytime.

My dreams were fading in the days leading up to the Lunar Party. When I was writing more poetry. But after my encounter with Walt—the worst version of the dream, yet—the dreams have returned in full force. When I go to bed, I hold my eyes open as long as I can handle.

Most nights I wake up in a sweat. I see her again. Sometimes she's holding my hand. Sometimes I push her onto the sand. Sometimes I only see the fear in her eyes. Now I know why. Now I know what she's running from. It's a white snake that erupts from the ocean. Then she's gone with a loud snap.

I try walking through the rose gardens. I try jogging on the spectacular coast. I sample treats at the weekly market. I repeat in my head. It was just a bad dream. We all have bad dreams.

Despite my efforts, my mind-body connection is getting worse.

I collide with a wall walking down the stairs to the kitchen. The wall is innocent. It remains in the same physical location it's always been. I close my eyes and move my arm towards it, then away. It's as if the wall doesn't exist—until my hand touches it. The dense taffy feeling of being close to an object, or a person approaching from behind you, is completely gone. How on earth will I move through the downtown markets without tripping over everyone? I'll expose myself as having dead intuition in a heartbeat.

I stub my toe coming up the stairs. The houseplants next to my desk are turning yellow. Any of these symptoms, individually, would be appropriate for dropping by the Sages for a tune-up, but then they would see my dream. They would know I'm a killer.

What would it be like to get a red flag before even becoming a mother?

The Amateur Art Show is only a few days away.

I can't write poems in this state.

I'm agitated

I'm spiraling.

I can't write.

Maybe Lolanda was wrong. Once, I read a book about dream interpretations in the Records. It said water symbolizes emotions, stairs symbolize personal growth, and poop symbolizes inadequacy. There must be an entry for snakes.

I hum a C to open the Records.

Nothing happens.

I've lost my intuitive access.

In the kitchen, I rub my hands together over a slice of apple pie Dad left cooling by the window overnight.

I take a bite. It's stone cold.

I spit it out into my hand and take the slice out to the compost bin. I'll be limited to fresh fruits and breads until I can resolve this imbalance.

The dearth of intuition is not the only way my body is changing. My night with Walt activated my reproduction. I have fertilized eggs, right now, in this moment, and I'll need to lay them by summer.

But I can't get on that spaceship.

I need to find a way to lay my eggs here.

When I was drunk at the Lunar Party, Omar told me something, but it wasn't about the phosphorus in the sand, as I had specifically asked. He'd said something else, something haunting, about the voyage.

Looking back, I acted like a child, drunkenly running past him to get in the maze. I should apologize for that.

He also made a good point at the cafe. Even if there are appropriate minerals here on Earth, the children still need isolation.

There is one place on Caleaf that could work, because it's naturally secluded by barriers of land and sea. It's a place where no humans have resided in centuries. I know, because I've been there—at least, in the Records. I've been there when it was a small shipping port. I've been there when it was a tourist destination. And I've been there as one of the last survivors, in the Great Earthquake aftermath, once Caleaf broke off from the mainland and any building still standing was on fire. The only question is whether it has appropriate foliage to feed the next generation.

Monterey.

THE SUN IS ALREADY hot under my feet the next morning when I run the clifftop path, my wooden surfboard balanced on my head, past Lava's treehouse to the ocean break.

I won't be riding any waves today.

I paddle just past the break and turn south. Going alone gives me the benefit of speed. It also means I must get there and back well before sunset to have time to return to town before nightfall. If I miss dinner, my parents will worry. If someone misses plans and is unreachable intuitively—the Code calls for a search party.

Other women are back on shore, trading gossip and braiding flowers into their hair. They're practicing their art for the Amateur Show. They're getting a head start on mating season, like Lava and Sequoia.

I want to peel my skin off, head to toe, to know what I am

beneath. I just can't find a way to do what's expected, without pushing for more. It's a beautiful island where everyone has what they need. How'd I get signed up for the chaotic role?

After an hour of steady paddling, I dunk my head in the water to cool my dark hair. I'm keeping my knees bent, my soft soles facing the sun. I've seen Pacific Ocean creatures in the Records. The only peace accord the Sages made with them was the boundary line between land and sea. Sharks, squid, and seals. They could all still be swimming these waters.

Paddling on the outer edge of the break, I am just on the border of the boundary of land creatures.

I pass the seaweed jungle I got stuck in with my friends. Beyond, there is a rocky bay. Further, a cliff that blocks my view of the coastline. To avoid getting slammed where the waves crash on the rocks, I have to paddle further out.

I pick up some speed. My fingers are numb in the cold water. The back of my neck roasts in the sun.

I'm almost past the rocks when I get pulled into a current toward a long stretch of rocky beach. First, a fight against it. I'm nearly worn out when I let it pull me diagonally towards the shore, still making some headway forward. The water is dark and I can't see how shallow it might be over the rocks. If I hit a rock and break my board, I won't be able to get back home.

Bigger waves roll in. The beach faces northwest. This swell is not like what we have on our home beach. I push through the whitewater of one wave, only to see the rise of another wave ready to break on me.

In the crash, I drop my board. My fingers are stiff from the cold water. Instinctively, I bring my arms to my face to protect my head.

When I come up, I'm facing a wall of water. This time, it's an even bigger wave.

I tumble in the whitewater and lose my sense of direction.

With each wave, the current is pulling me closer to the rocks. I don't know which way is up. I hold my break and let my body go limp, just like I taught in the Records one time when I took the role of a junior lifeguard instructor. I break the surface.

I have just enough time to gasp in another breath before a third massive wave pounds me down.

When I emerge, I see my board. The painted red stripe on the wood is a lifesaver.

I swim, thrusting alternative arms and kicking, pushing my board back to deeper waters past the break. I climb on and lie on my back to recover.

The hot sun defrosts my limbs. I wipe my forehead and feel a sticky substance. I squint my eyes open and see a red streak on my hand. It's blood. I have a gash on my forehead.

If I were at home, I would apply frankincense so it can heal without an aesthetically displeasing mark.

I'm not home. I'm in the ocean. Home to sea creatures that can sense a drop of blood from miles away. I lick the blood off my hand and dab my forehead again. It's probably too late.

The worst I can do is stay here in the water. At this point, Caleaf is further away than my destination.

I paddle on. Left, right, left, right. My arms burn but as I reach smoother waters, I pick up momentum. I pass coves I've never seen before, and the sun inches across the sky.

I'm in unknown waters, but the hills I see on land are starting to resemble the scene from the Records. There's a long sandy beach, and then a cliff point jutting out into the water. I come around the bend and I see it. The gentle bay.

I'm in Monterey.

THE SUN IS in the middle of the sky. That gives me a few hours on land before I need to paddle back.

I lean my board against a tree and follow a broken path eroded by floodwater and landslides up the embankment.

It's quiet here. The landscape looks more scraggly. There are no well-worn trails and no meadow clearings for large gatherings. Even the plants are different species. The abundant wild plants we eat on Sister Earth, wood sorrel and lamb's quarters, don't seem to grow here.

That's a bad sign. The reason Sister Earth is such an appropriate planet for our children is because its climate and terrain matches that of Caleaf. The vegetation is the same. Yes, we only eat wild plants and berries on Sister Earth, and we bulk up once we begin eating bread and dairy, after we come back on the Homecoming Voyage. But I wonder why Monterey, which is just down island from downtown, closer to central Caleaf even than South Caleaf, would have such distinct vegetation.

And the food is the lesser of my problems.

What I'm really here for is the sand. I lean down and scoop it up into my hands. The cool wetness of the lower layer is moist on my palms.

"How much phosphorus?" I say aloud.

The tactile senses on my hands and the vast processing power of the Records come together and produce a number instantaneously.

Well, they used to.

Judging by my facial wound on the trek here, my intuition is still off.

I try an easier question. The kind of question that ancient humans, with absolutely no intuitive proficiency, were still able to answer accurately. A yes/no question.

"Is this enough phosphorus for a human egg shell to develop?"

I feel into my gut. Is it a light, affirmative tingle? Is it a heavy no?

My stomach grumbles. All it's saying is, *I'm hungry*. I didn't bring snacks. I expected to be able to eat the vegetation here, but the first rule of foraging is to only eat a plant that you recognize by name.

There's one more way I can evaluate the sand. If I can get to a dark enough space, the phosphorus will glow. Like it does in the waves on Sister Earth at night. It's like a light show.

I pile a few handfuls of sand into the pouch of my swimsuit.

Old Monterey had a tunnel. There have been a lot of weather events across the centuries, but who knows—it could still be here.

Steel posts mark where the old buildings burned down. The ash from the fires has long since soaked into the dirt. Big boulders of white stone are smooth from centuries of rain. I touch one, and the edge crumbles into my hand. I cannot expect anything here to be solid.

I braid my tangled hair before the wind dries it into a frizz. Something I should have done earlier on this trek.

The ruins stretch over rolling hills. I walk across a grassy field to a higher elevation. From the unobstructed view, I see mountains like I do from downtown Caleaf, blocking the eastern coast that is many miles away.

I recognize the structure I want. I've seen it in the Records many times

In the shade of a tree is the dark opening of a stairwell. It will be filled with rubble and rainwater. There could be rotten remains of creatures fallen in. I use a tree branch to brush off each step ahead of me until I am fully in the dark.

At the bottom of the stairs, my eyesight adjusts. The wet air smells of mildew. The tunnel turns a corner and leads to another set of stairs, further down. I've already gone at least 10.

My face tickles with sweat. I brush my arms, unsure if I'm feeling a stray hair or crawling bugs.

I grab a fist of sand and hold it up. It's hard to tell. A stream of light angles in from above.

The next set of stairs would take me deeper into the Earth. I'm afraid of what I might see there, in the blackness, with my eyesight completely gone.

I imagine my mom gossiping, as if about a neighbor. "She went all that way and then stopped?"

For the first time today, I pause. It hits me. I'm alone and nobody knows where I am.

This was my plan. I was to discover the motherlode of phosphorus sand, then paddle back to Monterey's beach before voyage to lay my eggs here. Convince my friends to do it with me, even!

What would the Sages think of that? Would they let me enter my art in shows and build a residence, and collect the Motherhood Stipend? Or would they make me wait 20 years, to prove my eggs not only developed and hatched, but that my kids survived.

In the meantime, I'd be squeezing my fingers together, day by day, wondering if my child would know to forage food, walk uphill to freshwater streams, and nurture her intuitive abilities with the Records, without the guidance of older kids. She'd be secluded, yes. She wouldn't be safe.

"There's nothing here for her," I say. "Not even sorrel."

When I left home this morning, I was on the verge of some great discovery, worth fighting past waves and seaweed and even a facial scar.

In the dark underground, I feel as forgotten as this old city. I see who I really am. I'm a selfish woman who can't find my place.

I hear another voice in my head. This time it's Sequoia, whispering in Lava's ear.

"She went all that way and she could have just asked a Sage about the phosphorus?"

When I return to daylight, the air smells sweeter. I imagine the beauty of a sunset over Monterey's broad bay.

But I'll never see it.

TWELVE

The arts in rural South Caleaf are biased towards the Nature varieties: agriculture, animal sanctuaries, and flower gardens. Most men who traveled up for the Lunar Party return to their bosses right away. Their roles require it.

The women stay the full week to take part in the next stage of mating season: the Amateur Art Show.

Since returning from my failed trip to Monterey, I've been making up for lost time at the parties. Lava's mom, Primrose, hosted a guitar concert of the masters Kean and Jollio at one of her vineyards, an excuse for her dancer daughters to demonstrate their skills.

At a picnic hosted by the South Calefean women, I sampled their specialties Gala apples and date creams. In previous years, they blended their flavorful dates with ice cream, but they're subject to the ice shortage, too. Even at a neutral temperature, it's still delightful.

In all the bustle, I keep an eye out for Walt. He said he'd be staying around—at least until the art show.

I log four more mates. I jog the cliffs in the morning, work on poetry in the afternoon, and dawdle around town through dinnertime, tracing light and sound to the next sweaty dance party.

The days stack on top of each other. If I had let the dream after the Lunar Party derail my intuition again, I'm past it now. My intuitive skills are returning. Before I go to bed, I repeat the words Walt told me to get it to stop: *You're not real.* I haven't had the dream again, and I feel myself getting stronger.

Run.

Write.

Mate.

My mom avoids the kitchen when I stop in for a meal, and I purposefully stay out through dinnertime. She knows what mating season is like. She's been to parties just like these and knows how grueling it is to rack up mates. I resolve to find more.

Even with mating going so well, my poetry does not improve.

After losing my access to the Records, I'm getting better at writing from scratch, from pure willpower, without reading ancient masters like Mary and Anais to initiate the creative flow.

When I finally do enough exercises to get back into the Records, I realize how bad my work is, in comparison to what's been written in the past few millennia. Even my quest to be mediocre is hopeless.

I start to think I'm better off reading an old poem. If I at least bring to the show something Adollo reviewed, I'll know it isn't complete trash. But those old poems aren't exciting to me anymore.

I practice reading aloud, looking out the open window and assigning the sparrows on the patio fence as my spectators. My voice sounds flat. I can't conjure up volume. These words do not stir my emotions. If I can't feel my own poem, no one will.

I avoid the only word that does inspire me.

Piezoelectric.

After a particularly numb reading, I give in.

I say it aloud.

"Piezoelectric."

The birds screech. They flutter off the fence and swirl in a frenzy. Far away, other flocks return their calls. I take a sweeping bow. One by one, the birds settle back down into their places.

For once, I feel satisfied. It's the best reaction I could have hoped for, and it gives me an idea for the Amateur Art Show.

I'll do my exercises before the show to clear out my intuitive system. I'll go up on stage with nothing planned.

I'll improvise a poem in real-time, in front of a live audience. I won't have to conjure a performative delivery because I'll be a spectator and performer all at once.

I bet no one has done it before. This will be what makes me famous.

A smile ripples through my skin. It's something my mom would never do.

***

BY FRIDAY, I'm ready for the biggest moment of my entire career. I fold my bedding and shove it into a shoulder sack. I tie a pullover sweater around my hips, just in case. Even though early spring is warming up, it will be cooler in the Redwood clearing where the Amateur Art Show is held.

The walk to the Redwoods takes a few hours. Not everyone walks. Artists that are bringing heavy instruments, a tuba or a harp, get to borrow self-fueled buggies from the South Calefeans.

"I thought I had to tie my painting to my back," Sequoia

says. "If I had known someone would offer a space for it in their buggy, I would have used a bigger canvas."

"If I remember correctly, your painting is already as big as you," Lava says.

We take turns holding a big umbrella to shield all three of us from the glaring sun.

"Is it a life-size self-portrait?" I say. Her teacher is famous for her sepia-toned portraits.

"Why would you say that!" Sequoia is suddenly hostile.

"I didn't mean—it's a foundational exercise. I wasn't implying you're self-absorbed. Let me try again," I say. "It's Edgar."

"Close, but no further comment." Sequoia giggles. "I'm the same as you, Deer. I like to build some suspense for my art."

"Ha!" Lava says. "You Fine Artists with your mysteries. Everyone's seen my tricks already."

We move to the left of the path to let a self-fueling buggy pass us, carrying a cheesemaker and her cheese, piled high and covered with a reflective blanket.

"See?" Lava says. "Craft Artists have no secrets. I already know she's got goat and gruyere in there."

"But once she returns from voyage, she can age them for longer. She can make more varieties," I say.

"Nature Artists are the ones with no secrets," Sequoia says. "They have to produce whatever the Craft Artists demand."

Lava leans under the umbrella. "What they do is barely an art. It's the workmen who do the watering and pruning. My mom says she chooses her grapes based on weather patterns, not the talents of a farm boss. The real inspiration is in barreling and blends."

We cross a footbridge over a freshwater stream and into the shade of the forest. Sequoia closes the umbrella and slings it over her shoulder.

"Another half mile to the clearing," she says.

In the clearing, there are at least 10 stages. Some are designed for large displays like murals and furniture, and others for special acts that require props, like trapeze. The center stage is for food. The judges, older women of Grandma El's generation, review the work of the chefs first, so their debut offerings can double as what we all eat for the weekend.

Lava's dance is tonight, so we lay our bed rolls by her stage. My poetry reading is not until Sunday. Sequoia's painting will be displayed in the gallery section all weekend for the judges to review in between performances.

The clearing fills as maters and spectators pour in from the path. Sleeping rolls extend from the raised wooden stages to the tree line.

Some women climb trees for a better view of multiple stages at once. The men stay safely on the ground. Again, I look for Walt.

Lava ducks behind a tree to change her outfit.

"Edgar didn't want to come?" I ask Sequoia.

Her boyfriend still lives with his mother, like most men of age 20 who haven't chosen their role yet. He may not need to take work, if Sequoia chooses him as husband as early as the fall.

She chews the end of her ponytail. "He talked me into mating with other men. His mating skills aren't fully developed and he says it will be better."

"That must be a relief to know your numbers will be good," I say. "And a chance to meet a greater variety of men."

More mates will help her see that getting along as kids is not a predictor of getting along as lovers. If it was, then Omar and I would be perfect! I shudder.

"My mom was right. Mating isn't the same as lovemaking," Sequoia says.

I sense she needs comfort more than congratulations, but before I can find the right words, Lava returns.

"Whoa, who's that pretty lady and where's my friend Lava?" Sequoia says.

Instead of her usual flowing dresses, Lava is wearing a stretchy black body suit. It accentuates her every curve. The pants reach her ankles. It's snug around her neck but her shoulders are bare. Her single piece of jewelry is a string of white pearls, a bright contrast to the dark fabric.

"Is it too much?" she says.

"It's stunning," I say. The body suit fits her so perfectly that I know it is custom made to her precise measurements. The designer who is an expert on pants is Lolanda.

"But is it—"

"Yes. It's made by your friend Lolanda. To be honest, what I asked for was something unique. I didn't expect her to go in this direction. I hope ... it doesn't look bad?"

"Monochrome is interesting. Sometimes less is more," Sequoia says.

I imagine Sequoia revealing her painting, only to find the canvas is painted pure onyx all over. I stifle a laugh.

I've always admired Lava's curves, but this outfit is not her style. She's outlined like a two-dimensional silhouette. Earlier, she said she had no surprises. This certainly counts as a surprise to me.

Because Lolanda made the outfit, to admire Lava would be to compliment two friends at once. The words are easy. I don't know why I hesitate.

"Your dance will be unforgettable," I say.

LAVA'S TIME slot comes after dark. Even the stars are blocked by tall trees and clouds. To illuminate her movements, candles are lit on the edges of the stage and hung in leather pockets from the surrounding trees.

She chose to perform with no backing music. She doesn't need it. Her intuitive talent is rhythm.

Lava starts with her familiar hip swirls. She moves into spins. These are basic moves, the ones she leads with on the dance floors at parties because they're easy for everyone to follow. She shows her proficiency with grace and lightness. She introduces jumps, and the wood platform creaks on each landing.

The crowd murmurs at a daring backbend. The pleasant noise is overshadowed by a distant cheer—a percussion artist a few stages away is playing her finale.

Lava's hip shimmy is her most mesmerizing move, but it's not the same without her thighs exposed. The outfit lacks even a decorative fringe to enhance her movements. Still, she maintains the rhythm, continuously. She can do this one longer than any of her sisters. I try not to blink or breathe. She keeps going.

She claps her hands above her head and slides into the splits. The crowd erupts.

The front row stands, generating a wave of energy to the edges of the crowd as spectators jump to catch a glimpse of her smiling face in her final pose. Her sisters whistle and cheer.

If I had sat up there, with the dancers, I might have gotten a better view.

Sweat drips down her cheeks when she returns to our cluster of bed rolls. She kisses Sequoia's cheek, then mine.

"You did good," I say. "How do you feel?"

She giggles. "I ... don't know." She wraps a blanket over her shoulders and settles in to watch the next act, already halfway through.

I've never seen Lava shy away from attention. I think of the colorful dresses Lolanda's former mentor, the ones Lava was most drawn to in the downtown shop. Lolanda herself made dresses like that at one time. But she left it all behind. She returned from voyage, changed, and decided to specialize in men's clothing.

Just like her, we're in the midst of a transition. Something changes when we become mothers.

THE EROTIC EXCESS of the Lunar Party is contained to a single night. Now the mating continues, but at a slightly more balanced pace.

As if by silent communal agreement, the clearing stays quiet for sleeping. Duos trickle off into the tree line to get a round in.

Lava's male admirers huddle nearby.

She points them out to us. "Jules and Jay are cooks at the government building. And Stevie is a chocolatier's assistant."

"With that training, they'd make good husbands," I say.

"For someone," she shrugs. She turns her head and gives them a smile. They take the cue and come over.

"Look what Jules made," the tall one, Jay, says, patting his younger colleague's shoulder.

Jules, whose face seems settled in an eternal grin, pulls something from his pocket. He hands it to Lava. She holds it up.

"You made this?" Lava says.

"It's from an oak branch I found. I carved it with a butcher knife," Jules says.

Lava passes the wood carving around. It's smooth. I expected it to be in the shape of an animal, or even a kitchen utensil, but it just seems to be an amorphous lump.

"What's it for?" I say.

"For—fun?" Jules says. Suddenly his smile is gone and he seems unsure of himself. "I like carving things."

"So it's for pleasure," Lava says. "I mean, if it's not pleasurable, why do it?" She laughs.

"Your outfit looks so soft," Stevie says to Lava. "Can I feel it?"

The way men constantly ask for permission through the mating process is endearing, but at times confounding.

"Sure." Lava smiles and kicks her foot over to him. He touches her ankle. She's back to her usual, bubbly self. Jay joins in, running his fingers up her thigh and she giggles as he reaches her hip.

"That's enough," she says. They sit back.

I'm close enough to see that their hands are strong. Not rough like a farmer's, but not pale like Omar's.

"So the Queen gives you all the weekend off for the Show?" Sequoia asks.

"The full week," Stevie says. He puffs his chest. "We're expected to do our part. For mating season."

"For Caleaf!" Jules says. His grin returns, full force.

That means Omar will have this week off, too. I hope he's not using it to dig through top secret files on my behalf. I can't remember what I told him at the Lunar Party. I was too drunk.

Lava takes special attention from Stevie, the tallest of her admirers, and he follows her out past the tree line. That leaves Sequoia and I with Jay and Jules. Jules has a smooth face and I decide he's as young as Sequoia. I nod at Jay to leave with me.

Even though Sequoia feels conflicted about mating, I'm glad she's getting her numbers in. It's a sign of maturity.

Caleaf's stated goal is peace, but its silent drive is progeny. As the only human civilization left, the existential fear of disappearing lives in our bones. We must produce.

Jay follows me along the mossy forest floor, climbing around fallen branches and mushroom clusters. I lean against a tree. I only brought one dress. I don't want to get mud on it the first night.

I close my eyes, and as it's become my habit, I preemptively remind the girl in my dream to stay away, using the words Walt suggested.

You're not real.

Jay finishes so quickly that I consider stepping deeper into the forest to find a second round. The candles in the clearing are blown out, though, and between the song of insects and the darkness, I could easily become disoriented out here.

When I return to my bedroll, Lava and Sequoia are already sleeping.

THE NEXT MORNING, we switch stages so we can watch the stringed instruments, and in the afternoon, we leave our bed rolls to walk through the gallery space. It's our first time seeing Sequoia's work.

My guesses were close. Her selection for the show is a painting of her mother. In the shade of the trees, her choice of muted colors bring a pleasing peace to the eyes. Her technique is flawless. Her intuitive gift of photographic memory shines through. When the scores are read out, I have no doubt she'll rank near the top, even with a relatively safe choice of expression.

It's the equivalent of Lava's dance, had she worn one of her usual dresses. Or among poetry, an ode to the foremothers. It's respectful. Patriotic. Pure.

Another oil painter attempted a wildlife landscape, but the proportions of the animals are all off. There's a watercolor of a young woman in the Queen's robes. I recognize her as the

Queen, but at a younger age. The artist must have used the collective Records to become familiar with her youthful appearance.

I look for anything truly bold, like the single-color canvas I laughed about earlier, but the artwork appears to be standard fare.

No easel is empty. If I were to go up on stage and say nothing, what would happen?

Even at a show this big, someone has to be last. It might as well be me. This is a failure my mom has logged herself many times.

I don't expect things to go that way.

The improvised poem I share will be unforgettable. Wait until people find out about my never-been-done-before process. I'll get points for originality. If it works the way I hope, my scores will qualify me to judge shows as soon as this fall.

I'll be swept into an upward cycle through Calefean society, and prove I can carry on my Grandma El's legacy.

POETS AND SINGERS wear a heavy dark robe over their clothing to perform. Their art is a medium of sound. Not vision. It must be received in its purest form.

The singers line up first. We each get a swift five minutes on stage before a judge rings a sharp bell. But, we aren't required to fill the time.

The first singer belts a series of tones, showing off her volume, and then rumbles a low note, almost outside the audible spectrum. She sucks in a breath and ends with her highest note.

She leaves stage to a polite clap and hands the robe to Ivy.

The crowd returns to an eager silence.

Ivy's hair is fluffed out again, like a lion. It makes her face appear small. She sings a minor melody with long holds punctuated by pauses.

For the purpose of a judged show, the arts are not blended. Vocalists sing a cappella and don't enunciate full words. I can hear the meaning in her sounds. It could be inferred from her cartoonish facial expressions. I close my eyes. The song is tender. But it's not a love song.

"Wistful," I say.

I bring a hand to my mouth. I didn't mean to speak aloud.

Ivy pauses her song. One beat, then another, then another. Will the song continue? The crowd claps tentatively. She nods, indicating she is finished, and the spectators rise into a standing ovation.

She's the clear star of the singers. Her mom's reputation for a wandering husband eclipses her delectable pastries, but it cannot add or subtract from Ivy's skill. She's proven she is her own woman. I picture her in her downtown loft, above her mother's bakery, in hours of focused practice, not disturbed by the gossip or the long lines of pity.

I've had every chance to shake off my mom's failures. I could have been writing, all those years, not cramming it all into the final weeks before this show.

My stomach churns. If I come up short in my performance, I will be compared to my mother. I need true flair.

The last singer walks off stage. It's down to me and the other poet going on voyage this year. I know her mentor. She'll be proficient. Because I'm older, I go first. I take the robe and wrap it over my blue sundress.

Once I reach the center of the wooden stage, I flip my long hair behind my shoulders. I turn slowly, taking in all 360 degrees of eyes on me.

My lips feel stuck together with thick honey. My mouth doesn't open. I close my eyes and take myself back a week, to the party, to that first moment in the dance circle when I realized I was holding Walt's hand. That was before I even knew his name.

When I open my eyes, I pretend I'm speaking only to him.

Piezoelectric

Pizza

Peace

A giggle rises from my belly. I can't help it. I've barely been up here 20 seconds. I pause my turning so I don't make myself dizzy. I remember my exercises. I remember to trust the poem. This must be going somewhere.

Blessed are the peacemakers, may they multiply like bunnies

That line feels like it lands. A bit more. I continue, speaking slowly to enunciate each syllable.

Piezoelectric

Perspective

Pet peeve

Now, I'm struggling to maintain my confidence. I'm breathless. But the timer is running. I need to bring this all to some kind of conclusion.

Goddess have mercy on the peacekeepers, may they disperse like seeds

Piezoelectric

Procreation

Pi

May we all measure our inspiration against the sky.

I pause. There's more time left, but I can't find the next line.

I walk off stage and hand the robe to the other poet. She's on and I'm off, back on the dirt, my efforts complete.

I'm halfway back to my bedroll when I realize there was no applause. How could I miss it? Perhaps it was brief.

"Well done, babe," Lava says.

"Thanks." I lean in for a hug.

Sequoia squeezes my shoulder.

My friends are being kind, but I just exposed myself as a fool. Sequoia might even be thinking this, sitting right next to me. Lava will defend me against any gossip. At least, I think she would.

I can't go back and fix what I've just done, and I worry the repercussions will be permanent.

AT BREAKFAST, I hold a few logs of fire-roasted zucchini and lemon jelly to eat with my hands.

"The way she's looking at you, it's like she wants to pull you out into the woods," Lava says.

I turn my head to see who Lava's staring down.

"Don't look now!"

"Ah!" I bring my eyes back down to my breakfast.

It's Monday morning, the day we walk home.

Sequoia wipes her mouth after a gulp of orange juice. "It's the singer. Ivy. She's pointing. She's talking to someone and pointing at you."

"Don't look," Lava says.

"Isn't Ivy an only child, too?" Sequoia says.

"I mean, yes? It's not like we have a club and get together to talk about it," I say.

I don't doubt that Ivy is staring, but I want to see for myself.

"I bet she's threatened," Lava says. "You stole the night from her."

"Don't be silly," I say. "My poem was unmemorable. Even I hardly remember it."

"The audience was shocked into silence. I don't think anyone heard a word that other poet said." Lava bites into a block of cheese.

"She did a love ballad, standard stuff," I say.

Sequoia swats a mosquito off her arm. "Ok but what did that line mean about the peacekeepers? That gave me goosebumps."

- Since I pulled that line straight form the ether, I don't know myself.

"Does every poem need to mean something?" I say, a little too fast.

I can't decide whether to admit to my friends that I didn't write the poem in advance. My other option is to play it off like my work is some kind of unrecognized genius. It doesn't matter, though. What ultimately matters will be the scores.

I gulp some orange juice.

Without intending to, I look over my shoulder across the crowds eating and bagging up their belongings. I see her.

Ivy.

She's staring with tired eyes, like she's been awake all night. Her eyes widen and she looks away. She pulls a bread roll from her front pocket and tears off a bite.

I sigh. I know Grandma El was used to managing fans, but did she ever have to deal with negative attention? I recall her waving at friends outside the theater—selectively—only to the women she wanted to consider her friends. The most talented women.

That's what I should have done. A pleasant wave would show Ivy I'm not afraid of her gossip.

As we finish breakfast, the judges circle through the crowds, reading the scores. These are women my mom's age, some of them older, who have been chosen to judge this most important show. You have to be a really consistent artist to get nominated to judge the Amateur Art Show, and then you still have to help pay for the production. The food. The men who came to build the stages. We're not mothers yet, but the artists who get top scores will begin to quietly be booked for commissions before we even board the ship.

"Breezy, strawberry farm boss, nine points," a navy-cloaked judge reads.

Some cheers erupt from the other side of the clearing.

"Linden, muralist, five points. Sequoia, oil painter, eight points."

"Wahoo!" Sequoia lifts both arms triumphantly. She looks happier than I've seen her before. The time away from Edgar must have been good for her after all.

While the scores are read, we fold up our belongings for the long walk back. Lava and the other Primrose sisters all get nine points for their dancing.

When the judge begins announcing the singers, my heart pounds. Poets come next. The crowd parts for the judge to walk through and it looks like she might move into the next clearing over. I strain to hear.

The judge turns and her voice travels clearly. "Seven points," she says.

Could that be mine? A seven isn't bad.

"Deer, poet," she continues. "Two points."

Oh. So the seven was for the other poet. Who did that lame love ballad. And I got a two. Two points! Could I have just gotten the lowest score in this whole show? I haven't heard many scores under five.

I'm afraid to look at my friends, but Lava leans into my shoulder. "You're a ten to me," she says.

I force a smile. "Thanks." It's all I can muster. My whole career spans out before me, and it's not even a path. It's more like the climb up the face of a rock. I am starting at the bottom.

We head down the southbound road to return to downtown Caleaf. Ahead of us, I see a man with braids, a rare South Caleafean man who had permission to stay the full week for the show.

Could it be Walt? He said he'd be here. I wonder if he heard my poem. He didn't seem the type who would care about scores. I'm tempted to jog up to the man.

He turns his head to the side, talking to a woman. His profile, with a flat and wide nose, is not Walt's.

Our night together was a week ago, and it ended suddenly with my dream. Maybe he's forgotten about me completely. I imagine everything he's done since our night together, my face fading from memory. Taken a buggy back down to South Caleaf. Returned to a job harvesting dates for their date creams, still sadly with no ice. Or maybe he works for a dairy boss. He makes cheese. I never asked.

We walk slowly to pace ourselves, and with Sequoia still carrying her canvas, but other women aren't so wise. A group skips past us on the right, dodging a buggy, humming as they go. It's the vocalists, joined by a harp player and a garden boss.

"That lady has the voice of a queen," I hear someone say behind me. I turn around. It's one of Lava's admirers, Jay. The one I mated with. He stops chuckling.

I flip back forward.

The only queen-like thing about Ivy is her lithe lioness shape. I hope she does gossip about me. I'll reclaim my honor, even if it takes me the rest of my life.

THIRTEEN

After a valiant kickstart on mating, a full week of festivities, and the forest weekend trip for the Amateur Art Show, I expected to find relief in sleeping alone again, in my own bed.

And I do.

What I didn't expect was to be awakened before dawn to the sound of cymbals. This particular instrument, with its sharp, high-volume sound, is only used in emergencies.

Wildfires.

Earthquakes.

Land creature code violations.

The man clanging the cymbals pauses every four counts to holler an order.

"All Calefeans to the fields at noon!"

"All Calefeans to the fields at noon!"

The fields will be clear. For the past week, the fields have been populated with South Calefean tents, but the men left, and now after the Amateur Art Show, many of the women have packed up to return to South Caleaf for the rest of mating season, only to come back for the voyage takeoff at the start of summer.

I splash water on my face in the washroom. The workmen will be hurrying to finish a day's work in the next few hours, and women will be gossiping in the streets about what the emergency might be.

I'll skip my morning run on the cliffs and do exercises in my room instead. I'd rather wait for the real story.

THE ROADS ARE heavy with Calefeans walking in from the outer farms and gardens. The fields are filling up. The tents are gone, but I see piles of folded canvas. I also recognize a few South Calefean faces, women wearing stretchy pants instead of sundresses. Whatever's going on has delayed the South Calefeans from leaving.

Edgar's copper red hair sticks out in the bustle. I wave, and find him with Sequoia, hand in hand. We filter the crowd together in search of Lava. We find her standing with her sisters, who are helping a citrus farm boss hand out grapefruit wedges.

A baker carrying a basket on her hip pushes past us. "Croissants! Pound cake! Baguettes!"

The gathering is an opportunity for women to express their generosity.

"My gift," the baker says, handing me an almond croissant.

"Does this happen every year?" Sequoia asks.

"No!" I say. "This has never happened. Not in my time, anyway."

Lava leans in. "I bet it's the Nature Arts. My mom says when they have an accident, they try to pin it on the land creatures to avoid getting a red flag."

"I mean, why call everyone together for that?" I say. "The ice expedition lost 20 men and we didn't bother—look, even the women from the northern farms have traveled down."

The sun is bright in the middle of the sky, and the morning's marine layer has burned off completely.

"Wait," Sequoia looks horrified. "Are you saying someone was harmed?"

This is the part I hate, where the most compelling gossip is taken for fact and no one recalls what actually happened. People only remember what they want.

"I heard someone got lost," Edgar says.

"But that's silly," Sequoia says. "We all know how to navigate with the sun."

"At night," Edgar adds.

"Okay, so wait for the sun to come back up. Then navigate. Easy," Sequoia says.

Somewhere in the field, women start singing a celebration song to keep the mood lifted. We're all stuck here until we get direction from the Sages.

Who's more beautiful than my babe,
Who's more beautiful than my friend
Who's more beautiful than my mate,
The beauty of love will never end

Women clap and shake to the beat. The sound carries as more voices join in. My throat feels tight. I take a bite of the croissant and cough after inhaling powdered sugar. I mouth the words for a few rounds. Once the collective sound is loud enough, I join softly. My pitch is never quite right. After a few rounds, I catch the tune and my voice settles in.

The edge of the crowd pours into the streets and around buildings.

I've never seen so many of us in one place. The spacecraft takeoff is the largest annual gathering, but only mothers are allowed to go. More Nature Artists are passing around their produce. I take a few apricots from a bucket.

As easily as the song started, it dies off. There is a clump of brown hoods walking through a parting in the crowd, along the sea glass road. The men behind them step forward and place a wooden pallet on the ground.

A Sage steps up onto the pallet and holds a glass loudspeaker to her face.

"My beloveds," she says. "One of us has gone missing."

Lava nods at Edgar. He was right.

"When one of us is missing, it creates a tear in our collective tapestry. But through our intuitive brilliance, when we all focus our hearts on a shared outcome and connect as one—it must come to pass!"

When I thought I might not make it back from Monterey, I never imagined that a search party would be called. I find myself both disturbed and envious to think of this many people knowing my name and coming together to help me.

Despite all the ways I feel restricted by the rules in Caleaf, I have to say that life here is something special. There's beauty in interconnection. I may have a low poetry score, but I'm just as Calefean as every person on this field.

"Some of you know the man," the Sage says.

Lava looks at me. "Of course, it's a man," she mouths.

"As we sing together," the Sage continues, "picture his face in your mind."

The singers in the crowd hum a G tone to tune the crowd. Resonance matters when it comes to collective intuition.

"As you picture his face," the Sage says. "Notice what's around it. Plants, maybe a color. Shapes. Topography. These are all clues. Blood, bruises, a particular emotion. Whatever your particular intuitive skills, put it to good use, for all of us. Whatever you sense ... follow it like a scent."

Everyone is humming now. It's a continual flow with everyone's breath starting and stopping at its own rate. When you run out of air, you inhale and start again. Some women, already receiving inspiration, step away from the group.

I keep my hum going and turn to my friends. At least one of us will get an intuitive hit and we can search together.

"Oh—and if you don't know what he looks like, we have an illustrator making a drawing," the Sage says. "His name is Walt."

She steps off the wooden pallet.

I bend over, coughing. "Just powdered sugar again." "Wasn't Walt your Lunar Party mate?" Sequoia says.

I hold my breath. My cheeks poke out. How could she know —I didn't even know his name until later in the night. "I didn't ask for his name," I lie.

I want to believe this is a mistake, that the strong man I met at the party isn't mysteriously gone. I crouch to fan my face with my hand.

"Let's get you some water," Lava says.

She pulls me toward the edge of the crowd and pumps water from a fountain well.

Sequoia and Edgar, still humming the G, follow us.

I gulp from the communal mug. My hand shakes as I set it down. I suck in a deep breath and return to humming. "Hummmmmm..."

One of the illustrators, her hand shading charcoal at the speed of a hummingbird's wings, tears a sheet off her easel and tosses it to the crowd, immediately starting on another drawing. As the portrait illustration is passed from person to person, it's unmistakable.

The missing man is Walt, my Walt. My FM.

The last time I saw him was when he left my loft in the middle of the night. My mom's residence backs up to the eastern hills that mark the boundary of downtown Caleaf. The other side of the ridge belongs to the wildlife. It is the domain of the coyotes that hunt rabbits at night.

"I want to check the hills by my mom's residence," I say. "I have a hunch."

The group follows me down the familiar road, the same one Walt and I walked together after we left the Lunar Party. We pass the house where we kissed.

"Do you think he threw a rock at a wild animal?" Lava says.

"Or climbed a tree and couldn't find his way down?" Sequoia offers.

I shiver.

"Went into the water, past the boundary, and the waves crashed him onto a rock?" Lava laughs. "Maybe he tickled a coyote! Maybe he did a handstand too close to the cliffs! Maybe he tried to pet a baby bobcat!"

I turn back and glare at Lava.

"What?" Lava says. She stops. "Wait a second. Did you love him? Deer! I've never seen you so moody about a man!"

My face heats up. "I only met him that once!" I say. "I want to find him, like any of us would." I motion to the crowds dispersing down streets and fanning out in small groups.

My heart is tight like it's been shoved into a juice press. I barely knew him, but now that he's gone, the connection feels deeper than I realized. There was more to explore between us.

"Being moody won't help us find him," Lava says brightly. "Stay positive! Maybe he was playing *Lord of the Flies* and thinks he's stranded somewhere!"

We turn the corner past my mom's patio onto the grassy hills, following a trail up the slope.

"Eww, Lava, how is that positive?" I say.

"Because I'm saying he could still be alive." Lava turns back to Sequoia and Edgar. "Isn't that how you two met? Playing *Lord of the Flies*?"

"Why would you think that?" Sequoia says.

"Because I was there!" Lava says. "Remember, we'd query it in Records circles and take turns being Piggy."

"No," Sequoia says. She and Edgar have slowed their pace, still trying to walk hand-in-hand on the narrow path. Lava stops and turns around to address them.

"No, like you don't remember playing it on Sister Earth, or no, like that's not how you met?" Lava says, her irritation spilling through.

Sequoia is silent.

"I think *Treasure Island* is how we met," Edgar says.

"The lesson in both books is the same," I say. "They should have put women on the island," I say."

Edgar clears his through. "Well, uh, I think even men today are more intuitive than when those books were written."

"Whatever." Lava throws up her hands.

Sequoia cries out. I turn to see Edgar react swiftly to catch her from falling. "My toe," she says. "I kicked a rock."

Lava and I circle back. Sequoia sits on a small boulder to survey the damage.

"If only we had ice," Edgar says as he rubs Sequoia's shoulder.

"If I hear about that ice expedition one more time—" Lava says. "You should go home and elevate it. Maybe get something from the Sages."

"She's right," Edgar says. "You can lean on me so you don't put weight on it."

"But what about the search, aren't we supposed to search until someone finds him?" Sequoia says.

Edgar turns to me and pushes the bushy red hair off his forehead. "Deer, I truly hope your man is still alive. But if he's not, well, according to the Code, when they find his body, they can review his final moments in the Records to see what happened."

I feel a jolt in my gut.

"Why not do that now so we find him faster?" Lava says. "If he's transitioned, then his memories would be uploaded already."

In all my time querying the Records, I've gotten the information I knew I needed, information I didn't know I needed, and then some stuff that's just confounding.

"You need a specific enough query," I say. "The Records are vast. If you don't know he's transitioned, the Records could just return stories of men dying without ever showing you the one you want."

"When have they ever looked up a transitioned man's Records?" I ask Edgar. "I thought looking up a person was only something women did to practice a classic artist's technique."

"They did it for the men on the ice expedition," Edgar says.

Lava rolls her eyes. "Everything comes back to the ice expedition."

I'm replaying my final moments with Walt. What had I said in my sleep?

"Edgar," I say. "Precisely how long are these final moments they would review?" I am getting increasingly agitated. The Records could easily give a Sage a few minutes or a few hours.

"There's a loophole," Edgar says.

"In the Records?" I say.

"No, in the Code," Sequoia interjects.

"If he came to a violent end, the human brain would go into shock," Edgar says.

My stomach turns. I crouch down next to Sequoia. I had no idea Edgar was as much of a Code nerd as she is, but it makes sense why they get along.

"His final memories would be trapped," Edgar continues. "That's why unplanned transitions are so hard to investigate. Even while living, your traumatic memories are trapped, and so they're essentially expunged from ever going into the Records."

"So the loophole is, you can get away with murder if you make it scary enough?" I say.

"Eww, Deer," Lava says.

Sequoia coughs, bringing her hand to her throat. "This is gross, I don't want to talk about this anymore."

Edgar rubs her temple. "I just want to explain so Deer knows what happened to her man."

"Not really my man," I mutter. "But go on."

"So they would query back to his final days, even, to see who had final encounters with the transitioned person." Edgar shifts his feet and leans closer. "And if they don't get what they need from questioning you ... the loophole is that you don't have to wait until someone transitions to see their Records. A Sage can mirror you."

"Impossible!" I say.

"Then why did the foremothers bother to make it legal?" Edgar says.

His detailed knowledge of the Records is making me nauseous. This is what these two do for fun? My goddess, Sequoia could do better.

Sequoia grips Edgar's hand. "Can we go now?"

Edgar nods. He wraps Sequoia's arm around his shoulder to help her stand and the couple exits down the rocky path. Once they're out of earshot, I return to humming the G tone.

"Hummmmm," I exhale, closing my eyes, scanning my intuition for clues.

"What are you getting?" Lava asks.

I blink my eyes open. "We have to find him before anyone else," I say.

"What—do you think he's still alive?"

"I can't tell you," I say.

Hundreds of people saw us together at the Lunar Party. I don't know for sure that he went missing right after he left my loft. He could have gone to other parties, and had other mates, in the week after. But if he's found, and one of his final memories is me sleeptalking during my dream—I need to know what I said.

I walk ahead. We're a third of the way up the big slope. I've only been to the ridge a few times. There's probably a great view of the sunrise, but of course, the wildlife is roaming free on the other side. Wildlife that hunts between dusk and dawn.

Lava catches up with me. "Why won't you tell me what's going on? I thought we were friends."

I sigh. I already pulled Omar into my drama, I can't get my friend involved, too. "I want you to stay happy. And if I tell you, you won't. You'll be moody like me."

No wonder women shun women with red flags. My mere presence is projecting pain like a splatters of ocean spray.

"Okay, but you do want me to help you find your lost lover, and then not tell anyone. You're making me an accomplice without letting me choose," Lava says. "Deer. You only think about yourself. And the worst part is, you don't know you're doing it!"

My heart crumples. Truth be told, I don't want to find Walt's body. The Walt I met was strong and alive. He was running with me through the maze. He put his palms on my cheeks. His hands were not too rough, not too soft. I want to remember him like that.

"What's with you two," Lava says. "The ultimate perfectionist Sequoia's mind-body connection is suddenly so deteriorated that she's tripping and falling? And by the way, lying to a Sage can get you a red flag."

I look down at our dusty feet. Her nails are perfectly round, like little black cherries. Mine are long and narrow. Hairs sprout from my big toes.

Lava wouldn't report me. She's committed to her role. She's easy and fun.

"But more than that, Deer, it's hurtful," she says.

I'm not a Sage. I don't read minds. But even I can sense that Lava is radiating red.

Yet, I'm a walking liability. Whatever I said in my sleep clearly disturbed Walt and led to his untimely—if not violent—end.

"Pachamama," I say.

"C'mon, Deer, you can't just drop a word to change the subject."

I rub my fingers on a sorrel leaf. The words come to me without warning. This one is older. I sense into it.

The Earth is a mother and her creative power sustains life

Right. The power of the Earth mother flows through us all, but only a Sage can speak to the trees. This doesn't get me closer to finding Walt.

The good news is, my intuitive skills are on in full force. The bad news is, my unique intuitive gift is an utterly useless skill.

Just like my friends who became mothers before, perhaps Lava would be better off without me.

"This is just who I am," I say.

FOURTEEN

The remaining six weeks of mating season turn Caleaf's hills brown in anticipation of the summer solstice. The days grow long, stretching to the earliest sunrise of the year: launch day.

My body's capacity for pleasure finds new bounds. First, the food. Mating season parties feature an endless supply of chocolate cakes, strawberry cheesecake bites, and late-night pizza slices.

Then there's the mating. While I don't take men back to my loft after what happened with Walt, I explore new corners of Caleaf by way of visiting men's apartments downtown, in farmhouses, and on vineyard lands.

The domestic men who cook and clean have the softest kisses. The men who work with their hands, builders and farmers have the most gentle touch. They move slowly and rhythmically in bed. Their rough hands dance over my hips, tickling me until I moan and beg for them to come inside me.

The men are endlessly thoughtful with arranging pillows for comfort, and quick to adjust for any spoken or gestured request. Some have tricks. One man, a free energy cart mechanic, whispers dirty phrases in my ear that pique my imagination so hard I feel like I've gone into an erotic film from the Records.

Others struggle to finish. That would be fine if it were lovemaking, but we're mating. We're building our numbers. We need that flow of sperm to hit our eggs. We learn to avoid the men who heat up too slow, however cute and kind they may be.

The apartment building I avoid is the one downtown where Omar lives. I miss my friend, but I don't want him to get the wrong idea if I show up at his home. The few times I stop by the cafe where we used to chat, he isn't there, so I wonder if he doesn't want to see me either.

Sometimes I catch Lava gazing at me and I wonder if she's still mad at me for what happened during the search for Walt. The whole of Caleaf continued for three days. Even those down in South Caleaf looked through their beaches and hills to see if he might have taken the long trek home alone without telling anyone.

Though no announcement is made, I know that the assumption is that he's had an untimely transition. Perhaps the next time the Sages negotiate with the flora and fauna of the island, more will become clear.

The pleasure of long days napping and sweaty nights feeling my body crack open does bode well for my poetry. I pour it into my art.

My mom has kept the opposite schedule, skipping even the art shows she is invited to and going to her studio in the early mornings, still quietly isolating herself since Grandma El's transition. She pours it into her art.

So I'm surprised when I come home after a particularly good morning mating session to find my mother sitting in the armchair in my loft.

"Deer, come have a seat," she says. "Your score from the

Amateur Art Show was not good." She looks out the windows toward the hills.

In all the festivities, and with even some new poems penned, I had put that awful threshold behind me. Or so I thought.

"It's time for you to learn how to act. The women of Caleaf —" She spreads her hands. "They're nice women. We're not like other women. Don't give me that surprise—you've seen it. And with those rankings, now we know your talent won't protect you. You need to learn to speak well. Go ahead, then—give me a compliment."

The nervous energy rises from my belly. I start to laugh. "A compliment? You have a pretty—nose?" I say.

"No!" She shouts. "That's a fake smile. Feel it in your belly."

My laughter sinks.

"Say, 'I'm looking forward to your party,'" she prompts.

"I'm looking forward to your party," I say, enunciating slowly for emphasis as Grandma El once did.

"Okay ... try it with your hand on your chest. Yes. Close your eyes, and think of something that brings you joy, like being on one of your runs ... yes! You feel the corners of your lips turning up, don't you?"

I do.

"Now try."

"I'm looking forward to your party." My voice comes out soft and breathy.

"You have a true art with words," she says.

My heart leaps. Then I realize she is not talking about my poetry.

"You have to learn to accept compliments, too," she says.

This is practice. It's not even a real compliment. Now I know I'll never truly please her.

I massage my forehead with my hands.

"That's a lovely color on you," she says.

"Thank you," I reply.

"Now pretend we're at a concert," she says.

"I've never heard a prettier flute solo," I say.

"Walking down main street?"

Here's one I heard straight from El's lips. "I hope I see you at the theater again, soon," I say.

Life is not so different from what we act out in the Records. You just have to play the role you're given.

AFTER MOM LEAVES, I go to the kitchen to get some evening turmeric tea. My dad is rinsing dishes in the basin.

"Mom seems to have more energy," I say. While I didn't exactly enjoy our surprise lesson, it was the most I'd seen her since El's transition.

"She spent a few days in the desert," he says. "I think she came back with a few ideas. I haven't seen her this excited to paint since her early work."

He lifts a stack of plates to the built-in shelves.

"Early work?" In the seven years I've known her, she's kept to one distinct style. "What do you mean?"

"Oh, before—" He stops. "Well, it doesn't matter. A woman's art is always evolving."

This is true for most women. Every two or three years, they release a new format, a new color palette. Over a career, you can track the development of the artist in what she produces.

I've never seen Mom paint anything other than her ocean sunsets.

"I'm glad she feels better," I say.

FIFTEEN

By the final days of mating season, my appetite for frolicking slows. My belly is expanding. There are eggs growing inside, eggs with gelatin-like membranes that once laid in the thick phosphorus sand, will harden into a golden shell.

When I arrive home for an early sleep, I unlatch the front door quietly, in case my parents have gone to bed even earlier.

The ground floor is still. The floor-to-ceiling windows shine starlight into the kitchen, dining area, and living room. The living room is where we would host an art show, had Mom the impulse, but it sits unused.

Tonight, I see an unfamiliar shape contrasted against the beige upholstery. A brown hood pokes up above the headrest of an armchair facing the fireplace. Well, almost brown. Any textile designer would recognize the hood pigment as sage green. That's my first clue. The rest comes to me intuitively.

"Hello?" I say.

I know who it is and why she's here.

She knows that I know who it is and why she's here.

I don't need to pretend.

"Fine," I say. I walk to the loveseat and sit across from her.

The Sage's face is hidden in shadow of the deep hood. Only her fingers stick out from her loose long sleeves.

"I'm here about Walt," she says.

"Yes," I say.

"You know, some women still look for him."

"That's very generous of them," I say.

"Of course. Do you know that you were the last person to see him?"

"I—"

I bring my focus to my breath. What does she see, in this dim room? A light show of my thoughts? Can she smell my emotions?

"I haven't seen him since that night."

"And was he in any sort of emotional turmoil when he left?"

I remember my turmoil, the dream—and fast as I can, I redirect my thoughts to the pleasure of the beach.

"I don't think so."

"You know, men lack the emotional regulation of women." Her pace of speech quickens.

Without being able to see her face, my senses attune to her voice. I know she's smiling. She's bragging.

"Our ancestors, in the Pre-Intuitive Age, lived in constant fear of bad things happening," she says. "They had no peace accords with their fellow land creatures, so they had to run and hide. Even though our society has evolved beyond that, fear distorts your perception of reality. It can pull a person into a downward spiral, until he's running right into the thing he's most afraid."

"I see."

"Right off a cliff!"

I swallow hard.

"You know better. As for Walt—well, we'll find out. Deer, when was your last scan?"

"It's been—awhile," I say.

"Of course I already knew that. I brought you a bonus to make up for the skips. A dozen yellow roses for happiness." She pulls a vase out of a pocket in her heavy robe. The buds are still tightly closed.

"These will bring comfort. It's an important year for you," she says.

She means mating season. I'm not in trouble. I've done nothing wrong. At least, not yet.

"Thanks." I cradle the vase and inhale the sweet scent of the roses.

"Do you know why sorrel only grows near human civilizations?" The Sage asks, standing.

I perceive she's read my thoughts about the lack of foraging options in Monterey, but if she knows I went there in the flesh, she's not giving it away.

"It's a symbiotic species. It could grow in other places based on geological conditions. But it wants to be eaten. That's its purpose. As humans we live in harmony by nature by emulating nature. We become nature. So we proliferate, and we are at peace."

"I've done my best to mate widely and frequently," I say.

She nods approvingly. "I wish you the best, most abundant voyage!"

I glimpse her bare toes as she strides to the door.

"Oh, and you haven't had any strange dreams, have you?"

"Dreams?" I repeat the word.

I play it through my mind, feeling the hard D, how it leans onto the weight of the sturdy R. What a word.

"No dreams," I say.

She slips through the door, leaving it ajar. I watch her dark cape blend into the night foliage.

Lying to a Sage. It would get me a red flag.

It's also considered impossible.

My fear of the Sages and their mind-reading abilities is replaced with something far worse. Now I know that our society's supposed healers and peacemakers are fallible. Even the wisest of us don't know everything.

SIXTEEN

Before taking the stairs up to my loft, I cross into the kitchen to grab a mug of ginger tea. Mom stands by the counter facing the western window. The sun has long since set. I'm amazed to find her awake.

She's running her fingers over a fold of red fabric.

I gawk at her hands. "Is that a red flag?"

"And you thought the Sage was only here for you," she says. "It will be hanging above our home by sunrise. I suppose a few new watercolor pieces each week isn't enough anymore."

She lifts and shakes the heavy fabric. It's as tall as her. It's wide enough to be a bed linen.

"I'm sorry that happened to you," I say. From what dad said, I thought she'd turned a new corner with El's absence. Perhaps for her art, it was the opposite.

"Oh, stop being so snobby. I don't need your pity," she says.

I pour tea into one of El's handmade creations and warm it with my hands.

"I know you've been embarrassed of me ever since we met," she says.

"That's not true!" My throat tightens. "When I first arrived on the Homecoming Voyage—I went to the market with you and all the other moms wore matching dresses with their daughters and I didn't complain—"

"—oh, that's how I failed you?"

"No, Mom, listen." A hiccup bursts out of my chest. I try to slow my breath. "When we went to the market, that first time. I mimicked everything you did. I watched how you carried your bags. I memorized how you furrow your brown when you examine fruit. I mouthed along with you when you negotiated with the bread baker. I thought I could be exactly the same—" My breath finally evened out. "But it wasn't enough for you."

"No?"

She's gripping the red flag. I wish I could yank it away, run to the hills, and bury it somewhere to make this not be happening.

"When we were leaving the market, I asked you a question."

I can tell from her blank expression that she has no memory of this.

"I was trailing behind you. You were walking so fast. I just wanted to talk. I thought if I said something funny, or interesting, that you would pay attention to me. So I said, wouldn't it be fun to live at the time of the Great Earthquake?"

Her eyes widen. Her shoulders shake. She's laughing. She looks down at the red flag, and laughs again. Her eyes crinkle and shine.

"You can't say that kind of thing around here, Deer. The women will think you want to be a murderer."

"I didn't mean the violence! I meant the scientific advances at that time—not the war itself."

"Well, no one knows that, based on what you said. You said the Great Earthquake. You want to watch your friends die? That's what it sounds like. I hope I slapped you."

I rub my arm where she grabbed it all those years ago. After the bruise faded, I used to squeeze my arm to see if I could bring it back.

"I was fine—normal—before I came here," I say. "Now I hate myself."

"You've seen nothing. You should have heard what my mom said to me."

I'm letting it all out. "And I waited for years to take voyage because you said I would knew when I was ready, but no one ever feels ready, they just go!"

She sighs. "Oh, now that's my fault, too? Have I failed to teach you anything about Caleaf? You want my advice? It only takes one woman to turn against you."

She folds the flag.

"This isn't just a formality. I have to keep producing art. We'll get by on the motherhood stipend, but I can't socialize with the other women—"

"You don't have friends anyway!"

For a rare moment, Mom is speechless.

Then she starts laughing again. It's a free-flowing laugh that only emerges in private when she's telling Dad about another woman's embarrassment.

My anger boils up. "You don't have friends and you don't win shows. What does a red flag change for you, exactly?"

Her face settles into a smile. "You're right, Deer. I'll be just fine. Your dad will be fine. You go on to your career as a prolific poet."

We stare at each other across the kitchen. This is our last night like this, as mother and daughter. Tomorrow I take voyage. The next time I see her, we'll both be mothers.

Despite my attempts over the past seven years to have a real conversation, I don't feel like I know her at all. What does it mean to be related by blood, when we don't actually have anything in common? The mother-daughter bond is another

Calefean staple that seems off limit to only me. This residence, soon to be marked with a red flag, feels unwelcome.

"I'm sorry I won't get to see your launch tomorrow," she says.

But there is something I need to know. It's something only a mom can say.

"Wait, Mom," I say. "Back when you were in mating season, did you ever have a dream about me, as a child?"

"No," she says.

IT SHOULD BE my last night in my mother's residence, but I find myself on the other side of her front door.

Mom thinks I'm being absurd. I bet she thinks I'll come back to sleep in my bed once I cool down. It's not my bed anymore. I vow to prove her wrong. I'll stay out all night if I have to.

This is the last time I cross her threshold. The pain lingers. It's hung in this doorway for all these years. It always will.

I could turn south and follow Walt's path, to whatever doom he met. Or, I could go north into town and wait out the hot summer night. At sunrise, all the maters and mothers will begin walking up to the northern cliffs for the launch of voyage. That's only a few hours away.

It feels good to move. When I get to the business district, I'm overcome with nostalgia. There's the dress show where Lava bought me a dress. There's the late night pizza place, empty of the mating season crowds, but still open for another hour. The workmen have probably already cleaned up. On the side streets are the men's dorms I'd loiter through between parties, looking for a quick mate to boost my numbers.

There's one dorm I always avoided because Omar lives there. Our weird friendship isn't that different than the relationship with my mom. It never developed into anything real. Now it will evaporate. I doubt I'll come out for cafe visits once I'm a mother. The more I think about it, I might favor choosing a residence outside of town. I'll be filling my days with writing poetry and nights attending social events to boost my name recognition at shows.

I tell myself I only want to feel the doorknob to his building with my palm as a way of saying goodbye.

The problem with intuition is that your heart works faster than your head.

His entryway is dense with anonymized thoughts and stray brain waves. Habitual movements are carved in the air like a coyote's well-worn footpath. When you get really quiet, there's a lot you can know.

I see him stepping through this threshold and walking up the stairs, all in a blur, a year's worth of workdays merged into one. I see his door. He lives in Unit 5P.

Omar's face flashes into my mind. Now I'm seeing him in real time. He's getting up to answer the door. I know the feeling. When someone is thinking about you with emotional intensity, it sends a visceral shock of electricity down your spine.

I put a hand on my bloated belly. He knows it's me.

When I get to the top of the fifth flight, he's standing in the doorway. His fluff of messy hair brushes the door frame.

"I thought you didn't want—"

"I'm not here for that," I say. "I had a fight with my mom."

I follow him in.

"The penthouse?" I say. The room is bigger than I expected. It's not as big as my loft, but it's definitely spacious. His bed faces an eastern window, exactly as I would have arranged it, to wake up to the rising sun. A green couch and two plush papasan chairs create a small socializing space. At the western end there is a full kitchen.

The curtains are pulled shut, but an open skylight lets in starlight and a thick summer breeze.

"I told you about the promotion," Omar says.

"You didn't tell me it came with a penthouse," I say.

It's the closest I can come to admitting I misjudged him.

"You really are—prominent." Now I see why he wasn't around during mating season. It wasn't out of shyness. He was working.

"I'm an assistant to the Queen."

He's told me this before, but I heard it as embellishment. Now I see he was being modest.

"I'm sorry I ran away from you at the Lunar Party. I was not myself ... I had a lot of wine."

"I'm sorry the man you were with disappeared," he responds. Of course he'd know about that. Everyone must know.

"I just have to ask," Omar continues. "Do you think you'd be sorry—and here—if he was still around?"

Ouch. "Omar, we've been friends since childhood," I say.

"But you don't stay friends with everyone you've known since childhood. I've seen you end friendships for the sake of convenience."

His criticism hurts. I don't think it is actually true. But he's the only person I trust right now. And I need his help, again.

"I lied to a Sage."

He pulls me into a hug. He doesn't have the strength of Walt or the softness of Lava. Between us, I'm the soft one.

"I needed to tell someone," I say.

We sit on the couch and he wraps a cashmere blanket over my shoulders.

"It was about my dream. I was afraid she would see it. And it's—really disturbing."

"Try me. What did you dream?"

"A white snake came out of the water and ate my daughter. On the sands of Sister Earth. When she was hatching."

"The ocean on Sister Earth is too acidic to touch," Omar says. "What could survive?"

"Something without much pigment," I say.

He rests his hand on mine. "There's not a snake on Sister Earth. It must be symbolic. Perhaps it represents your fear about motherhood."

Of course a man wouldn't know what it's like to dream about your daughter.

"It was real," I say.

"Okay, but if there was some danger, wouldn't we all get the dream?"

I pull my knees to my chest. "What about the missing kid you mentioned?"

"The sensors on the Mothership do a sonar scan every voyage. The Sages will know the total count of kids by the time you land. But if there's some disease—"

"They'll leave us."

The two-month voyage suddenly feels much longer. In the dark room, the couch swallows me.

"The Sages have to do what's best for the collective," Omar says. "But it's unlikely. I'm sorry, I shouldn't be scaring you even more."

I wrap the blanket around my hair like the hood of a Sage and rest my head in Omar's lap.

"It doesn't matter now," I say. "But why didn't you tell me the phosphorus levels?"

"I couldn't get to it. That's only stored on the Mothership Terminal. Everything about Sister Earth is on the Mothership. "

"Even the space maps?" I say.

"What?

"You said we bought the space maps—"

"Don't mention that to anyone. I shouldn't have told you. I will lose my job."

He thinks I don't listen, but I do.

"Are you ready for this?" Omar says, more softly.

"Two months of space travel?" I exhale. "With all the advances we've made to innovate childbirth...sometimes I wonder if our technology is really such an improvement."

When I wake up with the sun, he's already gone to work, and my head is cradled by a pillow. Of all the beds I've woken up in through mating season, this is the warmest one.

SEVENTEEN

On the launch lawn, thick with a morning marine layer, the broad-shouldered pizza chef calls out orders to the gathering women.

"My fellow mothers! We do this every year. Sopranos, to the left! Altos, to the right! Musicians, into launch formation, please!"

It's just an hour after sunrise. While the air is damp, the summer solstice sun's warmth is already breaking through.

All the mothers have been to every launch since their own to support the spaceship's liftoff. My friends and I stand with the full-bellied maters off to the side. It's our first time.

The musicians tune their instruments. The great vocalist Osha, a woman with a shaved head, leads the mothers in vocal warm-ups. She continues, undaunted, as the pizza chef nudges and motions for the women to arrange themselves in a grid.

"You'd think they would be more coordinated," Lava says. She's always curvy, and yet, this is the most round I've seen her.

Even in the early morning air, the pizza chef's face is a warm pink. Lava's prediction about a season of flawless pizza was correct. She's proven her artistic value, but the pizza chef still seems to be running from that red flag from the fiasco with the blacksmith. She's trying too hard.

"There's my mom!" Sequoia points and waves towards her mother's distinctive petite frame among the sopranos.

Sequoia has the classic shape of a mater, with her bloated belly proportional to her butt. My belly seems small by comparison, but it's overshadowed by my breasts.

"My mom says we'll hear new songs today that they only sing at launch," Sequoia says. "Where's your mom, Deer?"

Last night's revelation still feels tender. I consider my words —specifically, how few words I can speak to adequately answer Sequoia's question. I narrow it down to five.

"Red flag mothers can't come," I say.

Sequoia gasps. "What!"

Some maters near us turn around.

I speak louder. "I said—"

"So it happened." Lava pats my arm. "I'm so sorry, Deer."

"It's okay," I say. "I'm my own woman now." I wish that were true. But I wonder if I'll ever truly be free of my mother's shadow.

Sequoia turns back to the chaotic crowd of mothers and waves in the general direction of the sopranos again.

A trumpet player pulls the pizza chef away from Osha, who throws up her hands in defeat. Her choral group disperses into the rest of the mothers, who have given in to the pizza chef's orders to arrange themselves by height.

"Maters!" A wise woman Sage holds a glass vocal amplifier to the flopped opening of her hooded brown cape. "Line up so we may begin the scans. Our launch window is only two hours, and we've got to get a couple hundred of you on board."

The flute players kick off a melody.

"Ow! Does that make your ears ring?" I say.

"Look at the ship," Lava says.

The silver outline of the spacecraft glistens through the morning mist. Even from far away, I can see the ship's subtle vibration as it's pushed out of the hillside bunker.

The flutes pick up volume as the massive ship responds. Visceral waves radiate through the crowds. I rest a hand on Sequoia's shoulder to steady myself.

Another Sage shouts directions to the male crew, donned in navy jumpsuits with the Calefean rose embroidered on the chest pocket. The spaceship is being rolled on its side over a bed of eucalyptus branches. At its widest, the ship's domed top is quarter mile in circumference, and the base is an inverted pyramid that encases the power crystals. The flute players walk alongside, playing the ship's resonance frequency, so subtle vibrations propel it forward with nothing more than a gentle nudge.

As the ship rolls, the dewy clearing fills with the aroma of crushed eucalyptus.

The crew is more pleasant to watch than the mothers.

I grab Lava's wrist. The ship picks up speed and careens toward the steep northern cliffs where the thick marine layer blots out ocean waves crashing on rocks below. "They're losing it!"

"Chill, babe. They know what they're doing," Lava says. "Trust the process."

Just as the ship reaches the edge of the cliff, the flutes shriek a staccato finish.

The ship halts. A saxophone activates the heavier base. With the grace of an acrobat landing a flip, the ship rotates so the pointed base drops into a cleft on the side of the cliff, and the ship door perfectly lines up at ground level.

"Wow," I say.

The Sages lay out a blanket with three pillows in the middle of the clearing.

From their position, the line of maters snakes along the ice plant bushes and onto the southbound path. We chase the end of it.

"You go first," Lava says to a cluster of women. They're South Calefeans, returned from their mating season on the lower tip of the island, wearing the characteristic black ankle-length bodysuits. It hadn't struck me before, but it's similar style to what Lolanda made for Lava's dance performance.

"No, go ahead," the raspy-voiced woman with hair in bronze braids says. The line keeps building. Five more women step into line ahead of us.

"You go," Lava says.

I lean forward, expecting the woman to make her offer again. Lava blocks me with her foot. The woman shrugs. She and her friends join the back of the line as it curves down the path. We tag along behind them.

From where we are now, I only have a distant view of the mothers, who are now humming together.

The Sages are starting their scans.

The first mater in line steps onto a wide tree stump.

The Sage seated on the first pillow, deep in trance, makes a hand signal. Next to her, another Sage records the mater's numbers with a calligraphy pen for the government files. A third Sage, standing with the glass amplifier, reports to the crowds.

"Petal, painter, daughter of Gem, the upholstery designer. 37 unique mates. 8 fertilized eggs! May your spawn bring abundance to all."

"That's a good proportion," Lava says. "I bet at least three of those eggs grow into a hard shell."

The next mater in line steps up for her scan. "Linnea, animal sanctuary boss, daughter of Daisy, the basket weaver. 15 unique mates. 3 fertilized eggs.

"Oof, the situation must be dire out in the country. She could have gotten that many mates at the Lunar Party and Amateur Show alone," Lava says.

I bring a hand to my belly. "Have you ever asked your mom how many she laid?" I say.

Lava laughs and mimics her winemaker mother's sharp voice. "She said, 'as many as I could, now go tell your sisters to get dressed for dinner!'"

Now that I'm gone from my mother's residence for good, without ever finding the emotional connection I craved, I wonder if my friends, the daughters of more prolific artists, really had it any better. Wearing matching dresses to the downtown craft markets doesn't guarantee you're getting the love you need.

The Sages call another woman's numbers, and the next. The line inches forward.

From the eastern side of the clearing by the spacecraft's cave bunker, Osha directs the mothers in a gentle melody. Guitarists are fingerpicking along.

The song stirs my heart. My whole body vibrates as if my own resonance frequency is being played. I feel buoyed by a swell of emotion.

"The mustard wildflowers. They always come in fall," I say.

"Don't worry, Deer, we'll be back in time to see them." A tear dribbles down Lava's puffy cheek.

The brass line joins in with a crescendo and the trumpets take charge of the melody. The trees rustle in response.

Small smooth pebbles rattle on the dirt path. A drum plays. The pebbles lift and lower, lift and lower, amplifying the beat.

Crows croon from above us, perfectly timed with the flutes.

All of nature is joining into the song.

The lyrics fade out, the musicians change key, and the

women start again. This time, faster. The drums play a four-count.

We charge our hearts
We charge our lungs
We charge our song as one voice
To send new mothers to space

They're crying. They're swaying. A woman kisses the tears of joy off another's lashes.

The line moves. We round a corner in the path to a better view of the mater scans. Once the Sage announces her numbers, each mater jogs west across the grass to the ship door. A crew member helps her into the spacecraft.

The Mothership is starting to spin from the kinetic energy of the song. Osha lifts her arms and the women's voices carry higher.

"Ivy, vocalist, daughter of Arnica, the pastry chef. 21 mates. 5 eggs. May your spawn bring abundance to all of Caleaf!"

"She didn't do very well," I say. Ever the overachiever, I thought Ivy would log more mates. If I counted my own mates right, I outdid my nemesis.

"Well no wonder, she's an only child—" Sequoia starts, before realizing her error and bringing her hand to her mouth.

It's a stereotype that won't fade, regardless of the proof. Grandma El was an only child, and a prolific artist. Breeding numbers cannot predict artistic talent. Yet, after what happened to my own mom last night, I don't want to argue.

Ivy jogs to the ship. It's spinning faster now. The full line of stringed instruments raise the volume of the song. Ivy waits for the ship to make two rotations before jumping safely into the doorway.

A breeze draws the marine layer south along the high cliffs. Soon it will melt under the sun. The water is pulling away from the cliffs, as if it's draining into a faraway sinkhole. Then I see the horizon. It's rising. The waters are pulling back into a massive wave.

The Sage who's been doing the announcing turns away from the line of maters and addresses the mothers.

"My loves, I need more charge from you, or we'll never get this ship off the ground," she says. Then, louder. "Put your heart into it! When it was your turn, mothers sang to power up your ship, and you'll do the same for these women."

She holds a fist to the hilly eastern horizon. "Our launch window is only 40 more minutes."

Osha motions, and the mothers begin a new song.

The spaceship itself oscillates up and down as it continues to spin. Its base rubs against the side of the cliff.

The Sage chuckles. "We are not about to send this ship halfway across the galaxy without enough creative power to navigate back home."

The Sage on the first pillow, who'd been in trance, turns her head. "You don't make that mistake twice," she says. The Sages burst into hysterical laughter with their shoulders shaking under their heavy robes, their faces invisible under their hoods.

Caleaf's greatest tragedy is rarely spoken aloud. The voices of the mothers falter, and Osha waves her arms. The song changes again.

Beauty is power

Bloom like a flower

The ship jerks to the side before stabilizing into position, spinning two feet off the ground.

"You are brilliant, Osha!" The Sage hollers. She settles back into position and waves the next mater onto the tree stump. "Next!"

Every instrument is playing. The musicians have their eyes closed, pouring all their power into performing at full volume. Some are unsteady on their feet, but when one falters, another reaches out a helping hand as the creative power passes between them like a closed circuit.

Osha drops her sweater to reveal bare shoulders as the musical energy heats up the clearing. Another big wave crashes. The spacecraft lifts higher, as if inching away from the splatter of saltwater. Just past the rocks, a school of dolphins leaps in unison. They hear our song.

A navy-clad crew member with tousled brown hair jumps down from the ship door and runs to the Sages. After he speaks to them, they each hold a palm to their forehead. They're communicating telepathically.

"We are almost at capacity," the Sage announcer says. "But do not worry! For any mater left behind, a woman will lay an egg in your honor."

"Capacity? Haven't they known how many women went out for mating season for months?" Lava says.

"There's what, 400 of us?" Sequoia says.

The South Calefean with the braids turns around. "450," she says.

I look back. We're in the final hundred.

The Sage who had been in a trance shakes her robes. "An impurity! Something is blocking our resonance."

She leaps to her feet and jogs over to the mothers.

"If you came with anger today, you must leave! Get out, if you are harboring regret. You are blocking the flow."

She starts scanning the musicians by pressing one hand on a woman's chest and the other on her back. She ducks under trumpets and around violins. The music slows. A jumble of notes comes out flat.

"Has this happened before?" I whisper.

"My mom never mentioned it," Sequoia says. The Sage is getting closer to where her mom is singing with the sopranos.

"You!" The Sage points to an older woman on guitar. "My

love. You have resentment. You need to take the holly remedy. Go home!"

The woman is gone before I can see whose mother it is.

The Sage marches back to the blanket.

I can't imagine the energy getting much stronger. I'm dizzy. The air feels hot as noon. Sequoia wipes sweat from her forehead.

Lava leans out of line and meets the gaze of her sister, Isla. Sisters have the best telepathy.

"Isla says they're only taking 50 more. That means—everyone behind us—"

"Look." Sequoia points.

The Sages direct the mater up on the stump to sit on the gravel. They don't say her name, but I've seen her during mating season, treating her friends to late-night slices at the pizza place. It's the pizza chef's daughter. She crosses her legs and drops her face into her hands.

They're culling us.

"Look alive!" the Sage yells. "We'll get this ship launched with as many of you as possible."

Sequoia nods to the pizza chef's daughter. "That's Linden. She's in my class. She's a talented muralist."

The next two maters are sent to the ship, and then another is directed to the gravel.

Five of the mothers, led by the pizza chef, are approaching the Sages. The pizza chef now has her stringy hair clipped up in a tight bun, exposing her thick neck. She's gesturing towards her daughter.

The two Sages seated on pillows continue, wordlessly, motioning some women to the ship and others to the gravel.

The announcer nods at the pizza chef and turns toward what's left of the line of maters.

The Sage answers. "No, the women left behind will not be

mothers, as there is no safe haven here for their children to develop. They will be honorary mothers. Godmothers."

I hear the low rumble of the pizza chef's words, but I can't make out what she's saying.

The Sage nods. She turns again. "Women maters left behind will not be mothers and will not receive the motherhood stipend."

The maters sitting on the gravel have their heads down. Their shoulders are shaking.

Isla is scanned and sent to the ship. The mothers' music grows louder, now echoing back to us from the big boulders further up the coast.

"This is bullshit," Lava says. "The Sages? Letting eggs go to waste? That's not abundance."

"Trust the process," I say.

She slaps me.

"You brat," Lava says. "I've only ever wanted one thing."

The women ahead of us look back, glancing between us, their eyes wide.

Lava turns her face away. She's crying. It's the first time I remember seeing a crack in her upbeat demeanor.

I put a hand on her shoulder. When she doesn't pull away, I wrap my arm around her.

"I know I said it was about numbers," she says. "But it's also about my daughter. I feel like I know her already."

Sequoia pats Lava's back. "You have so many eggs. You'll be fine."

"No," Lava says. "I want all of us to go. Together."

She's not worried about getting on the ship. She's worried about me and Sequoia. Is this why she was so adamant for us to all go the same year? I thought it was just her fun-loving personality, but now I see it came from a deeper place: fear.

The group in front of us steps up to get scanned. The Sage reads their numbers, with urgency.

"Oak. 27 mates. 5 fertilized eggs."

"Juniper. 31 mates. 7 fertilized eggs."

"Breezy. 50 mates. 10 fertilized eggs."

The last of them, in her sleek black outfit, jogs to the ship with the graceful ease of a gymnast.

"Whoa, ten," Lava says. "Imagine if all of hers hatched."

The Sage glances up at the dwindling line. "Next!"

I push Lava ahead.

"Lava, dancer, daughter of the winemaker Primrose. 48 mates and 7 fertilized eggs,"

The Sage sends her to the ship, but she's walking slowly. She doesn't want to get on until she knows we're coming, too.

I focus my attention on her and send the mental equivalent of a yell. "Go!"

She glances back. She heard me.

Sequoia steps onto the stump.

"Sequoia, acrylic portraitist, daughter of Hope—" The announcer stops before reading the numbers. The Sage recording the numbers shakes her head. The announcer shrugs. She points Sequoia to the gravel.

Only mothers can marry. She'll lose Edgar.

I step up.

I open my mouth to offer my space to Sequoia—if I've even earned it. I never wanted to go on voyage. I even said so, back at the treehouse. I only agreed to mating season because Lava pushed me into it.

"Deer, daughter of ... Rain," the Sage says. She clearly recognizes my mom's name as the recent red flag recipient. "25 mates. 7 eggs. Well done, my love," the Sage says.

I look at the announcer, her face shielded in her hood like the others. She motions to the ship. I can't place her voice. Has she done my annual scans? Is she the same Sage who questioned me about Walt? I didn't hear her compliment anyone else on their numbers.

My mind replays to the numbers she just read. It is a high proportion. There are no guarantees, but I doubt a woman who lays seven eggs will be the mother of an only child.

I am not my mom.

My bare feet press into the grass, following the footfalls of the maters before me. Lava is waiting for me by the door.

The spacecraft is spinning fast. It hovers several feet off the ground.

To make it through the opening, we have to get the timing of the rotation right. We also need to jump.

I sprint up to Lava. "Stand on my knee," I say.

Two crew members are leaning out the door, each holding onto a handle. The rotation is about eight seconds.

The door passes by.

Lava steps onto my knee, then brings her other foot to my shoulder. I hold her hips and stand up as I count.

"3... 2... 1."

I lift her as she leaps forward. The crew members grab her and pull her inside as the ship door spins west toward the ocean. I keep counting so I'm ready to jump at the next rotation.

I'm about to jump when I hear a scream.

I shouldn't, but I look back.

The line of maters has dissolved. Some mothers are still singing, but others have passed out on the grass from exhaustion. The trumpets are at their loudest yet, but it's not music anymore —it's just noise. The heat generated by the sound is overwhelming.

The ruckus is by the Sages' blanket. The pizza chef has pushed a Sage to the ground.

"Red flag!" the Sage yells.

The pizza chef backs away, holding her palms up, and turns to jog down the path back to town.

My mom built up her transgressions over decades of bad art. Other women stain their good reputation in a single fit of anger.

One of the Sages, with her hand pressed to her forehead, is hand-picking women from the line. She rounds up five of them and pulls Sequoia off the grass. The Sage corrals them toward the ship. Sequoia's numbers must have been close. She is going to make it after all.

When I look back to the ship, it's spinning even faster. Now it's on a six-second rotation. High tide at the base of the cliff sloshes like a whipped meringue.

The announcer has dropped her glass amplifier and is yelling. "You must go home to your mother, Linden. There's not enough fuel for even one more. This is for the highest good of all."

Linden, the muralist, has pushed away the other maters and is running towards the ship. Like her mother, she has strong, thick limbs. She's gaining on the group with Sequoia and the Sage.

There is no time to wait for someone to boost me. The door spins past me and I count backwards from six.

I leap.

My feet touch the floor. A crew member has a hand on my shoulder. I'm inside, on my knees, and as I turn to see the view pan from the northern cliffs to the western ocean horizon, I notice a hand gripping the door frame and a body swung long by the spaceship's spin.

It's Linden.

She lets go.

Her body is flung down to the rocks below. She must have known she wouldn't make it in.

I look away so I don't see her crash.

The injuries of such a grisly death will follow her into the next dimension.

Is it really such a bad life, what she was sentenced to? To remain an amateur in Caleaf—that's what I said I wanted, back at Lava's treehouse.

The Sage told me fear could bring a person to run right off a cliff, but I know that's not why she jumped.

It's because she felt her child in her belly, just like Lava. It was grief. She couldn't face life without her child.

When does an egg become a person? Perhaps—whenever the mother decides.

I haven't let myself think of my eggs as children.

You're not real.

I've watched my daughter die so many times in my dream. It would be better if she never hatches.

You're not real.

The last thing I need on this voyage is to bring my scream-inducing nightmares in a shared sleep space with 400 of my peers.

You're not real.

Omar asked me why I would be the only one to get the dream, if there was real danger.

Maybe the answer is in the question. I got the dream because I'm the one meant to do something about it.

EIGHTEEN

There is quiet sobbing on the ship as the story of Linden's gruesome ending is passed around. We knew that voyage was not entirely safe, that women get sick or can't emotionally endure the long journey in a closed space. We didn't know we would lose someone so soon.

And, we feel for the women left behind.

Lava gasps when Sequoia shuffles in behind me, still dazed from her final sprint and leap on board. Sequoia collapses in Lava's lap, and shivers as Lava strokes her hair.

On each chair there is a white waffle weave robe. I pull off my yellow sundress to change, and toss the old sundress into the bin on the aisle. We'll all get new clothes when we return to Caleaf as mothers. I wrap the multicolored patchwork quilt over my shoulders and take four drops of my voyage plant remedy to help my body acclimate to space.

The seats are arranged in a massive circular amphitheater with a small raised cedar platform stage in the middle. Aisles divide the seats into quadrants of about a hundred women each. From across the big room, I can recognize faces I know well:

Lava's sisters, and in another quadrant, the vocalists I recognize from the art show.

"This isn't the same ship as before," I whisper.

"Your mom didn't tell you?" Lava says.

My blank expression is my answer. She did not.

"This is the Mothership," Lava says. "This one has amenities instead of a second level of seating. We don't have a full class of men this time."

True. We've all been to space, but not like this.

The Sages have done their best to design the ship's interior aesthetics to be pleasing for the soon-to-be mothers. The aisles are carpeted with geometric-patterned woven rugs. Thoughtfully positioned peace lilies in woven baskets contrast with the gray matte walls. In the center of the ceiling, a crystal chandelier hangs over the center stage.

There is no privacy on the ship. We'll share the washrooms and our seats turn into beds. In the aisle seat to my left, Sequoia cranks her chair into the top bunk position for sleeping. The seats alternate. Mine is a bottom bunk, and Lava, on my right, is a top.

Our Sage—the one assigned to shepherd our voyage—walks up an aisle to the center platform. Her arms jerk as she moves, and even under the thick robe, her shoulders appear sharp. If I were to guess, she's a young Sage. She could even be Copal, the girl who overlapped with me on Sister Earth, the Records genius who chose to join the Sages instead of reuniting with her mother.

She lifts the glass amplifier to the shaded front opening of her hood.

The undulating chatter of the room—nervous laughter, moans, and already, some snores—quiets down.

"My beautiful women," the Sage says. "I am telepathically sharing a ship map."

I close my eyes and the visual dissolves in, each element sharpening as the Sage describes it.

"You'll see your nearest washroom at the end of each of the four aisles. The kitchen is the level below us. Above, you can sign up for time slots in the workout room, the massage center, and the salt water cold plunge—yes, that's one perk of being in outer space. Space is cold. We can make ice by funneling water to the outer layers of the spacecraft."

"Excuse me!" A woman waves her arm from the seating quadrant next to ours. "But is this evergreen remedy enough for two months in space?"

A dropper bottle usually lasts 30 days.

"A voyage is two months in Earth time, correct," the Sage says. "But time works differently in space." She laughs as if blissfully unaware that a joke is only funny to her.

Her voice comes out stronger, with more authority. "Remember that this ship is powered by creative energy. It will go faster if you don't think about it."

Two rows in front of us, a woman calls out to the Sage. "I'm sorry, but do you mean it will be faster or slower? Like how long exactly?"

The Sage tilts her head and her chin pokes out from her hood.

"Days that feel like years? Years that feel like days?" the woman continues, her voice getting more strained with each word.

Sequoia leans over to whisper. "She shouldn't keep asking. Sages always say what we need to know. No more, no less."

"Our advanced birthing technology may seem like a miracle of life, but this is only science! We are still subject to the laws of the universe," the Sage says. "Our only viable route to Sister Earth is through the Womb Tunnel, where there is no time and no space."

The Sage lifts her fingertips toward the soft light of the chandelier. "The Womb Tunnel is the birthplace of the galaxy itself. The ancient male scientists were regretfully uninformed about female anatomy and its parallels to the cosmos, so they nicknamed it a wormhole."

That one gets a few gratuitous chuckles.

"On your last voyage," the Sage says, "on the Homecoming Voyage, you rode a wave of the universe's expansion out to Earth's solar system. That's the route we will follow on our return journey. But to go to the center of the galaxy, we must journey through darkness."

"My mom didn't tell me that part," Lava says.

The chatter of the women picks up. Some are crying.

The Sage laughs again. "Time can't be measured where it doesn't exist! But nothing to worry, the food lab on the top floor will ensure we have enough oat porridge to live happily and harmoniously for whatever duration we are on board the ship."

A groan rumbles through the room.

"The food is the only part my mom did tell me," I say.

"You want to lay eggs? This is how it's done." The Sage leaves the center platform.

She takes a seat in a back row, directly across from us, next to the aisle by the entrance. She tilts her head against the headrest as if she's asleep.

"It's bad news when Sages speak in math riddles," Lava says. "I'm signing up for a massage. Want me to put your name down?"

"Please," I say.

I never thought I would appreciate it, but my mom's choice to not tell me many details about voyage makes perfect sense now.

Sequoia curls up on her bunk in the fetal position with her quilt over her face.

"Get me down for the cold plunge, too!" I holler as Lava exits the auditorium.

A FEW HOURS into the voyage, crew members in navy jumpsuits enter all four aisles with silver trays to hand out the first meal.

The Sage's heavy brown robe stands out in contrast to the sea of white mater robes. She's sitting in a back row seat with her head tilted to the side, and she's snoring loudly.

When a crew member in the opposite aisle over turns back to refill his tray, my gaze locks onto his long braids, pulled up into a ponytail.

It couldn't be.

Walt?

I get up. "I'm going to the washroom," I say to no one in particular, and squeeze past sleeping Sequoia on her extended top bunk.

There's no line at the washroom at the end of my aisle, but when I exit the amphitheater, I turn down the outer rim hallway that runs the full circumference of the ship.

According to the Sage's ship map, there's a stairwell at the end of each aisle. He was headed down the aisle across from mine, and then he'll take the stairs down one level to the kitchen. If I'm going to intercept him, I need to move fast.

When I approach the next aisle doorway, I slow to a walk. Once clear, I break into a sprint. I come around the curve just in time to see the navy of a crew member's jumpsuit disappear into the stairwell.

I turn in. A group of women block my path. They are coming down the stairs from the amenities, above us, where they were likely signing up for massages with Lava. I pause as if I'm waiting for them to clear the stairwell upward, but once they pass, I go the opposite way on the stairs—down.

One flight down is the kitchen. There are mixing bowls, already wiped clean, and trays of extra servings laid out on the wide counters. But no one is here.

I go down the next set of stairs. When I reach the landing, I'm face-to-face with him.

The man with braids.

A South Calefean, yes. But not Walt.

The top buttons of his jumpsuit are undone like he just finished his shift. The corners of his lips lift with amusement.

"You shouldn't be down here," he says. "The gravity converters will start making extremely unpleasant noises once we pick up speed."

I hear the low whir. It sounds just like the self-fueling carts.

I don't have an excuse for being here, so I try to stall. "How do you know? You've never been on the Mothership," I say.

"My older brother gave me all the tips. He's the one who recommended I sign up," he says.

Walt didn't mention a brother, and certainly not that he had been on voyage crew. But it's not just the hairstyle. This man is Walt's brother as clearly as Lava resembles her sisters.

"Is it hard—to get this—role?" I say.

"Hard? There is a series of psychological tests," he says, readjusting the tray in his hands. "It takes a certain type of man to want to do this."

"The type you and your brother are," I say.

"Someone who wants to go. Not everyone would," he says.

Every role has drawbacks. I never understood why Omar liked his desk job, until I realized that he's so good at it.

"What's that door behind you? It's not on the Sage's map," I say.

He's staring at me like there's something else he wants to

say. Why he's not more persistently pressuring me to leave a level on which I'm surely not supposed to be. He takes a few steps backward to nudge the door shut with his foot. "That ugly old thing? That's the Terminal. We don't only use intuition to navigate. We use it for the sensor data."

The Terminal!

Omar said everything about Sister Earth is on the Terminal. The phosphorus data. Not that I need it now. Now that I'm en route to Sister Earth, fertilized eggs in belly, white snake or no snake. A younger version of me would want to send Omar a message just for fun, but right now all I care about is getting through the voyage without losing my mind.

That'll begin with eating regular meals and staying in my seat like a woman should.

The crew member's tray still has three jars of porridge.

"May I?" I say.

I take one.

"Hey! Didn't I see you at the Lunar Party?" he says. "You were with—"

He stops. I know what he knows. I was the last one to see Walt alive.

"I—"

What can I say? I'm sorry?

I turn and run up the stairs, taking two steps at a time.

"Wait!" he says. The tray and dishes clatter to the floor. He catches me and grabs my arm. Tight.

"Ow!" I say.

He towers over me, standing adjacent in the narrow stairwell. The sharp exhale from his nose hits my face. "What did my brother tell you before he left?"

I shake my shoulder free from his grip. "What do you mean, he left? Are you saying he went somewhere?"

He brings his hands to his head, his elbows fanning out,

showing damp sweat marks on his canvas jumpsuit from running food up the stairs from the kitchen.

My mind swims between shock and awe as I realize what he's saying: Walt is still alive.

"He told me—a lot," I say. But my recall is not great. What did Walt tell me?

"Pachamama," I add, dropping the word I remembered when Lava and I were climbing to the ridge in search of Walt. "The word means the creative energy of the Earth mother."

"You can't tell anyone what he's doing," the crew member says.

"So tell me where he is."

Walt's brother rubs his neck. I stare him down.

"I was hoping you knew where he was headed. My intuitive messages aren't getting through," he says. "He could live in the wild for ten years if he wanted. Because he can talk to the elements, just like a Sage."

My eyes widen. "That's treason. Now you've just made me an accomplice. Why would you tell me that?" I say, shocked.

"You—you just demanded I tell you!"

My hot cheeks press upward into a smile. I shielded my inner world from a Sage, and apparently, Walt can sense like one. If Sages are not the only ones with advanced intuitive power, what gives them authority?

Why do they get to decide who gets on the ship and who doesn't? Who's scarred by a red flag for the rest of her life?

"I'll keep your secret," I say to the crew member.

Now that I think about it, I do want to see what else is on that Terminal.

NINETEEN

We're settling in for our first night—if you could call it that, with the spacecraft hurtling freely through the galaxy, untethered to any particular star's orbit. Women are cranking their chairs into bunk position and changing into their sleeping silk robes.

And apparently, I'm not the only one who's nervous about the first night sleeping in a room of several hundred bloated women.

"My fellow maters!" A giddy voice interrupts the side conversations from the center platform. It's Ivy. She's using the glass amplifier of the Sage.

"We are about to become mothers together, and in honor of this time ... what is time, anyway?" She gets a few polite chuckles. "I want you to know I think of each and every one of you as sisters."

I groan. "Spare me the sentimentality."

She flaunts her status as an only child to gain goodwill.

The chatter quiets down.

"Now let's settle in and make this the best Motherhood Voyage, ever! Our lovely Sage still needs to spend three quarters of her time sleeping to maintain her intuitive connection with the Sages back home. So it's time to nominate a volunteer voyage captain to relieve her of administrative duties."

The Sage is snoring loudly. I bet she's listening to us, even in her sleep.

"I nominate Ivy!" A high-pitched voice yells from the crowd.

"Ah, Lulu, I'm flattered," Ivy says.

She presses a hand to her heart. She scans the crowd. "Other nominations? No?"

I can't tell if her surprise is fake or real.

"I'd like to add one. For co-captain, I nominate … Lulu!"

Lulu leaps to standing. She's the acrobat who hung out with Ivy at the Amateur Art Show. "I would be—honored," she says.

"They planned this," Lava says with a yawn. "We're on a clown ship run by narcissists."

"Alright, we'll take a few more noms," Ivy says. "Then, we'll vote! Anyone else?"

"I vote Ivy and Lulu!" A voice yells.

"Really, no challenges?" Ivy says. She laughs.

"No one wants the job," Sequoia mutters.

"Alright, then!" Ivy lifts her fingers to her brow. "Your ship captains report for duty."

***

I WASN'T sure I would be able to sleep. And I suppose I won't have a choice. Ivy isn't done on stage.

"I know what will put us in the best mood," Ivy says from the platform, now gripping Lulu's arm. "Our favorite pastime from Sister Earth!"

"Cloud races?" I mumble to Lava. I look up at the crystal chandelier. "Putting clouds in here would violate the laws of the universe."

"Lesson circle!" Ivy says.

"She has a funny idea of fun," Lava says. "Watch us spend voyage learning calculus."

"Who wants to go? Mabel, I know you like those paranormal romances about shapeshifters and fairies … no? Lulu?"

Lulu nods solemnly. It's now part of her role as co-captain to pretend to like Ivy's ideas. She sits on the center platform and hums a middle C.

"Fiction," she says.

"Don't forget to tell us your query," Ivy says, kneeling at the edge of the aisle.

"Oh! I asked for the theme of our voyage."

"Good one," Ivy says, grinning.

"Ok!" Lulu stands up. "This is one we all know. I'm male. A regal shape, less farmer, more like pro wrestler? Gladiator. Aquaman."

Her eyes are shining. She turns, looking around, but she's not seeing an audience of maters. She's immersed in her scene.

"And I can fly," she says.

I'm only half listening. It's been so long since I did a lesson circle. Maybe I thought I could sit this one out. That's why I gasp when she rises from the platform, tapping the chandelier with her finger. She flies right through it, swooping up and down over the rows of women. The ceiling becomes white, fluffy clouds. Snow falls. My fingers are chilly.

Lulu gracefully drops into an aisle. The women near her are shivering. They are crawling out of their seats to be close to her.

"I brought you a gift," she says in a booming voice that is not her own.

The hall is dark as night. The only light comes from her hands. In her palms she's holding what looks like a mound of sand, tiny crystals that glow like lightning bugs.

A woman crawls on the floor in front of her, pulls her knees in, and becomes a pile of tree branches.

The room gets even darker.

Lulu squeezes her hands together and I hear the same whoosh I did when the spacecraft lit up from the crystalline base.

Her hands pull apart.

The tree branch woman lights up.

She's on fire.

"Whoa!" More women climb over the seats to get closer. I sit on my hands to warm them. Lava squirms next to me. It's tempting to get up, to get closer to the fire, but this is just a scene. The chill is not real.

Heat radiates towards us.

Lava jumps up, stepping on the armrests of the women in front of us, and kicking shoulders and heads and she stomps over the rows.

"Prometheus!" she belts in a deep baritone.

Oh. I do know this story. It's never quite the same when we do a repeat—the details play out differently based on who plays which part.

Lava dashes to the front of our aisle and up the next one towards the God of Fire. She's one of the Olympians. The others, Zeus and Apollo, charge down the aisle to the left.

The fire is spreading across the section to my right, but the other Gods have tackled Lulu, aka, Prometheus. A full quarter of the room is ablaze. Around me, all the women are trees. I'm even a tree. It doesn't feel bad, just like a stiff melancholy. My pine needles tickle and the heat of the approaching flames is overwhelming.

"Stop!" I hear Lulu's muffled yelp. It's her own voice, not the booming voice of a mythological God. "Let me up," she says.

The room returns to the cool lighting of the chandelier. My pine needles dissolve away.

Lulu stumbles back to the platform and drops into crossed-legs to close the Records.

Lava and the others who played Olympians walk back to their seats.

"What did we learn?" Ivy asks brightly.

"I had good intentions, but I was a traitor," Lulu says.

Traitor.

A person divided against her own collective. It's a word I'd rather not hear again. And that lesson is supposed to be the theme of our voyage?

Next to me, Sequoia hums loudly. She's still gripping her plant remedy. I take a few drops of mine to ease the disturbance of what we just saw.

Ivy raises her voice to be heard over the chatter. "Nice work, co-captain! So, who's next?"

"Wake up the Sage!" a woman yells. "My friend is sick!"

Ivy hesitates as if she doesn't want to stop the game. Or, she's afraid to. But that Records scene didn't end well, and she knows it.

"I'm going to throw up," Sequoia says.

"Come to the washroom." I guide her by her shoulders to the exit at the end of our aisle. She kneels by the toilet, dry gagging.

Traitor.

Who could possibly be a traitor? I would look like one, if I went digging around on the Terminal. I haven't done that. At least, not yet.

I wet a towel and wipe Sequoia's face.

"Is she okay?" Ivy stands in the doorway.

"I'm fine," Sequoia says.

Ivy's still looking at me. "It's the youngest class. We have a handful of them." She sighs and leans against the door frame. "Give me her bottle. She'll need a different tincture."

Sequoia wobbles onto her feet. I hold a hand to her back and fish her bottle out of her robe pocket. Ivy takes it and slinks off.

Back at our seats, I crank Sequoia's chair to the laying down position.

"What's her problem this time?" Lava says. Her husky voice lacks her usual warmth, almost as if she's part Lava, part angry Greek God. It's as if Lava's been logging her own version of a red flag—Sequoia's pine crown, her stubbed toe, and now this is the third offense.

Friendship is a funny thing. My friendship with Sequoia was always one of convenience because we both knew Lava. At times, I resented her. Now, I feel the need to protect her.

"Ivy's just getting her a different tincture," I say. "She'll be okay."

"Sequoia, do you want a bottom bunk?" I crank my own chair back and help her into it. I'll take her aisle seat.

Ivy's back on the center platform, now holding a healing tuning fork. She whacks it on the edge of the wooden platform and holds it up. The sound is not loud, but I feel the vibration in my skin.

"Quiet down," Ivy says. She's dropped the upbeat tone. "The first years are having trouble acclimating to space travel. We need to help them get their power back. In the spirit of generosity, all massage slots for tomorrow are reassigned. Anyone who was signed up can reschedule."

"There goes us," Lava says.

"Remember, the more relaxed we all are, the faster time passes," Ivy says. "Be like our Sage. Go to sleep."

AT SOME POINT during the night, I wake to see the Sage is coming around with her tuning fork. She spends a long time with Sequoia, asking about her physical symptoms and emotional disturbances. She asks about the timeline. Did it begin with the Records query? With takeoff? Or, something back in Caleaf?

I pretend to sleep.

"What about back at Sister Earth?" the Sage asks Sequoia.

She whimpers.

The Sage plays the tuning fork and leaves Sequoia with a new tincture, customized for her symptoms. She moves on to the next section.

Once her back is to me, I breathe easier. Still, I can't decide which is worse: the fear that she'll see the contents of my dream just by walking by, or that she is unable.

Our wise women do not have the power we've been led to believe, but several hundred of us have entrusted our safe passage through space to our Sage.

TWENTY

A few weeks pass. There's a particular comfort in maintaining a 24-hour day schedule even though we're spinning through space at least 20 rotations per minute. The only starlight that reaches us is filtered through the solar panel that powers the chandelier.

I doze through the day opening the Records to read old poems and the biographies of each poet's life. There's often a personal tragedy that sparks a new style and produces their best work. That's the theme.

I grow increasingly bored of the auditorium's nightly Records games.

Sequoia says she's feeling better, but I hear her slide past me to vomit in the washroom during the night. The Sage has swapped out her tincture three times. Including Sequoia, there are 10 first years on board. There would have been 11, had Linden made it.

Each night, after a few hours of Records circles, women take turns playing the tuning forks to immerse the room in soothing vibrations until we drift off to sleep.

I can see why women collapse mentally on voyage. I'm

thinking of my last words to my mom. Why was I so harsh? And why didn't I mate with Omar? It seems silly, in retrospect. It's just the pleasure of mating in the name of progeny of the human race. It's our contribution to society. Why was I so particular about it when it came to my longtime friend?

My emotions are amplified. Even sounds and smells seem to be turned up in volume. The flower tincture helps me relax.

I remember what Omar said about the snake in my dream simply being symbolism—not a real reptile. I never got a chance to look it up in the Records.

As the auditorium lapses into stillness, some women toss and turn. There are muffled laughs and sudden movements. Even after curfew, they've gone into the Records to play old books or movies. Once I'm cozy in my aisle top bunk, I set my own Records query: What is the dream symbolism of a white snake?

I'm shown a book with photographs of a white snake called an albino ball python. It does not resemble the snake I saw in my dream. Still, the interpretation provided in the book says a white snake symbolizes purity, transformation, and new beginnings. Scientifically, the white coloration is a recessive genetic trait resulting from heavy inbreeding.

It all sounds fairly positive. Maybe Omar was right. I'm just scared of the dream because I fear change.

I thank my Record Keeper and bring my consciousness back to the auditorium. The Records are a curious technology, existing both within each human and linking us all together. I suppose they have a way of traveling wherever humans go. They're accessible on Earth, on Sister Earth, and everywhere in between.

I snuggle into the warmth of my quilt and the softness of my pillow. I'm almost asleep when I hear the buzzing of a tuning fork near my head.

I open my eyes. It's the Sage.

"I sensed a disturbance in this part of the room," she whispers. "Be at ease."

"Oh!" My breath quickens. "Thank you," I say.

I count my breaths to lengthen them, inhales of six beats, and exhales of eight. The vibrations of the tuning fork tickle my heart. My body feels light, as if I'm floating. With my eyes closed, I see the whole auditorium, as if from the perspective of the chandelier up by the ceiling. The Sage is moving on to the next section.

Now deeply relaxed, I picture the freshly hatched toddler from my dreams in my mind. She's got my narrow oval face and matching downturned eyes.

I'm not in the Records. But the scene feels alive, like I'm facing a portal into my dream. Maybe if I enter it willingly, I won't be so scared.

Just like when we were kids playing on Sister Earth and someone wanted to switch the game, I cue the scene I want with a familiar, emotionally charged word.

"Run..." I whisper.

I'm at the beach. But this time, I have a wide view. There are broken shells of golden egg along the shoreline. The picture flutters into motion. Kids stumble around the shards of the shell from which they've just broken free and take their first few steps, falling onto the soft sand and getting up again. They look so small, with mostly hairless heads and chubby little limbs.

The freshly hatched toddler is in front of me again. This time, I notice a distinctive mole on her right eyebrow.

"I'm not who you think I am," she says.

She speaks!

"No?" I say.

She looks down the long shoreline, where hundreds of children are in all stages of hatching. Grunts, cries, and the slurp of embryonic fluids as wet flesh slides off stiff shells layer into a resounding backdrop. The noise drops an octave. The scene slows.

Behind the girl, the head of the snake rises in the white water of a wave. This is no python.

I've never seen the snake's face in such detail. It sparkles like mineral sand reflecting the sun. As it opens its mouth, I see rows of gleaming sharp teeth.

For a moment I wonder if I can finally save her. Maybe that's how I conquer my dream.

She interrupts my thought.

"It's not just for me. You have to save all of us," she says. She looks down the shoreline. There's not just one snake; it's a hoard. They're jumping out of the water and swiping up hatchlings in their extended jaws.

Time speeds up, as if the ocean tide cycles in and out in a time lapse. The shore is calm. Then, another class of kids hatch, with long snake necks zooming out of the water to peck off individuals. We're speeding through time, forward 5, 6, 7, 8 years, and then I lose track.

Time slows again. The snake's narrow face expands as it unlatches its jaw to reveal a purple-blue double tongue.

The cool exhale from its nose blows in my face. Its mouth snaps down over the child in front of me, and both of them are gone.

Everything is black.

My arms, my legs, and even my shoulders are tingling. I can't move. My eyes feel glued shut.

"Deer!" I hear Lava say.

"Hmm?"

"Stop hollering. We're trying to sleep," Lava says.

My throat is dry. I bring my hand to my neck. My eyes blink open to the dark auditorium. I hear whimpers and moans.

"Someone tell that poet to keep her mouth shut," I hear in a voice I recognize as Breezy. A few people laugh. "Get her off this ship," Breezy says.

I expect Lava to defend me. Maybe to comfort me. I realize it isn't going to happen. I am on my own.

What would Grandma El say to this?

I clear my tired throat. "Apologies, everyone. I was having a bad dream." At least it's the truth.

I dreamed of being a renowned poet. I've made myself infamous, and I am a poet. I curl toward the outer wall and pull my quilt up to my nose so I can cry into my pillow.

TWENTY-ONE

A few days later, I look up from my midday porridge to see the Sage pacing across the center platform. She's holding the amplifier, but hasn't spoken yet.

Earlier this morning, she moved the first years to the back row of the quadrant across from mine.

Everyone agreed the diarrhea earned them an exclusive washroom.

From a distance, I can make out Sequoia's face among the ten.

The Sage had tried singing to them. She had the crew make sweet oatcakes with cinnamon. Any other Sage might have given the whole group a red flag by now, deeming them a threat to society. Her hesitance only confirms my suspicion that the Sage is Copal. She's the only Sage young enough that she would have known the first years as girls on Sister Earth.

When the crew ran out of sugar and the first years still hadn't improved, the Sage climbed on a top bunk and screamed, "Do something, anything, that brings joy!"

Then, she slept in a closet for two days.

The first years took her order to heart, and what they came

up with was haircuts. Sequoia's ponytail is sheared off and her thick black hair falls just above her chin in a bob. As a side benefit, the visual identifier makes it easier for the rest of us to avoid the first years on the stairs.

Apparently fully invigorated from her closet nap, the Sage lifts the amplifier to the dark opening of her hood.

"Something is really wrong with this voyage."

"It's the first years!" Breezy yells. "Move them to another floor. They're putting us all in danger!" She's two rows behind me now. Lava scooted over one spot to take Sequoia's old seat, and Lava's sisters have joined our section.

"We are not advancing to the Womb Tunnel as swiftly as expected. Something is slowing us down." The Sage pauses. "Someone doesn't want to go."

Lava tuns to me. "You!"

No heads twist back to look, but I'm sure the women around us heard her.

"Why would you say that?"

"Back at the treehouse. You said—"

"Shh," I say. "That was—well, look, I'm here. I changed my mind."

"Fine. Whatever you say," she says.

I know being crammed into this spaceship with our sore bellies has made all of us more moody, but I worry the rift between Lava and I threatens to be permanent.

The Sage sways on the platform as if she's just received a message from the Sages back home. "I want everyone aboard this ship to understand the seriousness of our situation. Let me explain to you a little more about how the spaceship is fueled. We often call it free energy. The technical name for creative power is Cohen. It was named for a brilliant science teacher. Cohen is nonlocal, meaning it is everywhere at once. Any resistance to the flow of Cohen is also felt everywhere at once.

Creativity breeds creativity, but distortion propagates distortion. Someone on this ship is blocking our flow, and it's not only threatening an entire year of spawn, it's disrupting the peace back in Caleaf, right now. The women there are exhibiting similar symptoms as the first years."

She glances to the first years, seated to her left side.

"I've just gotten unanimous approval from the Sages that when we find out who it is, she will receive an automatic three red flags. Immediate transition upon returning to Earth."

My cheeks are warm. I feel Lava looking at me.

"What about her eggs?" Breezy calls out. "Can they be saved, for the greater good?"

"Caleaf is better off without them, eggs grown inside the body of, someone said it earlier?" the Sage says. "A traitor."

ADOLLO ONCE TOLD me the only rule of poetry is to tell the truth.

I may never become the iconic poet of my dreams. But I still have a chance to know the truth. I become increasingly convinced that the missing piece to the vision in my dream is stored on the Terminal.

Hour by hour, I alternate joining in exercises classes on the amenities level and sitting in the amphitheater. Each time I go up or down, I take a different set of stairs. The set closest to my aisle only goes up, and the stairs directly across from us are rarely used, at least by the women, because that stairwell only goes down—to the kitchen.

Over a few days, I figure it out. The afternoon is when half the male crew is upstairs giving massages, and the other half is two floors up in the food lab. The Sage spends most of the day sleeping, which means she will be awake for several hours of the night, but I try not to think about it.

I know what I'm getting myself into. And yet, the tradeoff is clear. I'm risking an already-ruined career for peace—peace of mind.

The little girl, now ever-present in my imagination, nods her head. She's right. This is the only way forward.

To mute the brightness of my voyage robe, I wrap my multi-colored quilt over my shoulders. At the end of the aisle, I go into the washroom, pause for a few beats, and then exit into the curved exterior hallway. If the ship is a quarter mile around, then it should take me five minutes to walk the full perimeter, or just over one minute between each of the four aisle exits.

When I reach the next one, I pause and watch for movement. Seeing none, I walk by, slow and steady, as to not alert any attention.

Once I'm past the opening, I speed up, keeping one foot on the ground at all times so my footfalls don't make noise.

The next aisle is the one with the washroom reserved for the first-years. I'm at the far opposite side of the ship from my seat. I turn into the stairwell, going down.

After one flight, I poke my head into the kitchen. There is a grid of extra oat porridge services on the table, one tiny raspberry pressed into the top of each, laid out in case someone gets hungry during the night.

I continue down the stairs.

The door to the room of the Terminal is shut. Walt's brother had so casually used his foot to shut it when I found him in the hallway that early day aboard the ship. I catch myself staring when I see him distributing porridge during mealtimes, but he keeps his gaze down as if a single glance will betray his brother's secret.

When I get closer to the Terminal door, I see it has no

handle, just a circle of cool walnut at waist-height where you would expect a handle to be.

I've seen this kind of door in some kitchens. It's convenient for cupboards. I press the wood. The door pops open.

The Terminal is in the back of a room no bigger than a matriarch's closet. The machine is taller than me, and covered with a large quilt. Even though it's kept behind a closed door, its unpleasant appearance is thoughtfully hidden.

I pull the quilt down. The surface of the Terminal is so shiny I can see my own reflection.

I squint at the machine.

Our Sage said free energy is called Cohen. I believe the word I remembered, *pachamama*, is referring to the same thing. It's the energy that connects all things. When I look at the ocean, my eyes sense its blue and gray color, but my heart senses the shape of the coming swell. When I look at a plant, I sense if its nutrients are a suitable match for my body's current needs. Even a cinnamon roll can tell me its flavor profile.

The Terminal is fueled by Cohen just the same, but it is not so forthcoming.

It's like the Records. It needs to be opened.

I hum a middle C.

Nothing happens.

I rub my hands together to generate heat and wave them in front of the machine.

The screen remains blank.

"Ah," I say aloud.

Omar mentioned he uses the Terminal to communicate with civilizations that lack intuitive skills. Of course it wouldn't respond to mental commands. If I were an early human, how would I use it?

I tap it with my finger.

The Terminal lights up like an ignited bonfire and makes the sound of several trumpets.

"Welcome!" A booming voice speaks from inside the machine.

I duck behind it and pull the quilt up to my face. Any moment a crew member is going to come running down the stairs.

A few moments pass. When I'm convinced I haven't raised an alarm—yet—I return to the Terminal screen.

The bright flash from earlier is gone. The screen has returned to a dark gray with one small tweak: a blinking white line at the bottom left. Omar had indicated the Terminal was loaded with information, but he never explained how you get into it.

Just because a technology is archaic doesn't mean it's easy to use. Sometimes, it's the opposite.

I take a deep breath. I came here for one thing, and then I'll be satisfied.

Omar said the Terminal runs a sonar scan of Sister Earth on every voyage. The data is only stored on this Terminal.

"I need to see the sensor logs," I say.

As I speak, my own words appear next to the blinking line.

A word comes to me.

Cursor

How quaint!

But quickly my luck deteriorates. The screen fills up with text. There are letters, numbers, and funky symbols. Most of these, I do not recognize, even as words.

The text is flying by much faster than I can read. When I'm relaxed in a hammock, reading from the Records, I can digest a textbook at 500 words per second. These words are going by way faster.

The worst part? There are no line breaks. A poet's nightmare.

If Omar were here, he'd have the patience to go back and read everything. I don't. I'm not sure I have time.

"I'm looking for a white snake," I say.

Again, my words appear at the bottom of the screen. Several hundred screens of text fly by.

That's something. That's more validation than what I got from Omar when I told him.

"I need to see it," I say.

"I'm sorry, I can't help you with that," the Terminal responds, audibly, in its loud voice.

The nerve!

"Omar said there were maps," I say back.

"Opening map view," the Terminal says.

I press my palms together in front of my lips. The cool gray screen is transformed into a paradise of color. Against a black backdrop, there is a constellation of planets, arranged in clusters, each centered on a sun. These are solar systems.

I recognize the one with Earth in it, with the familiar parade of planets I've watched pass through the night sky from my mom's patio.

The other systems vary in how many planets each has. One system looks like a hive of honeybees, with hundreds of tiny planets.

"Take me to Sister Earth," I say.

"Zooming in on your destination," the Terminal says.

The sun with the abundance of little planets gets bigger on the screen, then drifts off screen completely, as the view fills with a single planet.

In truth, the lines of the image looks like my mom's watercolors. The pictures are not even as clear as Sequoia's oil portraits. It's nothing like the visual clarity of the Records. The Terminal is not made for pleasure.

There's a menu to the side of the image with a list of categories: Minerals, Wildlife, Plant Life, Weather Patterns, Human Life.

I'm curious about the phosphorus levels, even though it can't help me now. But I will stay on priority.

I tap Wildlife.

More categories: Sea, Land, Air.

I tap Sea.

There's a massive list. It's alphabetized by species.

Luckily, this time the text is paired with line breaks—and images.

These are still the bad watercolor kind, but a quick scan suggests most of the ocean wildlife are tiny shell creatures.

I drag my finger on the screen to move the text. For each species, a grid tells me the total count, average dimensions, a color-coded health score, its diet, and its predators.

I'm reading so fast I almost miss it. In the picture, the white snake has its jaw shut with a serene look in its eyes. It could almost be a little snail that's lost its shell.

Its numbers tell a different story.

Called a Poon, the reptile has an average length of 30 yards and girth of 2 feet.

The Poon's health score, as of the sensor data from the last voyage, was rated 70, in the green.

And its diet? Human hatchlings.

"Whoa," I say.

My skin prickles. I back away from the Terminal. I have the urge to run upstairs, back to the amphitheater, back to where all my peers are sleeping safely, and pretend to know nothing of this disturbing information.

This snake isn't just a defensive wild animal, attacking a

human who dares cross boundaries. Its diet of humans is documented. The Sages must know.

Omar has access to the Terminal. I need to tell him.

Before I can speak, the Terminal does. "You've been inactive for 60 seconds. Shall I shut down?"

"No!" I yelp. Too loud. I glance at the door. Then, with authority, I say, "Please copy this screen and create a new message to Omar."

The image on the screen shrinks and moves to the left. An image that resembles a yellow notepad appears beside it. The cursor blinks on the notepad.

I speak and watch my words appear as if handwritten.

Omar, it's Deer. I found the snake from my dream. It's called a Poon. See, look at this photo! It does eat kids. What can we do?

"Please send," I say.

The yellow notepad disappears and the map fills up the screen again. Again, I consider looking up the phosphorus numbers, but decide it's unnecessary.

For me and my friends, we're mid-voyage with our bellies full of eggs. The only way to protect our children is to find out how to guard them against the snake.

My stomach churns. I tap the image of the snake. It gets bigger. Some large chunks of text appear next to it that are, to my relief, arranged in indented paragraphs.

I scan the section labeled "History."

The Poon has been on Sister Earth since its discovery. Upon the arrival of humans, it was attracted to the iron content in human fluids and developed a taste for human blood. The two species have co-evolved ever since.

Even with my quilt wrapped over my shoulders, I'm shivering. The embryonic fluid pours out of the egg as soon as the child cracks it open, running riverlets right into the ocean.

Further down, there is a mention of jurisdiction.

In 2667 AD, the Oxalis and Lombardos granted exclusive use of SEO046 to the civilization of Caleaf …

I stop. There's a name I recognize. Two, I don't. But the text is wrong. Our foremothers discovered Sister Earth.

"New message!" the Terminal announces.

The yellow notepad appears. It's from Omar.

Don't write our names on this. I deleted what you sent. I don't know how you managed to get on the Terminal, but we'll have to come up with an excuse of how we came across this material. When you're back we can request a meeting with the Sages.

My heart drops.

The Sages only act once all 40 members are in agreement. They still haven't decided whether to run another ice expedition, and it's been more than a year since the tragic death of those men.

And even if the Sages agree to do something about the Poon, the amendment contracts with another species don't always go well. What if the Poon is like the mosquitos? What if it refuses to change its diet?

My eggs will hatch in nine months. I can't leave them in a dangerous place. I can't let my friends risk their children like that.

I send a reply.

I have to tell someone.

I tap my fingers together.

Omar writes back. *The only appropriate channel for this information is to go through the Sages. You've already made me an accomplice to this. And if you expose yourself, you'll just get a red flag, but I won't ever work for the government again. They could reassign me anywhere. Even the ice expedition.*

You wouldn't survive that! I reply.

I'm pulled between protecting my eggs and my friends' eggs —and the safety of my childhood friend. I imagine his floppy hair and his soft brown eyes. Electricity runs through my body. I've always cared about him. Now with the fear of losing him, I wonder if I've been blind to my own feelings.

Omar's response appears. *You act without thinking. And at the expense of the people closest to you. But whatever happens, I won't regret helping you, because ... I love you.*

I care about Omar. I tried to keep him in the dark, to protect him from my full motives. To preserve the friendship. But why? Because I love him, or because that was the only way to get him to do what I wanted? His accusation is the same as what Lava said on the hillside.

Maybe I am selfish.

I don't think being selfish is always bad.

I write back. *I wish love were enough, but I have to do what women have done for millennia. I have to save my child.*

TWENTY-TWO

I sleep late the next morning. Someone's put a jar of breakfast porridge on my bunk, by the looks of it, several hours ago.

"Deer!" Lava says. "It's our turn in the spa. They've finally given up trying to heal the first years." Lava's already folded up her quilt. She's as perky as I've seen her this entire trip, and I hope this means her old self is back.

My shoulders are sore from a restless night. My nightmares were the moments I woke up in the quiet amphitheater and remembered what I saw on the Terminal.

I crank my bed to the seated position and tuck my jar of oats into the pouch with my plant remedy.

We take the stairwell at the end of our aisle up to the amenities floor where women with their robes tied snugly are using the exercise area for a workout class from the Records.

The woman playing the workout instructor hollers, "We're gonna squeeze those cheeseburgers outta those hips—alright, and those French fries—and that carrot cake!"

Behind the exercisers, some women have set up a tetherball court, but instead of playing a game they're just taking turns riding on the ball like it's a swing.

We walk along the outside perimeter. The massage rooms and cold plunge take up half the floor and are walled off from the exercise area. Lava crosses our names off the clipboard with the calligraphy pen, and we go into adjacent candlelit rooms.

While I undress and climb under the sheet, I consider what excuse I could use for accessing the Terminal. What would be appropriate to my role? Some roles are official, others inferred by the dynamics of the group, moment to moment. Who makes the joke? Who gives advice? There is an uncomfortable schism when anyone steps out of the group's expectation.

To not be in your role is, in a word, selfish.

I lay on my side and arrange the pillows around my belly. When the crew member enters, I look up. I'd hoped it would be Walt's brother, but, no braids on this man.

"Deer, the poet?" He looks at his written schedule. "The Sage recommended dandelion oil for you," he says. "It's vitality-boosting. Does that sound good to you?"

"Sure," I say. I've been given dandelion at my annual scan before.

"How's voyage going for you?" He presses into my shoulders and feels around for tension.

"Oh, uneventful," I say.

His hands pause behind my lungs. "Take a deep breath," he says. "It's okay to feel anxious. You're certainly not the only one."

I comply, and sink deeper into the pillows and soft table as he works down my spine.

"Bringing the next generation into the world does something to your body, not to mention the strain of space travel," he says.

"Why did you take this role?" I ask.

"It's an honor." He moves down to the middle of my back and my kidneys. "I helped my mom at her avocado farm for a few years, but she struggled. She had one good crop, and then transitioned early."

Agriculture requires a high level of intuition. Like a Sage, an agriculture boss must not only sense the patterns of plants, but of the wind, the rain, and the insects. Though that is not the same as talking to the elements, as Walt supposedly can do.

He continues. "So, I suppose, my taking voyage is a way to honor my mother. She didn't have daughters."

"Oh? I've never heard that," I say.

"It's rare. Because of the sand temperatures, the first egg to develop is usually a girl, but not for us."

He reaches a tender muscle on my low back. I take a deep breath. I know his prodding is what will make my body feel better, but it's too much.

"Softer," I say.

"Of course." His hands lighten.

I grasp for a distraction. "So no sister. But how many brothers?"

He holds his thumb in place. His hands zero in just where I need. Can a man have intuition this good? I breathe into the pain. It radiates through my body as if exhaling its way out.

"None, just me."

He's an only child. He could be about my age. His mother struggled with her art. Ivy's mother struggles, too. I remember the pastry chef's dry scone crumbling in my dress pocket.

On my third exhale, the pain dissipates. A weight drifts through my body and down into the floor.

When he moves his hands to my arms, behind my closed eyes, I see the girl from my dream again.

Just like always, she's a mirror image of me, except for the distinctive mole on her eyebrow.

Whatever the masseuse had kneaded out of my obliques

released a veil from my inner vision. Now it's so clear, I don't know how I could have missed it.

The girl isn't my daughter.

She's my sister.

———

AFTER THE MASSAGE IS OVER, the masseuse exits the room. I curl up in a ball on the floor. I want to cry, but the tears don't come.

"Mom knows about you, doesn't she? She always knew," I whisper.

My sister doesn't reply.

A few minutes pass. I know they'll want the room for the next person. When I exit, I keep my gaze down and beeline to the end of the hallway for the cold plunge. The pool itself is a large oval, ringed with a line of rose quartz pebbles that refract the dim light with their welcoming geometry.

The pool isn't empty. A disrobed woman floats on her back in the center.

I hang my robe on a hook on the bamboo-lined wall, and wipe the massage oil from my exposed body with the provided eucalyptus-soaked warm towels.

I dip my toe. "Ow!" I say.

The woman in the pool tucks her knees in and turns to face me. "Hurts so good, right?"

It's Ivy.

"Even the Pacific isn't this cold during the winter," I say.

"It could be colder. Actually, the pipes would freeze solid if they were even a few inches closer to the surface of the ship, because—"

"I'm aware," I say. I didn't ask for a science lecture.

Ivy flaunts her status as an only child to earn sympathy. Is that why she reported her own dad? To boost her mom's art? What a way to get ahead. I'd like to ask her. I'd like to ask her a lot of things that aren't appropriate to say aloud.

What's it like to report your dad to the Sages?

How does it feel to get a perfect score at the Lunar Party?

Do you worry your career has already peaked and the rest will be downhill?

Is it exhausting to be nice to everyone, all the time?

Gratefully, Lava will be entering the room at any minute and will save me from saying something stupid.

Ivy swims along the outer edge of the pool, using the wall to pull herself along. When she comes back around to where I'm sitting on the lowest stair step, she pauses.

"You know, Deer, we're not that different," she says.

I sink down off the stairs so the water level covers my breasts.

"We're both only children. Only daughters."

Well, she's wrong about that.

I can still see my sister's eyes, and the unhinged white jaw snapping around her. The different variations of the dream blend together. I often wake up yelling, "Run!" But was it her who said it? Or was that me? Did she grip my hand? Did I push her away, right into the jaws of a bloodthirsty predator? Even with the cold hard sensor data of the Terminal, I do not know the truth of who I am.

Ivy continues. "It's not just that. You're not the only one who remembers."

My mouth drops. Does she know about the snake, too? Has she been having dreams about her sister's death? Finally, someone will understand me.

Ivy leans in so close our noses almost touch.

"My intuitive talent is like yours, but instead of remembering words, I remember sounds."

I swallow hard. She's so poised—I can't imagine her blurting out a sound in the middle of a conversation, the way I do with remembered words. Though it would be funny, if she did.

"You made some beautiful sounds at the Amateur Art Show," I say.

"Well, these are different." She pushes herself back and her wake ripples to the edges of the pool. "These are—you'll see."

Her lips barely move. Her face contorts.

What emerges sounds like a mix between a rooster's crow and a dolphin's whistle

I shiver.

"See? On its own, it's terrifying. But with words ... what you shared at the show really made me feel something. To be honest, I'm not sure I understood it, and it doesn't look like the judges did, either."

To say the judges simply did not understand my poetry is probably the kindest compliment I'll get. If only it were true.

Ivy sighs. "I just feel like these sounds need to be expressed, and I was wondering."

I look back at the door, willing Lava to come in.

"Would you want to do a collaboration?"

My teacher Adollo never bothered with collaborations because she didn't want to split the cash prize. To her credit, her residence had a room of just trophies.

I flick the surface of the water with my thumb. There is no perfect art. There is no easy art. The Nature Artists, like the masseuse's avocado farm boos mom, depend on the whims of the weather. The Fine Artists, like my mom, are bound to the whims of women. The Craft Artists balance style and utility, and are perhaps more secure because of it. If I could go back and become a glassblower instead of a poet, I would.

"I can't sing," I say.

"Oh, you don't have to do that part. I'll sing."

I see how this plays out. We write a song together, enter it into an art show, and split the prize money. She gets all the attention for her performance and goes on to be in high demand for events and stage productions. My input is quickly forgotten.

But, being associated with Ivy's spotless reputation boosts my appeal. After a promising win, the women might forget about my Amateur Art Show scores. Completely.

And if I turn down her collaboration offer, I'll have trouble even getting entered into shows. She's the popular one. Her friends won't want to associate with me.

If Grandma El were here, what would she advise?

"I'll do it," I say.

Ivy stands just as the door opens and Lava walks in.

"I can't wait," Ivy says. She takes a robe off the wall—my robe—and wraps it around her wet body.

It doesn't matter. Even my poetry is not my own anymore.

TWENTY-THREE

The peace lily in the wicker basket at the end of our aisle is turning brown. The blossom droops. I notice it each time I go to the washroom. I can't be the only one to see it.

I take extra doses of my plant remedy. I volunteer to play the tuning forks at night. In my bunk, I open the Records, just to be sure I still can.

I've seen what I've seen on the Terminal, and no conscious intention can overpower my inner will. I can't lay my eggs on Sister Earth.

Surely, I'm the one who is slowing us down. I don't want to go. I don't want to go to Sister Earth and lay my eggs on a beach only to leave them vulnerable to a bloody confrontation.

This is the part Omar, a man, would not understand. Keeping this information inside of me is putting us all at risk.

I return to my amphitheater seat from two hours of yin yoga on the amenities floor.

"Lava," I say.

She looks up. "You missed it. Your bestie Ivy led another lesson circle. The question was, how can we speed up the ship? We watched Jonah be thrown overboard and eaten by the fish."

"Did they say it was a true story?"

"Does it matter? Isla got to be a sexy Queen of Nineveh."

"Did you have a role in it?"

"I was on the pagan ship crew who tossed him into the sea."

Lava's warmth has evaporated. I've lost a friend. But, who am I to say she can't change roles. What makes bubbly Lava the true self, versus who she is becoming now? If I'm honest, with myself, I've changed roles too.

Maybe it started with me. Still, I can do what I failed to do during the search for Walt. I can tell her the whole story.

"I need to talk to you. Privately." I grab her arm. "Come to the washroom."

Once we're inside, I check all 10 stalls. We stand by the sinks and wait for two women washing their hands to leave. Then, I move the potted peace lilies to block the door and tie a robe belt around the door knob. The women will assume we're pleasuring each other.

"There's something I haven't told you, and I want to start at the beginning," I say.

"Ok." She nods.

I take a deep breath. "The night after we met up in your treehouse, I had a dream. In the dream, a white snake came out of the water and ate my child, just as she was hatching from her shell."

"Argh, Deer!" Lava leans over the sink. "Did you tell that to Sequoia? I feel sick."

I crouch down to a squat and rub my temples. "Well, this is why I didn't tell you," I say.

Lava runs water over a towel and dabs her face.

"So, that made me scared to come on voyage. I didn't want it to happen. I thought I could stop it, and I tried. But then Omar told me there were space maps on the Terminal and it literally says right on the Terminal that there is a sea snake on Sister Earth, and that it eats hatchlings—"

"—I knew you were up to something, going up and down the stairs—" Lava says, interrupting.

"But it wasn't my daughter, after all. It ate my sister. That was the dream. It was a memory."

Lava bolsters herself up to a seat on the countertop.

"You're getting ahead of yourself. Didn't you ask the Sages?" Her, too?

"That's the problem. I think they know," I say.

"But why—out of hundreds of kids—would the snake choose your sister?" Lava says.

I hesitate to tell her. "There are lots of snakes. Think of other women you know who are an only child. Even men. There's a crew member—"

"So wouldn't they have the dream, too?"

I take a deep breath. "That's what Omar said. Why am I the only person to have the dream? The answer is, because I'm responsible to do something about it."

Lava laughs, but it's not her old gleeful laugh. It's sardonic. "Oh, sure. You are the same old Deer, aren't you? You've got to be special. This is just like when you wanted to go to Monterey and we nearly drowned."

Even my best friend doesn't believe me.

"Lava, I'm telling you, I saw a picture of the snake on the Terminal. I read all its characteristics. It's real. And the Sages know about it."

In the mirror, I see a huge knot in my hair. I look insane. I haven't combed my hair for probably a week.

First Omar, and now Lava, don't see this as urgent. They think I'm being rash. Sure, in the past, I have made hasty decisions. But this is different. This is trouble that's been brewing for months.

If no one will believe me, then I have to show them. I have an idea.

"You'll see," I say. "When we lay our eggs, I'm going into the water. The Terminal said the snake is attracted to human fluids, like the egg runoff at hatching. My sweat and blood will bring the snake to the shore and everyone will see something they cannot deny. Then the Sages will have to do something about it."

Lava rolls her eyes. "You really think you're something? This is what you do. You're desperate to be important. To the point of harming yourself? You know the water on Sister Earth will burn your skin."

"You don't believe me." I paddled to Monterey. I'm not afraid of any water.

"What does it matter, if I do?" Lava says. "If this is true, then it's done with the cooperation of the Sages, for the greater good. If you challenge their consensus, you get three flags in quick succession and you're sent to isolation. Deer, we live in paradise. All our needs are taken care of. Not a lot is required. But you go around acting like every polite smile is an insult to your very being. Why can't you just be happy?"

"I don't know, maybe because I lost my toddler sister? If you thought you might lose a daughter—"

"Would I go against the Sages?" Lava wipes the corner of her lip. "She's gone. Live for both of you. Write twice the poetry. Deer, I'm telling you, it's not that hard to just blend in."

"You're a Primrose sister. I wouldn't call that blending in."

"Think about what you just said! We look alike. We're all dancers. No one can tell us apart. Most days, the unique role of Lava doesn't exist."

I fold my arms.

"Deer, isolation is not for you. I have an aunt who was sent there."

"The treehouse architect?"

"She was talented," Lava says. "She had a team of workmen, but she liked to handle the most complex constructions herself. She was nailing in the wrought iron frame of a balconette addition to second-floor French doors, and lost her balance. She landed on the shrubs below. It was a red flag right away. The woman who'd hired her didn't want the residence anymore—claiming it was tainted—so it was dismantled. Her lovers stayed away, not wanting their reputations tarnished. The treehouse was her last true inspiration. She quit making art after that and the next two red flags came quickly."

I'm reminded of how I treated my mom after her red flag. Would she rack up two more so quickly, and be in isolation before voyage even returns? I never thought that would be the last time I see her.

"So she's in isolation?"

"She was. I've heard pieces of the story only when my aunts and cousins are gossiping, a few bottles in. I'm afraid to ask my mom directly. But one time my mom finished a bottle of her favorite vintage after winning a show." Lava ruffles her tightly coiled curls. "My mom said the Sages quit giving my aunt the tinctures because they were having the opposite effect. They were making her more angry, not more compliant. But my mom said that's by design. Sometimes tinctures bring you to health by making you vomit. In my aunt's case, there was something she needed to release, but she never got the chance."

I look down at the floor tiles, squares of black tourmaline set in a hazy golden paste.

"Isolation is not a nice place," Lava says softly. "They give you all kinds of delicious food in hopes it will refresh your happiness. They'll tell the family, 'She responded well to cinnamon today!' But no one comes out of isolation. There's no human interaction because the Sages don't want to put anyone else at risk. All women choose transition."

I rinse a towel with water and dab my forehead.

I'm a poet. It doesn't make sense that it would be my role to defeat a vicious predator. At the same time, I know I'll be haunted by the dream if I don't, and that is a fate worse than isolation.

"I lied to a Sage—"

"Deer! I can't talk to you if you're going to be like this."

"Okay," I say. I am alone.

But at least now I have a clear intention. Once we reach our destination, I will surrender to my fate. I'll leave my eggs on the beach. And to give them the best chance at life, I will withdraw into the water, and die the same death as my sister.

TWENTY-FOUR

"Fellow maters, I have the best news." Ivy is back on the center platform, with her white voyage robe somehow looking crisp and clean even after many weeks in space.

"Not another lesson circle," I mutter.

"Our Sage—" Ivy motions to the hooded woman sleeping in a back row chair, sitting upright. "—says we made up for lost time. We'll be at the Womb Tunnel in just over a day."

What a relief. If I was the one slowing down the ship, the decision I made to go into the water must have freed my stuck energy.

"It will propel us into Sister Earth's solar system so we can land. Who's ready to lay some eggs?"

Not a single person makes a sound.

The first years have hung quilts around their bunks to make a fort. Women have made strict rules about use of the exercise room, reserving it for friend groups for hours at a time, no walk-ins allowed. Any hope of camaraderie was lost earlier in the voyage.

"I know it's been a long voyage. To commemorate this momentous ... err, moment—"

Ivy struggles for words. I would break down in front of such a tough crowd. I admire her resilience.

She smiles nervously. "Let's have some collaborative art to capture the range of emotions we are all feeling. Okay?" She nods on stage. "Let's start with—"

I keep my head down. Going on stage is the last thing I want now. I'd be almost guaranteed to expose my plans. And then they might actually eject me into space.

"—Lisa the acrobat, and Ellen the portrait sketcher!" Ivy announces.

This one is going to take some effort to set up. Lisa is digging through the hallway closet for hanging silks. Ellen finds some paper and leans a folding chair against a bunk as an easel.

Lisa climbs onto a front row bunk to hang the silks from the ceiling, a few feet away from the chandelier.

"Let's give them some ambiance," Ivy says. She hums a G to tune us. The sound surrounds me and my shoulders release as I join in with the group.

Ivy begins singing a Calefean classic—"Adeline." It's about a woman who finds an emerald city in the forest and can't get back home.

She runs, oh oh
Climbs the tallest tower of them all
But Adeline can never go home

Lisa swings and twists in her interpretation of the collective mood. Ellen does a few sketches of the mythological Adeline and the emerald city, then sketches a more literal interpretation of Lisa's movements.

The whole room is filled with the song. Tense faces of women dissolve into relaxation, and some women sway, side to side. The chandelier bobs from Lisa's movements.

Ivy has a talent for shifting the emotions in a group. I can see her, one day, replacing her teacher Osha and leading the mothers to a successful voyage launch.

No one else even wanted the responsibility of ship captain. She has the rare capacity, and more importantly, desire, to be front and center. Without a doubt, what's been a challenging voyage has gone more smoothly with her leadership. If I get a chance before we land, I'll thank her. It's the least I can do, since I'll obviously not be alive to follow through with her proposed collaboration.

The next duo is a drummer and a cheese maker. Since we do not have milk on the ship, the cheesemaker describes her process and shares food pairing recommendations, to the drummer's pounding rhythm of bare feet on the wooden platform. My mouth puckers as if I'm tasting each variety she describes.

"Deer."

Ivy said my name.

My heart pounds. I stand.

"And I'll collaborate with sounds," Ivy says.

This isn't a judged show. What the others displayed were casual, messy versions of their chosen art. Everyone's expecting me to share a poem.

I walk up to the stage and look around the amphitheater at my fellow women—my fellow almost-mothers.

They don't know their children's lives are at risk. The best I can do for them is to die. Has it really come to that?

The girl from my dream flashes into my mind with a response.

"That is not the only way," my sister says. "You can speak."

I step onto the wooden platform. The drummer's barefoot beat still reverberates through the wood.

The old saying that people fear public speaking more than death wasn't so far off.

I've come to terms with death.

"This isn't going to be a poem," I say to Ivy. "But it's something I need to say."

She clears her throat. "I'll follow you," she says.

I address the room. "This is a true story. It's not from the Records, well, not exactly."

Ivy hums softly.

The best I can do is to tell them everything. At least, everything except for the part about Omar and the Terminal. My one last favor to him can be to protect him. I want to own my role and all the mistakes I made along the way.

"This white snake is still on Sister Earth. It is a predator of humans. It ate my sister, and it will feed off our own children when they hatch come spring," I say.

Ivy's voice rises into a piercing scream. This must be one of her remembered sounds. My skin erupts into goosebumps.

The first years peek above their quilt fort. Whispers travel through the amphitheater. In the back row, the Sage's hood no longer tilts to the side. She's alert.

Breezy, two rows behind my seat, hollers out. "That's disgusting. Why would you disturb us with a horror story when we're a day away from laying our eggs?"

Ivy starts humming again but breaks off into a cough.

"It's true," I say. "It's not a made-up story."

I turn to Ivy. My best theory tells me, as an only child, that she lost a sibling, too.

"Don't you know it's true?" I ask.

A baritone voice comes from the end of the aisle. It's the crew member who gave me the massage. "I remember," he says. "I've had a dream like that—every year during mating season. It's why I never went to the Lunar Party. It depressed me too much, to put anyone through that."

"Stop the nonsense," Breezy says. "Be like the first years. Cut your hair. Take another plant remedy. Stop making the rest of us sick!"

A few voices call out in favor. The noise in the amphitheater rises. I feel smaller and smaller.

"We can't lay our eggs on that planet," I say. "Our children will die!"

The amphitheater explodes into chaos. Women are yelling. The chandelier swings from side to side as if the spinning ship has hit some turbulence. I'm tempted to pull myself up onto Lisa's silks so I can retreat to the ceiling. Being upside down would give me perspective.

"Well, where can we lay our eggs, if not on Sister Earth?" Ivy says.

I want to tell her there are other planets. I think of the space maps. There were so many planets in the same solar system as Sister Earth. Surely one of them would have the right nutrients. But, who knows if it would also have natural threats.

If I say anything about the Terminal, I expose Omar.

The crystals on the chandelier rattle. The Sage shuffles up the aisle to the center platform where Ivy and I stand. She's shorter than either of us. Same height as my old classmate, Copal.

"My loves," she says, speaking into the glass amplifier. "We are approaching the Womb Tunnel. It is the birthplace of all creativity. In the Womb Tunnel, you will not be somebody. You will enter the dark. When we exit, your identity will return. You will be the same particular arrangement of subatomic particles that you are today."

The crowd rustles. Women hush each other, straining to hear every word the Sage says.

"The Womb Tunnel is a place of pure potential. It is where

all creation begins. Thoughts become things. If any of you lacks purity, the results will be ugly. "

There's an audible gasp.

"Keep your thoughts pure, and you will be safe."

She sets down the amplifier. The Sage turns to me. Her floppy hood obscures her face and neck.

"Expect a red flag when we're back in Caleaf," she says.

Ivy stares at the ground. Our first and only collaboration has come to a quick end. I know what she's thinking. If she hadn't called me up to the front, none of this would have happened. Maybe she's thinking, she should have known better. The Amateur Art Show judges were right about me, after all.

But me? My worst fears have been cleared. I've seen something that's only visible on the other side of speaking up.

"My poetry, your sounds," I whisper, "they're coming from the same place."

Down the aisle, one of Lava's sisters has taken my seat. My quilt and other belongings have been tossed across the aisle. I don't belong there anymore.

Deep within, I feel okay. Even if it takes 500 years for the Sages to resolve the atrocity of the Poon, and all of us here are long transitioned—I know I did my part.

I EXIT the platform into the aisle. I'm not sure what my place is now. There must be a vacant seat somewhere in the amphitheater, but in the past few minutes, everything has shifted.

Ivy's co-captain, Lulu the acrobat, steps onto the platform. "I believe Deer," she says. "I don't remember much about hatching, but I remember being afraid. Especially whenever I'd get a glimpse of that beach."

"That's because the water stings your skin!" Breezy hollers.

Murmurs ripple through the crowd.

"I don't want to go back, either!" someone among the first years yells.

The Sage shakes her robe. "We have less than an hour, beauties. If we don't go into the Womb Tunnel with a clear, collective intention, we won't come out at all."

A line of women is building in the aisle opposite me. One of them steps onto the platform and picks up the glass amplifier.

"My mom told me she laid five eggs. And I only have one sibling. Everyone tells us that some eggs just don't develop, but we always felt like someone was missing."

She hands the amplifier on to the next woman. It takes me a moment to recognize my friend. Sequoia's face looks more round with her short bob.

"I have a story I need to tell, too," Sequoia says. "When we left Sister Earth last fall, it was different than most of you remember. There was a story in the Records we used to play called 'The Lottery.' It's about a character who gets killed by a mob. I played Mr. Summers and Edgar played Mr. Harry Graves and our friend Eddie—" Sequoia's voice descends into a sob. "Eddie would play Mrs. Hutchinson. So we were throwing rocks at Eddie just like usual, but we really killed him. Somehow we dropped out of the Records without knowing it."

The first years are arguing. Someone nearby shushes them down so Sequoia can finish.

"I'm the one who did the query that day. I didn't—learn the lesson."

The first years stand up in front of their fort. "Eddie was my friend!" one of them yells.

Sequoia continues. "We tried to bury him, but the rabbits dug him up. Some of the kids wanted to light him on fire, some wanted to throw him in the water."

Her voice is barely audible from the sobs.

"Someone wanted to eat him," she whispers. "The kids split up into opposing teams. They were sharpening rocks and making bows and spears. They were planning a real-life battle. And then voyage showed up. We boarded, and left, and I thought if I could get back to Sister Earth on the Motherhood Voyage, maybe I could fix it. All of it."

Sequoia crouches down and vomits on the oak platform.

"I've spent the past year digging through the Code of Caleaf for loopholes," she says. "But the truth is, I deserve isolation. When we return to Caleaf, I volunteer to transition immediately."

She drops the amplifier to the ground. Tears drip down her chin, and nasal discharge shines off her upper lip.

All this time I thought I was the one slowing down the ship. All the while Sequoia was sitting on a secret. She was the so-called traitor.

Sequoia turns to the Sage. "Please don't leave me in space. I just want to say goodbye to Edgar."

"I'M SORRY, but we can't lay our eggs in a war zone," Ellen, the illustrator, says. She's crying.

"We can't lay them on the ship," Ivy says. "I don't know about you all, but mine feel like they're going to break out of me any minute. I can't hold out for much longer."

I'm still standing in the aisle. "Ok, bear with me. We land the ship. We fill some buckets with phosphorus sand. We take it back to Earth, and lay our eggs in Monterey—"

"Deer, no," the Sage says.

"It's secluded! By land and sea."

The Sage shakes with laughter. "The amount of sand we'd

need to pack onto this ship, for the eggs of several hundred women," the Sage says. "We'd need a fleet of ten ships this size."

My shoulders slump.

The Sage sits cross-legged on the platform with her hand on her forehead. She's telepathically communicating with the other Sages back home. If I thought she might have mercy and change her mind about my red flag, it's too late now. Word has traveled.

I grab the amplifier. "There are other planets," I say to the crowd of women. The room goes quiet like a dimmed light. "Hundreds of them."

The Sage breathes heavily as if she's downloading a lot of information. Her shoulders twitch. I'm not sure she likes what she's receiving.

"There are space maps," I say. "On the Terminal."

The Sage jumps back to attention. "We can't just show up on a planet, uninvited, and lay our eggs there, with no respect to the existing wildlife, the geological balance—we need permission for that kind of thing." Her hands are briefly visible as she waves her arms. Her skin is pale from being shielded from solar light.

My heart pounds. Somehow, I have to convince enough women on this ship to violate Sage orders. What will she do, give out hundreds of red flags?

"And it's not just the wildlife we need to petition," the Sage says. "We would need permission from the Oxalis."

"What—what's an Oxalis?" Ivy says.

The Sage brings her palms together in front of her face. "The Oxalis are our human neighbors on Earth. They hold dominion over many galaxies. The space maps belong to them."

"I thought we were the only ones left?" Ivy says. She's crying now, too.

The Sage says, "We agreed to mutual isolation generations

ago. Now, we may not even have translatable language. There's been no communication."

Maybe I don't need to convince all the women. Just the one who happens to be a Sage.

"The Queen has a different story," I say. "And I know someone who can help."

TWENTY-FIVE

The Sage and Ivy follow me into the stairwell. We leave the co-captain, Lulu, in charge of preparing the women for the Womb Tunnel, which none of us have actually been through and we're all horribly unprepared for whatever it will require. Downstairs, in its small room, the Terminal is covered up with a colorful quilt once again. I activate it and the trumpets play.

Both Ivy and the Sage jump back in surprise.

I fill them in on the voice commands and how to find the maps. In the process, I reveal that I've been snooping around on the Terminal—an act worthy of a second red flag. If the Sage is logging the offense, she doesn't show it.

The Sage taps her forehead through her heavy brown hood. She taps, faster, then a little harder.

Her shoulders slump in defeat. "I can't get through," she says. "I would need unanimous approval from the Sages to change our destination. But without a connection..." She clears her throat. "My oath is to shepherd this voyage of women to lay their eggs, for the abundance of Caleaf. I'm afraid to ask, Deer, but—what do you have in mind?"

I pull up the maps. "Everything about Sister Earth is on this

Terminal," I say, repeating Omar's words. "And we can send a message back to Earth, no intuitive connection necessary. Or—to another civilization."

"Wait—those tiny dots are all planets?" Ivy says.

"They are the other Sister Earths. It's an entire solar system of planets with comparable environments to Earth. I don't know if they're all ideal for egg laying like ours is. Well ... was."

When I tap on a planet, the screen brings up a grid of information about it, just like the map did for the wildlife species on Sister Earth. The images are blurry, like before.

There's a swampy planet with frog-like creatures.

There's a rocky planet that has no visible vegetation.

There's a planet that's entirely underwater, with an extensive list of sea creatures.

"These don't look like very good options," Ivy says.

The Sage paces behind us. "Less than 30 minutes to go before the Womb Tunnel," she says.

"Show me the best planets for laying eggs," I say to the Terminal.

A new list appears.

The first one is our Sister Earth, tagged in the Terminal as SE046.

"See?" The Sage says. "We are already using the best planet."

"But aside from the Poon, what if the kids have continued making weapons?" My throat catches.

I tap on the next one, below it. SE107. It's got red dirt and deep canyons. A river. No trees. Only bushes.

"There!" I point to the section on jurisdiction. "It belongs to the Oxalis. They use it for their eggs. It must be okay."

"Just because the Oxalis are an advanced civilization does not mean they are peaceful," the Sage says.

Ivy groans. She's making one of her remembered sounds.

She closes her eyes. "I can't believe we're not alone," she whispers.

I know how she feels. The existence of another civilization is better than a miracle and worse than a threat, because we don't know which they will be.

I compose a message to Omar.

I'm with our Sage and ship captain, Ivy. The first years alerted us to a crisis on Sister Earth and we need to lay our eggs on another planet.

Omar's message comes back, seconds later.

The first years here are quarantined. The Sages pieced together what happened on Sister Earth when they did Edgar's intuitive scan. But they are struggling to find a flower tincture to treat the issue. All our Sages have gone searching into the wild.

The Sage sighs loudly. "And I thought the bad connection was on my end. If I can't get through to the other Sages, I'll have to make the decision myself."

I open the next planet on the list. It has a lot of waterfalls, and elephants. It also has the Poon.

"Nope," I say.

The fourth planet has blinding white sand and the only wildlife are insects.

"How is this good for eggs? What would the kids eat?" I say.

"Co-evolution takes time," the Sage says. "Do you think the beautiful climbing trees, and the tart berries, and the abundance of reishi mushrooms, were all there hundreds of years ago when we started laying eggs? Do you think any of the eggs from that first laying survived their childhood? It takes years—generations. Our human species evolved to survive on that specific Sister Earth, and the planet itself evolved to harbor us. Its topography and climate matches our Pacific island home. It is Calefean perfection."

"Even the Poon?" I say.

"Even the Poon," the Sage responds.

Ivy gasps. "Are you telling me that you knew about the Poon this whole time?" Ivy says to the Sage.

"It keeps us peaceful," the Sage says. "Every thriving population has a natural predator to keep its numbers in check. Why would humans be different?"

"Good goddess." Ivy turns to pace around the room. "We've been scrambling for more mates, more eggs, just to have our reproduction limited—by an outside force?"

"The Poon coevolved with us," the Sage repeats. "For mutual benefit."

"If what the first years' said is true," Ivy says, "it's not working. Deer is right to question it."

"If you knew the things the Sages know!" The Sage says, chuckling.

"So tell us," I say. She is silent. I point to the Terminal. "We are not going anywhere with a Poon, but what's our verdict on white sand planet?"

"We can't leave our eggs there," Ivy says. "The survival rate will be low. Really low. I wouldn't even be able to forage food there. I doubt many hatchlings will."

The fifth planet on the list is covered in snow.

"The Terminal's analysis may be correct that it is appropriate for eggs, but the children who grow up there would not be well-equipped to live in Caleaf," the Sage says.

"Our best option is with the Oxalis," I say.

Ivy's face glows in reflection of the Terminal screen. "But, leaving our children to grow up on a planet belonging to another civilization? They'll be outsiders. How do we know if the other kids are peaceful—"

"Obviously, we can't guarantee that of our own!" I say.

"You don't know the Oxalis," the Sage says. "You don't know their values."

"Do you?" I ask.

"The women will not like it," Ivy says. "They won't, but they won't want a vacant planet either. Maybe we go upstairs?" She looks at the Sage for approval. "We can all think about it some more? Take a vote?"

"Consensus takes too long," the Sage says. She would know.

I write to Omar.

We need permission from the Oxalis to lay our eggs on their SE107.

We wait.

Omar's message comes back.

Absolutely not. The Queen is in the midst of a sensitive negotiation with the Oxalis. This would derail years of effort.

The Sage leans in towards the Terminal. "Years?" she says. "This is not good. Whatever she's up to—the Sages will not be happy about it. The mutually-respected isolation was a safeguard against extinction—"

"Wait," Ivy says. "If we're not alone, I need to know how many other civilizations there are on Earth."

The Sage scratches her head through her hood. "Can't say exactly. It's a big planet."

"It's our intuition that keeps us peaceful, not the Poon," I say. "And if the Oxalis have intuitive technologies, I just can't believe that they're bad."

I dictate a message to Omar.

The Oxalis planet is our best bet for these eggs surviving. We need you to translate a message to them.

"Even if he does, the Oxalis will certainly say no," the Sage says. Then, louder. "We have mere minutes before the Womb Tunnel! I see it!" She holds a fist out in front of her face like she's measuring the sun's distance from the horizon.

"But what do you say ... Sage?" I'm tempted to come right out and call her Copal.

Omar's response appears.

Do you think this is a game, Deer? An adventure? There is too much at stake.

Ivy puts her hand on my shoulder. "He doesn't understand what it's like to have eggs in your belly," she says.

I think back to that last night with Omar before I boarded this ship. Maybe I was wrong. We could have worked as lovers. I told him about my dream before anyone else. I felt safe with him. Was that love?

But now I see why Omar couldn't get a cloud to budge in those childhood races on Sister Earth. Intuition is not just sensitivity. It's willingness to risk. It's confidence in the outcome before there is proof.

I don't think he'll love me anymore after what I'm about to do.

"Terminal, new message to the Oxalis," I say.

"Deer, I already gave you one red flag," the Sage says. "Remember your role. I don't want to give you another—"

A yellow lined sheet of paper appears on the screen.

I dictate a message.

Oxalis, my name is Deer. I am a poet, daughter of Rain the watercolorist, and granddaughter of El, who was a great ceramicist in Caleaf. My voyage is in crisis and needs an alternate destination to lay our eggs. May we use SE107?

I press send.

All three of us step away from the Terminal.

The spinning ship wobbles. In the stairwell, crew members jog to their seats on the lower level. The Sage has her hand to her forehead and I know she's pulling the brakes to slow us down and give us more precious time. We stare at the Terminal, waiting.

The Terminal speaks. "You've been inactive for 60 seconds. Shall I shut down to conserve power?"

"No!" I yell.

The ship, in a continuous spin since we boarded on the clifftop meadow, jolts to a halt. The three of us are thrown to the ground.

WITH MY FACE pressing into the rug, I pull my plant remedy from my robe pocket. To go against Omar and the Queen. What will we tell the women?

I consider an opening line: "We're choosing between an old place we know is bad, and a new place that might be good."

For me, all that matters is the Poon. But every woman is living a different story.

They'll worry our children will look different than the Oxalis kids. That they'll be treated like outcasts and when they return to us in 20 years, they'll show up broken on the inside. We've seen enough historical stories in the Records to know it is dangerous to be different.

I take another dose of evergreen. Four drops, under the tongue.

My limbs are pressed down into the rug as if we're spinning faster and faster. My body feels like it's being pounded with pressure from every direction. The silence is loud.

Then, I'm floating. I'm nothing. I'm a single photon of light and everything around me is light. It is pleasant. I wouldn't mind staying here.

But there's movement. I'm sucked into a vortex, with all the other little photons, and we're rushing down a drain, getting closer and closer to a tip that never arrives.

Just as I give up, my eyes pop open.

I remember who I am. Deer, age 27, a soon-to-be mother

who belongs to Caleaf. I'm in the spacecraft, on voyage. I move my arms and legs. All of me is intact.

I SIT UP. The Sage is tapping on the Terminal.

"We made it," she says. "We're in the solar system of the Sister Earths. The sensor data is coming in."

Ivy crawls to her knees, and pulls herself up to standing. Still wobbly, she wraps an arm around the Sage to read what's on the Terminal.

"We have crystals inside the rocks on Sister Earth that collect data throughout the year," the Sage explains. "When we get close, their information is uploaded to the Terminal. It's faster than me scanning the entire planet."

Ivy's mouth gapes. She points her finger to the screen.

The human population on Sister Earth should be in the upper four figures. The current count is 250.

The Sage sighs. "Last year, when we were one child short, we worried there might be a disease on the planet. A disease that could wipe out the population if it spread. That would wipe out Caleaf if someone brought it home. And I suppose that did happen, in a way."

I climb to my feet.

A new message appears on the screen. It's a response from the Oxalis. We did it. We got through.

It's a single word, but it's not in our language. The characters look like hieroglyphs.

"That's a word I don't know," I say.

Ivy says, "Can't you sense it?"

I gaze into the word and take a few deep breaths. "I'm not getting anything. I bet Omar would know the translation."

Just as I'm about to turn away, the Terminal speaks. "This

message is in a different language than your default setting. Would you like me to translate?"

"Please!" Ivy and the Sage say together.

Below the strange characters, an intelligible word appears.

Affirmative

"They said yes!" I raise my arms in victory. I grab the caped arm of the Sage. "Please," I say.

She grunts. "I know I'm going to regret this, but ... fine."

The ship tilts as she intuitively updates our navigation, and we spin past our old childhood planet into unknown territory.

TWENTY-SIX

As we land on the planet of the Oxalis, the alternate Sister Earth, the spacecraft's pointed base burrows into the hard ground. I follow the line of women and jump from the spacecraft door onto the sand. The aridity of this strange planet envelops me.

Every movement activates a new sore muscle, the result of so much time sitting still. The crew hands each of us a thumb of blue cohosh root, but I don't think I'll need it. My eggs feel ready to slide out the second I drop into a crouch.

Several hundred of us are asking the same question—where to crouch? This isn't the beach of our own incubation and hatching. We can't smell our way to our point of origin.

If we were on Sister Earth, the women would move chaotically at first, feeling into the magnetic field and scent trails from decades ago. Lava and her sisters would lay their eggs a few feet from each other. I would find the exact spot I was hatched, and my mom before me. The whole ordeal would take no longer than an hour.

Here, we feel the planet's magnetic field, stronger than the one on Earth, but it's unfamiliar. It offers no guidance.

The sand on this beach is not soft. The grain is colored pebbles. The water, though vast, is too still to be an ocean. I saw a river on the maps, but this must be a lake. High canyon walls wrap along the water as far as I can see.

When the kids hatch, where will they go? There's no sandy hill to fumble up on hesitant hatchling legs, an essential stage in building bodily strength.

The Oxalis mothers have already been here. Their gelatinous eggs poke out among the pebbled sand. I dodge these living mounds as I stumble along the shoreline.

The women radiate out. Everyone's looking around and waiting for a cue. I haven't seen a single woman crouch.

I wipe my face with the sleeve of my robe. The rocks pinch and poke my feet. I sink to my knees and dig my fingers into the sharp rocks. The intelligence of my body is taking over. I can't hold back any longer.

I excavate a shallow ditch. With my feet placed on either side, I crouch with my knees wide. I inhale and then moan as the first egg drops to the ground. The vibration of my voice opens my channel. I put my palm between my legs. Another one is coming right behind it. I relax my belly and pump my hips up and down a few times. Two more eggs plop down, piling on each other like dumplings. Four to go.

A pleasant humming drifts down the beach. It wouldn't surprise me if it's Ivy. She could be having the most miserable egg laying experience of any of us and still think to encourage the women around her. Like a true Calefean, she always considers the group's needs first.

I hum along. It helps. Another egg slides through me.

I move my hips in a small circle, then switch directions. I rub my low belly. The final eggs drop out. I have done it.

With my hands, I push the rocky sand over my eggs, creating a small mound like the ones I saw earlier. I drop to a seat and roll down to my back, with my legs still spread wide on either side of my mound. I drift into sleep.

When I wake, light shimmers off the still water. The sun is rising over the lake. It's big. At least our kids will get a blue horizon, even if it faces the reverse of our ocean sunsets.

A few women tentatively dip their toes in the water. It doesn't sting. Our children will get to swim.

I recall my plan to dive into Sister Earth's acidic water as a sacrifice. I would have done it.

With the help of my sister and my dream, I've protected my children from the one thing I most feared. Whatever I've left them vulnerable to, I don't know, and I won't find out for 20 years.

TWENTY-SEVEN

On the return trip, the ship feels lighter. Our bellies are free from the pressure of eggs, and, riding the wave of the universe's expansion, the ship flows with the outward spiraling current.

It's not all good news. Everyone is sick. Nausea, excruciating headaches, dizziness, and bodily aches and pains. We continue taking the flower tinctures the Sage provides, but sometimes, it makes the vomiting worse.

"Sickness is common on the Motherhood Voyage," the Sage says, in an attempt to comfort us.

But we know this voyage is not like any other voyage before it.

On my way back to the amphitheater from a particularly productive expulsion over the toilet, I encounter Isla in the aisle. She looks so much like Lava, I can't believe I'm not looking at my friend.

"Lava says you can have your old seat back," Isla says.

"Oh! That's nice," I say.

We haven't spoken since the egg laying—since our last heart-to-heart in the washroom when she told me about her aunt. I'd figured she had written me off as halfway to her aunt's fate, but maybe there's still hope for our friendship.

I pack my quilt and tinctures into my arms. When I'm halfway around the outer hallway, I'm accosted by Breezy.

"You!" Breezy pushes me into the wall. "Even if the Poon got half my eggs, I'd still have five. That's better than zero," Breezy says, motioning to the amphitheater, "Now we've lost our entire class of eggs, because of a nobody poet who thinks she knows better than everybody." Breezy's nose is inches away from my face.

"Hey." I hear Lava's brusk voice. "Get off my friend."

Lava's smile can brighten a room, but her frown has even my least favorite South Calefean cowering.

Lava wraps her arm around my shoulders and walks me back to our original seats. Sequoia's is still empty.

Once we're seated, Lava takes my hand. "To be honest, Deer, I agree with her," Lava says. "With my egg counts, I would have been happy to take on the Poon. And what I saw of that other planet—I don't like it."

I know she's saying what women are thinking. Most women on the ship, anyway.

"But what I've been thinking about since we reboarded," Lava says, "is what it means to be sisters. I share everything with my sisters. My mom. My clothes. My art. Nothing is really my own. You understand what it's like to have something of your own."

I nod.

Lava fluffs the back of her tight curls, pressed flat from her pillow. "For the women who have fewer eggs—they deserve a chance. It's not just a numbers game for them."

I reach up and wipe an eyelash off Lava's cheek. "I've been so shady to you. And Omar," I say. "The pattern is, when I get too close to people, I get scared."

I pull my robe tightly around my chest. "I think it has something to do with losing my sister. I'm afraid of losing people, so I push them away."

"It makes sense why you would do that," Lava says.

"Did I really mess things up with Omar?" I say. "I don't know what's going to happen when we land. He was kind, even when I literally ran away, and that's what matters, right? Now I just wish I had given him a chance—when I had the chance."

"Omar's a good man," Lava says. "But not your man. Listen to yourself. If you have to talk yourself into it—" Lava makes a face like encountering a bad smell. "Don't."

She's right. "The only romantic connection I've felt was that South Calefean who ran away," I say.

"Ran away?" Lava says.

"Disappeared," I correct myself. "Who will ever understand me? I hardly understand myself."

The crew enters the auditorium with trays of oat porridge. I spot Walt's brother's long braids, but he keeps his gaze straight ahead.

"I thought I did," Lava says with a sigh. "I used to think there was more between us than friendship." Her voice drifts into the sound of glass jars clanking onto tables.

"Babe!" My mouth spreads into a silly grin. I wrap my arms around Lava and drape one of my legs onto her lap.

"Thing is, I'm always trying to stand out from my sisters," Lava says. "You stand out. I don't know if I wanted you or just to be more like you. Maybe both."

"You're by far my favorite Primrose sister," I say. "Friends again?"

"Friends," Lava says.

"Best friends?" I say.

"Don't push it!" Lava jokes.

When Walt's brother hands us our oat porridge jars, I let my finger graze his hand. He's my only tether to Walt, a man whose intuitive skills go beyond sensing the elements. He can talk to them. There's one more secret I want to tell Lava, which has implications for both my heart and the future of Caleaf, but it's not my secret to tell.

I'M GETTING my last massage of the voyage when I overhear Ivy talking to her co-captain, Lulu. I wrap myself in my robe and follow the sound to the cold plunge.

"I believe you," Ivy says. "There's no shortage of proof the Poon exists. Even the Sage admits she knew about it. What I don't understand is why, as an only child, I wouldn't have seen it. I mean, isn't there a good chance I lost a sibling?"

I walk in.

"Oh!" Ivy says. "Hi, Deer."

"Your sibling could have been a Sage," Lulu says. Possible, but unlikely. Ivy was not the same year as Copal, and I don't remember anyone else in the years near us who joined the Sages.

I dip my feet into the cold water, sitting on the edge.

"Wouldn't we have seen the Poon attacks when each year was hatching?" Ivy says.

"No. The beach was gross," Lulu says.

"Why?" Ivy says.

"Well—" Lulu pauses.

"We couldn't swim in the ocean there," I say, wigging my toes in the Mothership's space-chilled salt water. "Kids even used to joke—if you misbehave, we'll throw you in the ocean by the egg beach."

"It was a gross beach," Lulu says again. "I mean, I suppose it's beautiful, but we all had a memory of hatching there, which is primal, and not entirely pleasant, so we didn't want to go there."

"Primal," I say. "What a word. Both beautiful and raw."

Ivy stands to exit. "If it was that scary, I just think I'd remember it."

My skin erupts into chills. I pull my feet from the water as if just realizing it's toxic. "That's it!" I say, loudly enough both Lulu and Ivy jolt backwards.

"It's something Sequoia told me about memories," I say. "They're hidden if they're too scary. So much that they are never uploaded to the Records when you transition." I pull my knees to my chest.

"But my memory came back to me when I decided to become a mother. Why was that?"

THE SAGE ADDRESSES the amphitheater as we approach Earth's orbit.

"I've received an update from the Queen's staff." She's talking about Omar. "The women back home have been struck by the same illness. There will be no welcoming party when we land. The Sages on Caleaf are still roaming the wilderness, searching for an appropriate plant to make a new tincture. I'll be joining them."

Throughout the room, women whisper, already speculating on what's happened in the past few months since we left.

The Sage says, "Traditionally, you would each begin construction on a new residence, now that you've become mothers." A few voices holler a halfhearted cheer. "The construction projects will be on hold until our collective health is back to normal. Please return to the residence of your mother."

I groan. "We're going to have too many red flags for one roof," I say.

Lava pats my hand. "But who knows? If it turns out you saved our eggs, maybe they'll reverse the red flag."

"I don't know that I'll survive long enough to be sure of that," I say.

The Sage turns slowly, taking in the room of women from the center. "If your flower tincture is making your sickness worse, you don't have to keep taking it," she says. "We'll have a new solution for you soon."

"To be honest, I've vomited so much I feel better," I say.

"So it worked," Lava says.

"The tincture?"

"I know you don't know me for my extensive knowledge of plants," Lava says. "And I don't have Sequoia's photographic memory of Code quotes. But when I'm in my aunt's treehouse, I wonder if she wasn't really crazy," Lava says. "They say the flower tinctures bring harmony to your energetic system. So if they're making you sick, maybe that's what you need. Maybe the only way to get better is to eliminate the bile."

"So to follow this analogy, your aunt's rickety treehouse, which will surely be the cause of your untimely transition if you stay there through a windstorm..." I say. "It was eliminating—something broken?"

"It's not just a treehouse. It's an art installation," Lava says. "I think what she was trying to tell us is, the beams of this place are not stable."

"I can see why the Sages would be spooked," I say.

TWENTY-EIGHT

The Mothership lands on Earth in the late afternoon. Humid air of late August meets us as we climb down the rope ladder onto the dry brown grass of the launch lawn.

My walk through town back to my mother's residence is not so different than my first time showing up there in a voyage robe. This time, the terrain is unfamiliar not from novelty, but from change. There are red flags on residences that didn't have one before. The blacksmith's residence is completely gone. Including her patio chair. She must have transitioned. The home is demolished so a new mother can custom build her residence to some new trend or personal style. There is always work for builders. Always a residence under construction on every block. Caleaf's streets are ever-evolving.

The red flag above my mother's residence flops in the breeze.

"You're back," my mom says with her arms crossed.

The living room, perpetually dim and empty all my years living here, is warmed by a fire in the fireplace. Easels with half-completed canvases are scattered behind the couches.

"You brought your studio upstairs?" I say.

"Oh, that? I'm experimenting with new colors and the garden level didn't have enough natural light."

Dad comes out of the kitchen with three mugs of drinking chocolate.

"There was no party," I said. "The Sages didn't show up to do the residence selections."

"We heard your voyage was unsuccessful," Mom says.

"Is that what people are saying?" I ask.

"The queen announced that your Sage on board lost control. She'll be assigning two Sages to the next voyage," my Dad says. "It's terrible to hear you lost your eggs, but once they shared the sensor data from Sister Earth—well, one voyage of lost eggs is nothing compared to an entire generation exterminating itself."

My mom squints, taking in the disheveled voyage robe I'm still wearing. "You wouldn't believe what's been happening here."

My dad glances towards our garden. "The Sages are up north at the farms dealing with wildlife contract breaches. The pests are taking over yields, threatening a food shortage. I'm adding in carrots and potatoes with our usual vegetables, just in case."

Some gray stubble foils his dark skin. The remnant of a small cut exposes him. His intuition is waning.

"And haven't been able to get in for our annual scans," he says.

Mom puts a hand on his shoulder and carries on, swinging her mug around as she delivers her melodramatic update.

"The cotton's been totally destroyed by a fire. A big rain came through and some women in town had to relocate because of black mold. Then there was the first years' diarrhea—"

"We had that on voyage, too."

"And what else was on your voyage, some moron who

thought you should leave your eggs on a foreign planet? You poor thing. If only—" She reaches her hand to my cheek.

"That was me."

Mom's voice trails off.

All those years I tried to be what I thought my mom wanted. Now it occurs to me that she rightfully has no idea who I really am.

"I got a red flag," I say. I look towards the kitchen as if the red fabric might be folded on the counter, where Mom's was just two months ago, before Dad climbed onto the roof to hang it for our neighbors to see.

"That won't be coming anytime soon," my dad says. "Tell her about the wool—"

"Oh, there's a dispute between the sheep boss in South Caleaf and the weavers," Mom says.

I throw up my arms. "My career is over before it even started, and you're telling me rural gossip?" I say. "The women on my voyage hate me."

My dad sets his mug on the coffee table. "But now you've landed, and your mother is catching you up on what we're all dealing with—here."

"Fine," I say. "Fill me in."

"The sheep boss wants the Sages to send an emergency voyage to Sister Earth because they're worried about their kids."

Jacara knows the sheep boss. Her dairy farm is in the same region.

"But, the weavers say bringing back any kids who survived the conflict will make the health here worse than it already is," Mom continues.

Lolanda knows the weavers. She collaborates with them to make fabrics for her dresses.

"We can't just leave them there," I say. "Both Jacara and Lolanda's kids are on Sister Earth. Well, they were."

"Some women think we should. They think they're dangerous," my mom says.

"This isn't exactly paradise," I say.

"It would get a lot worse," my mom says. "And how do you think the women will power up a ship if they're all filled with anger?"

My dad shifts his weight. "The Sages will choose the best decision."

"So we just wait for that?" I say.

"Three women were taken to isolation last week," my mom says. "The health here is precarious. Some women have lost their intuitive abilities completely."

Mom turns to her canvases and flips one around so the wood-paneled backing is exposed.

"Mom—what gave you the idea to switch colors?"

Her unfinished paintings are too abstract for me to recognize forms. A blotch could be a cheek or a flower petal. A shadow could be a figure or a nose.

"Oh, you know how your dad is always saying, energy cannot be created or destroyed. Once I quit having to enter shows and be around other women, I wasn't angry anymore. I finally had energy for new ideas. Oh well, it doesn't matter. It's too late to save my reputation."

The fire crackles. My mom's wrinkles have set in deeper since I last saw her, but the outline of her skin glows a warm gold.

"My eggs might be okay," I say.

Mom cups her mug and inhales the frothed chocolate steam. "On the planet of our sworn enemy?" she says.

"Where did you hear that?" I ask.

"Why would our civilizations stop talking if we were friends?" Mom says. "They must be extraterrestrial hybrids or something." She makes a face. "That's why they're not in the

Records. And that's what's so unnerving about it, now that they have access to Calefean eggs."

"I did it to protect my children. From the Poon," I say. Of all people, my mom should be on my side. She'll understand—she has to. "I did it because of what happened to my sister."

My dad clears his throat. "You're an only child, Deer."

I keep my eyes on my mom's face. "I've been having dreams about her. I know you built the Residence with a fourth floor because you expected two of us. Didn't you?"

"Deer, it should come as no surprise to you that my mating numbers were not especially good," Mom says, nodding to her partially painted canvas.

"And you're an only child. Did El ever tell you how many eggs she laid? Because at hatching, you would have seen your siblings—"

"Hatching is not something I choose to think about," Mom says. "Why, why do you insist on making life more difficult than it already is?"

I slump my shoulders.

"It's better for me to not remember," she says.

I keep thinking if more people remembered the Poon, they would understand. They would make sure we never lay eggs on that planet again. But their memories are stuck because it's too painful.

THREE DAYS LATER, a message arrives. It is intricately folded into the shape of a rose and garnished by a gold ribbon. I unfold it. The text is hand-calligraphed on the Queen's letterhead.

To all of Caleaf:

My beloveds, we are on the verge of extinction.

Questionable circumstances on Sister Earth have greatly diminished our numbers. It will take decades of Motherhood Voyages to replenish our offspring. Meanwhile, a sickness from that same conflict has crept its way home, leaving many of you ill beyond the support of our flower tinctures.

I know the question on your minds is what we will do about the children on Sister Earth, who are our children, but also pose a threat to our entire existence.

According to the Code of Caleaf, every child receives an intuitive scan by the Sages on the Homecoming Voyage.

We will double the number of Sages on the next Homecoming Voyage. Upon scan, we will isolate those who are beyond repair, scheduling them for transition upon arrival to Caleaf, and treat with the best intuitive remedies those who are stable.

We will continue to run Motherhood and Homecoming Voyages, on the usual schedule.

Secondly, after conferring with the Sages, I have agreed to cut off all contact with our Pacific mainland neighbors, the Oxalis. It was my decision to break many generations' commitment to mutual isolation in search of advanced technologies to serve you, my beloved people. The negotiations were exponentially more tense than those with even our sharpest-toothed wildlife. Now I see how my actions have put us in danger.

With our diminished numbers and weak state, we simply cannot risk external conflict. It will wipe us from the face of Earth and demote us into the Records of history.

I have agreed to retire as of the next dark moon, and live out my twilight years in the countryside as a new woman rises to lead our island civilization. It has been my honor to serve a long and peaceful reign.

What I leave you with: Anyone who attempts to contact the Oxalis, now or in future, will be subject to immediate transition due to the danger it causes every person within the borders of this island.

For now, do what brings you joy, to bring Caleaf to its full power and expression to fuel every voyage, now and into the future.

The letter is signed in glittery gold ink, *Queen Ande.*

I read the queen's letter three more times. It's my fault the queen is transitioning? Because Omar and I exposed her attempt to talk to the Oxalis?

I feel dizzy. But, I cannot agree to this. I won't live out the rest of my life, always wondering what became of my eggs. My friends' eggs. The Sages may be afraid of the Oxalis, but I messaged them, and I'll do it again.

There must be a way to challenge the Sages. It's not right for them to have authority, even over the Queen.

But the mischief I pulled on the voyage to win over one Sage isn't going to work on an island of women who hate me. I'm going to need to find a loophole in the Code of Caleaf, and I need Sequoia's help before she destroys herself out of guilt.

———

THE NEXT DAY, on the way to Sequoia's mother's downtown residence, I pass through the daily market.

When I reach downtown, the main street looks empty. I worry I'm too late. Then I see the stalls are compacted close to the government gates. My usual favorite bread baker is not present. Neither is the apricot boss, the berry jam chef, or the pizza chef. It's the early-career mothers who are missing. These are women my age or slightly older. Women who have kids on Sister Earth.

On the edges of the market, there's a woman sitting alone in tattered clothing, her face baking in the hot sun. The vendors look bored. A few people mill about, but no socializing. No joy.

Ivy's standing at her mom's pastry table, wearing a pink apron with the Calefean rose embroidered on the front and her mom's name underneath. When she sees me, she averts her gaze. Oh yes, I have a red flag. I suppose our agreed collaboration won't materialize outside voyage.

I walk slowly past her. She's only got her usual scones, and a few fruit-filled donuts. My shadow from the afternoon sun crosses her face. She stares at the single chocolate-frosted donut out on her tray. I'm close enough I could grab it, and I'm tempted to, just to see how she reacts.

Some tables are not vendors at all. An acrylic painter has an art installation on display. It's an intricate painting of a white snake against a blue background, with the words drawn in a fancy typeface, "Peace on Earth."

The Poon, as a symbol for peace? If they'd seen what I saw in my dreams, they'd never think it.

"What does this mean?" I ask her.

"The Poon helps siphon off the troublemakers. Like you and your mother," she says.

My mouth drops.

"That's not true!" I say. "My mother keeps to herself—even to a fault."

The sparse and quiet market is interrupted by drumroll.

"And—action!" a woman hollers.

I turn to see a woman in a long burgundy dress sprint into the market, chased by two more women, dressed only in gray swimsuits, with feathered wings strapped to their shoulders. The coarse wings, intricately woven with thread and seagull feathers, brush my face as they go by.

The winged women tackle the lady in the dress as she cries, "Help! The Oxalis!"

It's a performance piece. I suppose extraterrestrial hybrids isn't the only rumor about the Oxalis going around. These three seem to think they're part bird.

After lying still for a beat, the three performers rise and bow. A few vendors snap in appreciation.

I decide to grab a snack and get over to Sequoia's house before another artistic expression has me giving up all hope. I approach a bakery stall.

"I'll take two baguettes," I say, motioning to the long sticks poking out of her covered trays.

"No more baguettes today," she says.

"Oh! I meant those." I point.

She's looking over my shoulder. "All out, sorry."

I step back. The stall next to hers is the pastry chef.

The bread chef from the adjacent stall is watching, though. Ivy won't talk to me. She wouldn't sacrifice her own reputation. Word has already gotten out. Even without the wool to hang in display, they know I have a red flag.

I exhale. As I walk towards the far exit, women peel away from me as if I'm a mole splitting a path in the dirt with my body.

The last stall adjacent to the government gates belongs to the pizza chef. I haven't seen her since our launch. She has a red flag, and while she's not banned from the market, no one is lining up for her delicacies the way we did all summer.

There is a silver-haired woman yelling in her face. "I am the only surviving member of the ice expedition," she says. "Yeah, no one likes to talk about why a woman got sent to the mountains."

Vendors leave their spots to listen in.

"I watched those men fall to their deaths," the woman says. "But I don't belong in hard labor. Once, I was a harpist. I went on my Motherhood Voyage just like the rest of you, and I laid five eggs, and none of them came home to me!" She slams her hand on the counter.

"The Sages took my residence. They took my stipend. I'll never meet my babies, but I will kill the Poon with my bare hands."

The pizza chef leans forward. "I wish I could change what happened to my daughter. But we all make sacrifices for the greater good. To lose a few children each hatching? It's for the best."

The pizza chef sees the gathering crowd. It energizes her.

"People were killing each other for thousands of years," the chef says. "Do you want us to go back to that? Let the Poon live."

The crowd cheers and groans in equal volume. I glance through the government gates, wondering how much of this is being watched by the queen's staff. Or the Sages.

I inch closer to the pizza chef's stall. "I'm sorry about your daughter," I say. Surely, having been on the wrong end of Sage decisions, she too would question their authority?

She nods at me with recognition. "Linden sacrificed herself for your voyage. And you made it a waste."

My heart pounds. I have so few friends in Caleaf. If even a fellow woman with a red flag shuns me, I'm completely alone. I glance at the baguette woman, and the pastry chef beyond her.

"May I?" I motion towards her sliced green olive pie.

"I won't deny you. Take a slice."

"Thank you," I say.

I could warm it with my hands, but it doesn't feel right.

I back away, and in the process, bump into someone.

"Watch where you're going! If your intuitive sensing is off, stay home!"

I turn around. The woman is old enough to be my mother. I don't know her, but she has a baguette in her basket.

"I'm sorry," I say.

"Get out of here before you harm someone," she says. She drops her gaze and walks away.

Along the fence of the government building, a long line stretches into the neighborhoods. It's women and men waiting for their annual scan from the one lone Sage who hasn't gone north to deal with the agriculture crisis. No one looks healthy. All of them have a visible ailment—a limp, a wound, a rash, a cough.

The Sages don't have a remedy for what's befallen Caleaf. And if we're not healthy, there's no way we'll be able to sing with enough harmony to power the next voyage.

SEQUOIA'S SECOND MOM, the assistant calligrapher, answers the door. Sequoia's five brothers are lounging in the living room.

The last time I was here was the afternoon of the Lunar Party. I hadn't paid much attention to the common spaces. There are patchwork quilts draped over every couch and chair. Quilts hang on the walls. Quilted cozies wrap around the mugs on the bar-height marble kitchen table. Sequoia's mom must be a quilter.

"They're upstairs," Sequoia's second mom says. They? I imagined I might find Edgar here, too. The more the merrier.

"Sequoia?" I say, drumming my fingers on the entrance to the third level of the downtown residence.

"Deer, come in!"

Sequoia and Edgar are pretzeled on a bean bag, her head on his chest, his arm over her waist, her fingers in his red hair.

"You look great," I say. "I was worried—after how things went on the voyage."

"Actually," Sequoia says. "I am glad you pinged me." She unwraps herself from Edgar and sits up. "I was so miserable, and sick, and as soon as I told everyone what really happened on Sister Earth—I felt better." She tugs her ponytail loose. "And I only did it because I saw you share your story. So I have to thank you for that."

My eyes fill with tears. "I'm so glad you're okay," I say. "And I hope you won't go through with—transitioning."

"No." Edgar pulls Sequoia into his chest, wrapping both arms around her shoulders. "We'll deal with a punishment from the Sages if it comes, but especially with everything else going on, I imagine they'll be debating the origin of this for quite some time."

"That's what I came here for," I say. "I disagree with the Sages. On the Oxalis. Whoever the next queen is, we need her to establish open contact so we can be sure our eggs are okay."

I crouch down to sit on a quilted stool. "What does the Code of Caleaf say about the Sages' authority? I need a loophole."

Sequoia crinkles her nose, and begins recalling text from her photographic memory. "Our matriarchy was designed after analyzing the weaknesses of many millennia of fallen patriarchies," she says. "Caleaf stands for motherhood. Reproduction. Care. Future generations. Collaboration. Compassion. Generosity. Consensus."

She returns her gaze to me. "The Sages dialogue about every decision. The reason the queen backs them, and the people trust them, is because they take as much time as it needs. They only act when consensus is reached. And the cornerstone of every decision is they're always going to choose the greater good over any individual."

Edgar adds, "It's a really good system."

I stare across the room, past Sequoia's bed and dresser, to

her open studio space. She's got stacks of blank canvases and a triad of easels set up, each with a stunning self-portrait. She must be feeling a lot better—to paint herself in such glory.

Edgar clears his throat. "There's also an emphasis on tracing issues back to the source," he says. "That's why Queen Ande took the fall for communication with the Oxalis. That's why Sequoia and I will eventually have to answer for the great loss on Sister Earth."

"So what does that mean for the Oxalis? These are your—both of your eggs, too!" I say to the pair.

"They'd intuitively run predictions and determine a probability," Sequoia says. "Based on all of history. If it's, say, a 30% chance of war, that's not worth it. They will protect the collective in the name of peace for future generations."

I remember why I disliked Sequoia when Lava first introduced us. She doesn't care how something makes you feel. She just wants to be right.

"I'm not just thinking of myself," I say. "What about the Poon? How is it care for future generations to lose hatchlings every year? We should kill it."

"Hmm," Sequoia says. "I imagine it's been debated. But again—most of the kids survive. An expedition to attack the Poon would be an act of violence. The antithesis to peace. Ultimately, I don't think the Sages could get on board, in keeping with these values."

I feel like I'm in a particularly lively Records learning circle. Social science was never my favorite subject.

"Okay, okay, no acts of violence," I say. "But the ice expedition, which we've always known was dangerous—"

"To lose a few men each year so the collective can have better food preservation and enjoy properly chilled date creams?" Sequoia says. "Debatable. That's why it's taking the Sages more than a year to decide."

"Ugh," I say. "This just feels wrong. What about when an act of violence is care?"

"Can—can that be possible?" Sequoia says.

"You want my take?" Edgar says. "If you want people to get on board with a new way, beyond the Code, initiate a great act of care. Outdo the Sages at their own thing."

"Intuition?" I say, thinking of Walt.

"Healing," Edgar says.

Sequoia turns and squeezes his cheek. "Wow, you're so smart, babe!" She looks back to me with a grin. "Can you believe him? That's what you do, Deer. What you pulled on the voyage, but now, with everyone. Get them to tell the truth and then the illnesses will go away."

I consider it. "Okay, so it'll be a confession circle? Would anyone come to that?"

"Maybe call it something different," Sequoia says.

I TAKE the long way home on a path west of town. Along the way, I see miniature rock formations and leaf art. Flower crowns hung on the knobs of trees.

Women are artists, through and through. We're not ourselves if we do not create.

I arrive back at my loft, invigorated to workshop the idea I got from Edgar and Sequoia. When I am at loss for direction, I turn to the Records, and this will be no different.

After moving through my exercises, I try an old trick Adollo taught me. She called it the non-query.

I hum a C. The Record Keeper appears.

"Tell me what I need to know," I say.

My room dissolves into a crisp breeze. Brown leaves crunch under footfalls on concrete. I'm leaning back on a Victorian park bench. The wood slats are worn smooth. My hands are stuffed in coat pockets.

"True story," I say.

I'm female.

My character is gazing up at a bronze statue of a man on a horse. There's a plaque by his feet, but she's not close enough to read the caption.

Whoever this man was, a lot of care was put into preserving his memory with this art installment. In this moment, though, she doesn't know who he is, and neither do I.

It's funny, then, that many centuries later, it's her story I am seeing.

I settle into the character and feel the tightness in her chest. Dry skin on her nose flakes from being wiped with a college cafeteria napkin that she's still gripping in her pocket. She's been crying.

It gives her solace to look at this old statue and not know who the man is. In him, she sees both significance and mortality.

A squirrel scurries on the top rail of the fence wrapping around the grass. It stops to face her. The animal can feel the reverence of this moment. She's about to make a decision. I can feel the build of emotions rising through her chest to her throat. What she's about to do could ripple through time and space, and change everything.

She wants to change her major from pre-law to fine art.

Her smile is my smile.

"What happens next?" I whisper.

The scene goes dark. The Record Keeper slides the book back on the shelf and I'm back in my loft again, alone.

The lesson is clear: While the Code can convince minds, only art can win meaningful devotion.

I poem drops into me, as if it's been hanging in the air above my head. I see a string of words and mouth along. I can't help but think this one would be better with music.

And dancing.

***

THE NEXT MORNING, I'm on the rooftop of Lulu's mom's residence, a drinking chocolate mug in hand.

"This is the eucalyptus wood set she designed for a tulip garden boss," Lulu says, pointing to her patio furniture designer mom's samples. "And this slat bench was a hit for entryways."

Ivy is the only one standing. "I'm not sure I should be here. My mom is loyal to the Sages."

"It's just a show," I say. "Aren't they always quoting the fore-mothers, *beauty begets beauty*? Art is how we heal. We have to pour our feelings into the art," I say, quoting Grandma El's advice. "Right now, anger isn't a symptom—it's the cure."

Lava crosses her legs on a wicker chaise lounge. "That was the worst voyage in recent memory—no, not because of you, Ivy, you were a great ship captain. But look. We came back healthier than most of the women who stayed behind. And we have Deer to thank for it."

Lava's got fresh toenail polish on, and I can smell her lavender oil. Lulu's hair is in an intricate braid. We're each holding onto what will boost our own moods, trying to choose beauty, but it's tough, among all the bickering between neigh-bors, the paralyzing grief, and the illnesses.

"And you think this poem you wrote will help all of Caleaf?" Ivy says to me.

"Not just the poem," I say. "What we need for this show is for everyone to bring the art they're most afraid to share. What feels offensive or disturbing. The rage, the anger, the guilt. What you worry will get you shunned. Your sounds. Lava's dancing." I grin. "It's going to be so ugly that it's beautiful. And we'll call it the Great Purge of Shame."

Lava adds, "I bet we can get some more women from voyage—especially if you help us, Ivy. The women trust you."

Lolanda rummages through an oversized canvas bag in her lap, from an acrylic bucket seat. Her bangs are trimmed to brush her eyebrows just like always, but her freckles have faded since the last time I saw her.

"When I heard what happened on your voyage I was inspired to work with black velvet," Lolanda says. "These samples are like the outfit I made for Lava's performance, but with more texture."

Lava reaches over to feel the fabric. "I have an idea for a dance that will be different than anything you've seen." She claps her hands. "Lolanda. Can you make some of these to fit men?"

I turn to Ivy. "If we can recreate the emotional release that happened on our voyage, we can help everyone process the grief of what's happened. What's still happening. This is how we help. This is how we contribute."

TWENTY-NINE

A few hours later, women from our voyage are building a stage on the fields west of town. A woodworker has borrowed her mentor's tool set. Triangular arrangements of beams are connected with canvas to make a big tent that doubles as a backdrop. Another team of women are taking self-fueling carts to deliver hand-calligraphed invitations to the residences in town and beyond.

I don't have to look far for the poem I'm going to share. It's the one that's been inside me all along. The initial lines made it into my notebook months ago, and now I've expanded it.

Ivy should be warming up with the singers, but she finds me leaning against a tree, watching a butterfly.

"I worry it isn't enough," Ivy says. "You said you've got something special for the end?"

"It's going to be an outpouring of emotions like Caleaf has never seen," I say.

What kept me up last night was contemplating how we can truly recreate the alchemy we experienced aboard the Mothership. My dream had been with me in the months prior, but the impetus to take action was only mid-voyage.

The turning point was watching Linden fall. Her loss was the loss of my sister, all over again. Memories, even the stuck ones, come back into the light when the same painful emotion is triggered.

Sequoia is wrong. Sometimes an act of violence can be an act of care. I need to break the peace to expose what's rotten.

That's why I'm bringing more to this show than my poem.

"Good," Ivy says, "because I got the voting machine from the government building."

My visualization of women crying and hugging in joyful relief fades.

"You did what?" I say.

I follow Ivy to the stage. We walk up the center aisle, outlined by small rocks stretching all the way across the field, and bigger rocks that mark rows where women can lay out their blankets to sit on the grass.

Right in front of the stage there is a golden scale with the Queen's rose quartz crystal weighing down one side. It's surrounded by dozens of tall vases, each one overflowing with long-stemmed white roses.

It would be a beautiful decoration if I didn't know which section of the Code of Caleaf outlined this particular arrangement.

The voting machine works like this: Women may vote by plucking a single white rose petal off one of the buds, and placing it in the empty bowl of the scale. If the Queen's quartz crystal is outweighed by the accumulated petals, she is overthrown.

"But Queen Ande already agreed to step down," I say. "What—what does this accomplish?"

Even Sequoia didn't suggest this route. Because it's not going to fix anything.

Ivy stands with her nose inches from mine and talks low.

"We still have a few days before the Queen's transition party. We need to send a message to the next queen. We're not abandoning our eggs."

Lava's counting off the dancers in the tent. She shrieks with delight. They're learning her choreography fast. Some workmen are rolling in a statue as big as a horse, covered by blankets. The women have been creating. Their expressions are to be revealed soon. This show was my idea, but it's like an accelerating wave that's grown outside of my control.

"She says she had a peaceful reign, but it's not true!" Ivy says. "Look at what's happened on her watch. She doesn't deserve a transition party, or twilight years on some other woman's goat farm. She deserves an immediate transition."

Caleaf has never overthrown a queen. If Ivy turns the women against Queen Ande, she will not only lose the throne, but she'll be sent to transition—alone. Her final destitute moments will color her existence in the next realm. It is needlessly violent.

"Are you sure about this?" I say. The show was my idea, but I can't get the women to come without Ivy's support.

"If I'm going to make my sounds in front of all these people, I want it to count," Ivy says. "Last night, I talked to my mom. She was an only child, too. Neither of us remember the Poon, but the more I think about it, my theory is those of us with the most pain are least likely to acknowledge it. We had it worse than most women."

I had intended to use an act of violence as an opening—to return us to peace. With my heart pounding, I worry each small rebellion sparks a fire that will grow to such height none of us can control it.

AT SUNSET, women trickle onto the clearing. Some saunter in as if they're just passing through. Others approach the scales right away, with urgency. They vote.

Lava and I are huddled in the tent with the dancers and props.

"Who are these beautiful women?" I say. I recognize some women from our voyage, and others I can't place.

"It's our crew," Lava says. "And some old friends. You remember Jules from the Amateur Art Show?" A woman with purple-dyed curls winks at me. The men are wearing wigs.

"I always thought men's strong bodies would make for some spectacular choreography," Lava said. "But I was afraid to try it because I had never seen it done. Surprise, these men have an instinct for rhythm. I may never go back to solo work."

A harp soloist plays on stage. I peek through the entrance of the tent. Some women spectators have brought their husbands, as requested.

"We gave invitations to red flag women, too?" I say.

"Everyone was invited," Lava says. "The first years, men, everyone."

The audience doesn't number much more than the performers in the tent when we light the stage candles. Ivy steps up and greets the small crowd.

"This show is imagined and produced by the members of the latest Motherhood Voyage. The style of art may be different than what you're used to. Clapping is not necessary—crying is encouraged. We are here to feel."

I step onto the freshly-sanded wood platform, to my mark, on stage left. In the fading sunlight, I see expressionless faces angled up at me. I begin my poem.

I want beauty

I want power

I want to see things as they really are

I want to look past the self-doubt
and self-loathing
and know the real me.

As I finish, I keep my feet glued to the stage. I'm not going to rush off and miss the applause—or lack of it—this time. What I see is something different. Women and men hold their palms to their hearts. A few snap their fingers. I know I've done it. I've written something true, and they can feel it.

I bring my own hand to my heart, and bow in gratitude.

As I exit, Lava is lifted on stage by two crew members in shaggy wigs. Her freshly-trained dancers wear Lolanda's design of black velvet jumpsuits.

One dancer twirls Lava, and the other lifts her up by the waist. She's propped up onto both their shoulders while they do footwork, all the while keeping her steady. More dancers join them, all in the same dark suit, with colorful banners attached to their arms.

The first song begins. A procession of guitars emerges from the tent. They sit on the edge of the stage, just behind the vases of white roses.

Lava holds her arms out in a T shape and the dancers lower her to her feet. She leads choreography with the music. The dancers clap and slap on beat. Each fourth count they slam their feet on the stage so hard that I'm afraid someone will split a beam. The music speeds up. They all jump at once. They land on their hands and knees, then split, rolling off the stage to the left and right.

A dancer brings a pole onto stage and slides it into a carved-out base in the wood, then twists it so it anchors into the dirt below.

Lulu is up. She somersaults onto stage, landing with her legs straddled and her cheek to the pole. Without flinching, she uses the strength of her arms to inch up the pole, then flips upside down, holding on with only her legs. Then, only one leg. The audience snaps their fingers with awe.

The dusk has quickly faded. I see movement far out in the field and realize people are still arriving and arranging their blankets in rows beyond where the rock markers are laid. Lines form on either side of the stage leading to the voting machine. A few petals have joined the Queen's quartz crystal—votes for the Queen to live.

Ivy and her singers step to their marks on stage right to accompany Lulu's dance. They hum. She lifts her arms and looks up at the night sky, then dives forward and kicks up into a handstand. The sole of one foot leans against the pole and her other leg points straight up. She bends her knee and grips the pole with the back of her leg. She lifts her arms to a light applause. She curls up into a ball at the very top of the pole, then adjusts her legs and swings around it, picking up speed, 3, 4, 5, 6 rotations before she reaches the ground. In the candlelight, her velvet jumpsuit exposes the definition of her dense thigh muscles.

Women are whistling and snapping. Their shadows pass in front of the stage as they cast their votes. A mound of petals forms but still has a long way to go before it will defeat the Queen.

Ivy's singers move to the center of the stage to accompany her sounds.

Ivy holds both hands in front of her face. This is the first time she's performed her sounds for an audience. It sounds like a low note of a trombone but something about it reminds me of a tree falling in a wind storm.

Some women gasp. A few get up and jog away. It doesn't phase her. She continues on. More women pass the front, casting their petals for the Queen's demise.

The dancers do an acrobatic number where they toss a flyer

into the air and catch her at the last second. Lava does a solo while being sprayed with water, with the candlelight illuminating the rainbow mist. A few candles sizzle out.

I read more verses. Ivy sings my words and punctuates with her sounds. I've heard whistles, some laughter, and gasps of surprise, but none of the emotional outpouring we had on voyage.

As the singers leave, the stage hands bring a series of easels onto the stage, each covered with a quilt.

My belly turns. Sequoia had told me she didn't want to come. She was afraid of being confronted by angry mothers.

The lights flip on, and she pulls the quilt off the first easel. It's a stunning oil portrait of Linden. The crowd gasps.

Expressionless, she moves to the next easel, revealing a portrait of a child. "These are the kids." Her throat closes up. "I will never forget their faces."

As she pulls the covers off the rest of the pieces, Edgar sets smaller canvases out along the edge of the stage. She's painted the children. All of them. The applause from the crowd starts small, and rises like a wave.

"I have one more thing to tell you," Sequoia says. "Many of you know I have photographic memory, which is true. But regrettably, I'm a mediocre painter."

She brings her hand to Edgar's shoulder. "Edgar painted these. He's done all my work, actually."

Sequoia waits for the muffled whispers to settle down.

"His intuition has always been stronger than mine, and he always compensated for my lack. So when we got here and he wanted to paint—well," she shrugs. "It was the least I could do."

I see the couple, side by side, linked by not one, but two secrets. That's a bond not even mating season could break.

As carefully as they were set up, the easels are refolded by the stage hands. No doubt Edgar's paintings will win awards, though whether a man's art can be sold for profit is something even the Code does not address.

In each performance I see why the artist felt it was a risk, but everything is beautiful. The art is raw, it's erotic, it's so ugly that it invokes pleasure. Each woman is experiencing the freedom I did when I told the truth on the voyage. The freedom to be herself.

The lump in my front pocket, sagging the hem of my dress, is my finale.

I need every woman here to leave crying. It's the only way they can break into stuck memories and release the emotions so we'll be strong enough to power up the next voyage.

The final dance leaves a prop on stage—a tall tree stump. It's the perfect height.

I place the sleeping animal from my pocket on the stump. It's a small white bunny I captured in the hills this afternoon. I grab a serrated construction tool that was pushed under the stage. The Nature Artists would know better what I'm about to do. They recognize when an animal has chosen its transition to the next dimension. The rabbit didn't exactly approach me, but now, it sits serenely on the stump.

I didn't think it would be appropriate to practice. In the candlelight with hundreds of women watching, I realize I only have one shot.

I raise the tool above my head and slam it down.

The bunny is smashed. Before I register the splatter of blood on my dress, I feel the small animal's current of energy flatline. We share creative power with all of nature. It's like losing access to a circuit.

I feel the loss.

I feel the loss of my sister, of Walt, and Grandma El.

The tool clatters to the ground.

Ivy pushes me off stage. Tears stream down her face. "Why, Deer? The show was almost perfect."

She feels it too.

Women in the audience are yelling. "Where are the Sages? She's broken the peace accords!"

Someone shoves past the white rose vases, knocking them to the ground, and presses her cheek to the dead rabbit's guts, shrieking, "Don't go!"

One of the dancers blocks the woman. "No, look. It rests peacefully."

Another woman picks up a glass vase and throws it. It lands on some rocks and breaks. They're lighting candles and trying to pick up the pieces, but now the blood from their hands is staining shoulders and arms. A man picks up a rock and throws it at one of the vases by the stage. It shatters, the long-stemmed roses flopping to the ground.

Women who haven't cast their votes yet are pushing to the front, grunting and groaning. Two women collide and push each other until they both stumble to the ground. They're hollering and kicking. They're wrestling and rolling on the grass. A circle forms around them. One of their husbands pulls them apart but two more women take their place, throwing punches and kicks while an expanding group looks on.

A sourdough chef, one my mom once purchased from regularly, grabs my arm and pulls me into the chaotic circle. Ivy yanks me the other way and pushes me into the tent.

Lava squats on a cushion. She stares at her bare feet. "I know why you did it," she says. "But I don't think you needed to."

I wipe my dripping chin. It's blood from the bunny.

"We needed more—"

"No!" Lava looks up at me. "You always think it's not enough, whatever you do. But it was. It was plenty."

I want to cry but I feel numb. The night's gotten cold. A trail of smoke wafts into the tent. The stage, only constructed hours earlier, is on fire. The women's yelling is overpowered by cheering. Ivy pulls the tent door to the side to get a better look.

"The voting," she says. "The scale tipped!" She turns around. Her face lights up with a smile. "We just overthrew the Queen."

I want to tell her that we are not different. She's killing our government head. I only killed a rabbit.

Women break off a slab of wood from the burning stage and light the end of it to make a torch. They hold it up high and the remaining crowd marches toward town. They're headed for the government building, right now. They're chanting.

Save the children

Save the children

I'm not sure if they mean our eggs on the Oxalis planet, or the remaining kids on Sister Earth. But, this is a statement all can get behind.

Then someone yells, "The Queen must take responsibility!" The chant changes.

We want justice

We want justice

BY THE NEXT MORNING, the scene looks straight out of the Records. Hundreds of Calefeans are splayed out on the ground in front of the locked gates of the government building. We've spent the night here. The women will not leave until the Queen acknowledges the vote.

This can't be Caleaf. We've never challenged our government.

"I wish we'd wake up back in your treehouse and find out this was all a lesson circle of some long-ago event," I say to Lava.

"No," she says. "I feel it in my belly. We're mothers. And this is real life."

The sun is rising over the wildflower hills. On the sea glass-lined pavement, in flower beds, and down side streets three blocks deep, women look like cinnamon rolls curled up next to each other. The chants from last night died off around midnight, but some stand up as if they might begin again.

"Someone's coming!" A whisper spreads through the crowds.

I jump to my feet with everyone else and strain to see the figures pacing down the stairs of the government building. It's a line of government workers in burgundy polo shirts, embroidered with the Calefean rose. They're coming down the grand front steps of the tower.

When they reach the gates, women step back. They slide the gates open and stand on the outside. The front row of women crouches down, and those behind them follow suit, so more of us will have an adequate view.

The government worker in the center holds a glass amplifier to his face. It's Omar. His curly hair is pushed to the side and matted down. Their clothes are fresh, but all the men's eyes droop like they haven't slept.

"My fellow Calefeans. It is my responsibility to share with you that, in response to the results of yesterday's vote, Queen Ande has made her transition, closing out a lifetime of service to our peaceful island nation."

He leans his head to the side and coughs.

So that's it. The official report may be that Queen Ande managed a peaceful reign. But what appears to be peace is actually suppression.

The women start softly. They're clapping to the beat and repeating the chant from last night.

We want justice

We want justice

Omar begins to speak again, but he's interrupted by the holler of someone on a side street. "Where are the Sages? We need to choose a new queen!"

The stomping gets louder. Some sections of the crowd are a half-beat behind, and others are too fast. The combined noise makes the continuous sound of a rattle.

"The Sages—" Omar speaks louder into the amplifier to be heard over the women. "The Sages have left."

The chanting stops.

"What do you mean, left?" a woman says. "Like they're out searching for new flower tinctures?"

"I am reporting all I know," Omar says. "The door to their wing is normally secured, but this morning, we found it wide open. Their treatment rooms are empty. Not a Sage can be found. And it seems, they've taken their supply of tinctures with them."

I lift my fingers to a scrape on my shoulder from last night. I'm low on frankincense. I meant to pick up another bottle from the Sages. What will I do without it? The tinctures are our foundation of health and wellness. What will so many women do without their daily drops of tincture?

I'm jostled by someone pushing backwards through the crowd.

"Stay calm!" Ivy yells.

"Excuse me! Pardon me!" Women are pushing through, trying to return to their residences to secure whatever remedies they still have.

Omar speaks again. "Myself and my fellow government

workers are loyal to Caleaf. We pledge to serve the next queen with equal devotion and effort."

His words are affirming, but his tone is void of enthusiasm. The men beside him watch the crowd with hesitant curiosity.

Ivy pushes her way to the front. She takes the voice amplifier from Omar. He steps to the side and leans back against the rungs of the gate.

"Alright, Calefeans. The Code says the Sages pick the Queen. So how do we choose without the Sages here? So I have an idea: Who is the oldest woman present?" She looks around. "Is there someone who remembers how they did it last time?"

Queen Ande was a year older than El. El did a late transition. A woman who is older than Ande would be very old by now. The women I see around me are younger. Many of them were on voyage with me.

More women slip away from the crowd, still reeling from the departure of the Sages.

"Over here!" Someone yells. They're propelling a woman through the crowd with raised hands. She's wearing a thick gray dress with long sleeves. I wonder if she's hiding a sore like El did, out of stubborn desire to release just a few more seasons of art.

At the front, she's lowered to her feet and Ivy wraps an arm around her to steady her.

"You're Marigold, the cross stitcher, right?" Ivy says. "How do we proceed?"

I'm amazed by her memory of names.

Marigold squints at the crowd. "It's like anything else. We take nominations. Then we vote."

Women's heads turn back, to the side, and over to a friend's ear to whisper. The excitement is palpable. The new queen could be any of us.

"And," Marigold adds. "You can nominate anyone, but you can't nominate yourself."

"You heard her!" Ivy says. ""Nominations?"

Lava and I look at each other. I'm about to joke that this is the voyage captain scene all over again, but she bellows in her low growl, "I nominate Deer!"

Ivy nods. "One nomination for Deer, the poet."

"I can't—I have a red flag," I say to Lava.

"Do you?" Lava says with mock horror. "Because I heard the Sages ran out of red flags, and they're not here to give you one."

Someone yells, "Ivy!"

"Yes? Who would you like to nominate?" Ivy says.

A chant begins.

Ivy

Ivy

Ivy

She looks puzzled. Marigold chuckles. From a distance, I read her lips as she explains to Ivy what's happening. "They're nominating you," Marigold says.

"Oh, right," she says. She brings the amplifier back to her face. "A nomination for myself, Ivy, the singer."

"I've never seen someone so popular try so hard to be popular," I say. "I keep thinking it's a humility act, but she really doesn't know that everyone loves her. Believe it or not, it's genuine."

A member from our crew climbs on another's shoulders. The wigs from the production are gone. I'd forgotten there were some men in the crowd.

"May I make a nomination?" he hollers.

Ivy looks at Marigold. She shrugs.

"Go ahead," Ivy says.

"I nominate Omar. He's worked closely with the Queen for years now. His reign would provide continuity."

There's a low murmur. "Continuity is what we don't want," I hear someone say.

But people are stomping and clapping.

"Can a man be queen?" Ivy says. She looks at Marigold again.

Marigold leans on Ivy's shoulder. "Sure," she says.

"A third nomination for Omar, the government worker," Ivy announces.

"Not like he'd win, anyway," Lava says.

"It's obvious who it will be," I say.

The women beside me are stretching their arms. Ivy senses the restlessness.

"Don't forget that some of us are struggling with their intuitive abilities. Watch where you're going—with your eyes," she says.

"Voting opens at dawn," Ivy says. "Results will be announced once we receive the votes from South Caleaf."

"Wait!" A woman yells. "How will we navigate the Homecoming Voyage without a Sage? Our children are trapped!"

Ivy lifts the amplifier up again. "That will be for the next Queen to decide."

She drops the amplifier and disappears into the crowd. I don't envy her. She's about to step into a pivotal role, and I can't think of anyone better for the job.

THIRTY

In the evening, I cross the threshold of my mother's residence. It's not like my parents to leave the front door unlatched.

The cozy fire in the living room has been put out, but a figure in a brown robe is seated on the couch, facing me. Her hood hangs down around her shoulders, exposing her pale face, glowing in the dark like a ghost.

I'm entranced by the familiar features. It's my Grandma El, but donned in the robe of a Sage.

I walk closer. "Who are you?"

She chuckles. "I'm your great aunt. Or, I was, before I abdicated my maternal lineage to join the Sages."

I bring a hand to my mouth. El had a sister.

"Don't look so surprised," she says. "El and I knew each other as girls on Sister Earth. She resented me when I chose the Sages instead of going home with her to meet our mom. Mostly, because of the ding to her reputation, seeming to be an only child. But she didn't mind the little career boosts I gave her, here and there."

"You helped her," I say. "She had privilege."

"As you know, it isn't always enough." She nods upwards, to the floor above us. My mother.

I sit on the couch across from her, watching her as if she might disappear in a blink. With Ivy as queen, I can see us negotiating with the Oxalis. Even killing the Poon to make Sister Earth safe for the kids. But we won't be able to navigate a voyage without the Sages.

"They said the Sages took the remedies and went to live in the wilderness. Why are you here?"

"Because I have an offer for you."

She pulls an object from the inside pocket of her robe. It's a rough stone the size of two fists, marked with soft lines like it's been smoothed by centuries of flowing water.

"We Sages operate as if we are one mind. We haven't forgotten your red flag. You made many selfish choices on your voyage. You lied about your dream."

"If I hadn't said something, we would have landed on a war planet," I say.

"You didn't know that. You didn't know that until Sequoia spoke up. You only cared about your selfish desires."

She closes her eyes.

"I see your grief about your sister," she says. "When you learned my identity, you experienced a little yellow bubble of hope. You thought maybe your memory was wrong. Maybe your sister lived after all, and is among the Sages. I'm sorry, but that is not true."

Her eyes open.

"As you know, the Records store only human memories. This is just a small part of the infinite shared knowledge of the universe. There is creative power in every animal, plant, single-cell organism, droplet of water, photon of light—a single atom. Even rocks, like the one I am holding, can store information."

She sets the rock on the coffee table.

"This particular rock was retrieved from Sister Earth a few years ago, after spending many centuries there, perched on the beach where we lay our eggs. It may look simple and dingy, but it holds more information than all Terminals ever built—combined. One need only to query it with a particular date and time to get a vivid, 360-degree view of what it saw. Perhaps you'd like to see the day of your hatching?"

"I've seen that beach in my dreams too many times," I say.

"But your memories are murky. Remember what I told you last time? Fear distorts reality. This is what I learned in my many years as a Sage. When fear is invoked, multiple versions of the same memory exist, and it's unclear which to trust. Sometimes we can't find the memory at all."

I realize she's referring to the questioning tactic Sequoia taught me about: mirroring.

"You don't know what really happened to your sister," the Sage says.

My sister. I remember the mole on her right eyebrow. That was a constant. In some versions of the dream, she tells me to run. Other times, I tear my hand away because she's holding me back. My legs are like spaghetti. I push her, not knowing my own strength. By then, it's already too late.

"I'm not a killer," I say.

"In a civilization so carefully curated to be peaceful, you're a troublemaker. You're the only one on this island with the constitution for conflict. Look: You've both caused a standoff with the Oxalis, and fashioned yourself as the answer for it."

She makes it sound like I orchestrated everything, but I was just trying to resolve my dream.

"Don't take my word for it." She nods at the table.

I sit in silence and stare at the rock. Entering the memory through it would be a way to see the scene objectively. I don't know if I'll dream of my sister again, now that I'm safely back in

Caleaf, never to travel space again. The fear I had of voyage has now passed.

I didn't just lose a sibling. I lost part of myself. Now, it's time to move forward.

"You can't give me my sister back," I say. "I know who I am."

"You don't," she says. "You don't, because you still don't see that the Poon is essential to our peace. It's coevolution. The Poon has a particular taste for human blood. But through the centuries we have observed a pattern. The kids who run away survive. It's the ones who fight back who are eaten. That sort of disposition is unwelcome in our peaceful civilization. We will never reach 1,000 years of uninterrupted peace if we eliminate the Poon, as you are proposing."

Out the window, the breeze blows the grasses on the dark hills.

"What do we get, when we reach 1,000 years of peace? Some sort of special thing in the next dimension?"

She laughs. "You want a gold star? No, nothing superstitious like that. We get 1,000 years of peace. Isn't that enough?"

I look away. "But if the kids on Sister Earth dissolved into conflict, the Poon isn't even working—"

"For someone who's spent so much time in the Records, you are a hard sell, Deer. Don't you wonder why the men here are so docile, compared to so much of recorded history?"

"Because intuition helps them be in touch with their feelings," I say.

"No!" she says. "Because the Poon has cleaned bloodlines for generations."

I shift in my seat.

"You want the truth? Here, query this rock. Maybe you did push your sister, like you've speculated. Yes, I can read your thoughts even as I'm speaking. Maybe the Poon got the wrong girl. The only way to know..." She holds out her hand.

"I know I'm a fighter," I say.

In my imagination, I see the old beach scene, but in a new way. This time, I'm charging toward the snake, a rock in my hand, I'm throwing it at the snake, making it right in the nose, and sweeping my sister to safety.

That didn't happen.

I can't change who I was then.

But I can choose who to be now.

"Sometimes violence is essential to peace," I say.

"No, dear," the Sage says. "As the foremothers have written, *beauty begets beauty, and violence breeds violence.* To bring harm to the Poon would be to introduce violence onto the planet, and it would reverberate in violence being seeded here, too. The Sages know the only way to remain at peace is to be peace. That's why we are leaving."

"If we fight with Calefeans, even in attempt to help our people, we are merely fueling conflict! This, this will cause more harm than it could relieve. The mess here—it may take centuries to clean up, and we are well-equipped for it. But, we will remain in hiding until we trust we'll be properly received. Only then will we return with our tinctures."

She lifts her hood to cover her head. "I imagine we'll be back sooner than you realize."

THIRTY-ONE

A week later, I shake out my yellow sunflower sundress in my loft. It's still my favorite of the three. My hair is in tangles. I split it in thirds for a braid, but then, on second thought, I begin the braid from the side so I can wrap it around my head.

Before walking to town, I heat a mug of sipping chocolate over the wood-fired stove. I like the creamy mixture off my upper lip and rub my fingers over the mulberry stained mug. It's one of Grandma El's creations.

I wonder if she would have offered the same advice, had she known I'd live in a time of conflict and not peace. I wonder if she'd even know what to do, herself.

A parade of self-fueling carts with baskets of rose petals speeds to the town center, carrying the votes from South Caleaf and some rural areas. Instead of using a voting machine, the petals will be evenly laid out in three rows. The longest row wins. The new queen will be announced at noon.

The government gates are wide open. Older women walk in the Queen's gardens, mourning Queen Ande. The late Queen's carefully curated floral selection serves a secondary purpose. It has a healing effect, with the absence of plant remedies.

Lava meets me on the corner of the sea glass-paved main road.

"You look regal," she says.

"I don't know why I'm nervous about this," I admit.

The dress shop we shopped in together has a new sign in the window, advertising mosquito poison. Lava nods towards it. "My mom is thinking of getting some for our porch. With the Sages gone, the mosquitos aren't honoring the boundaries they set."

"We resort to violence so quickly," I say. "Where will it end?"

A vocal quartet to our left sings an original song.

No such thing as a male queen

No such thing!

Lava says, "It's catchy, right?"

"It is," I say. "But I just picture your male dancers in a chorus line. I don't think they're making the point they think they are making."

Lava laughs. "Isn't there a word for that?"

"Ironic," I say.

Some first years I recognize approach to cast their votes. They're carrying white petals. My heart flutters. That's my color.

I grab Lava's arm and whisper. "They're voting for me?"

"The first years predict you'll be the most fair because of your experience with the Records," Lava says. "And the Nature Artists, mainly because they see death and don't mind what you did to the rabbit."

The quartet finishes their song. "We love you, Ivy!" they holler.

Lava continues. "The Craft Artists have a bias toward Ivy because she promised them she'll bring the ice expedition back right away, so their cheeses and date creams can be presented at the right temperature."

I nod. "She is a crowd pleaser."

"And," Lava sighs. "The older women are voting for Omar because he says he'll uphold the final decision of the late Queen."

"Wait—was I supposed to make a promise?" I ask.

Lava stops and turns to me. "I think you did, at the show. When you killed the rabbit, I think people understood that as a promise to kill the Poon."

I gaze down the street. White, yellow, and pink petals stretch out down the paved road.

"The show didn't have the outcome I intended," I say. "Though I can't deny it brought women together."

IVY AND OMAR are already seated on pillows at the top of the government building staircase when I arrive.

Ivy taps her knee with her fingers, drumming them to a song she's humming. Her eyes gaze up in the cloudless sky as if her mind is elsewhere.

I lean forward to look at Omar, seated on her other side. Up close, he looks older than I remember. The pudge from his cheeks is gone.

"You know, Omar, if it wasn't for you, I wouldn't have known about the Oxalis," I say.

He sits with hands folded in his lap. "Don't shift the blame on me," he says. "You are the one who sent the message. I said to wait for the Sages."

Ivy leans back, as if to steer clear of the confrontation.

"I still think I did the right thing," I say. "And we can do better than the Sages."

The carts carrying the votes are all lined up. Government workers in teal polos marked with the Calefean rose stand by to begin the counting. The cross-stitcher, Marigold, volunteered to read the result. She waits at the bottom of the steps with her daughter, a horse sanctuary boss.

"The white roses are votes for Deer, let's put those on the right," Marigold says, pointing to the stones laid out to mark rows on the sea glass-paved road."Yellow for Ivy, in the middle, and pink for Omar."

The government workers pull baskets from the carts and pour the petals into a single layer in the three distinct rows. For each man with a basket, three more follow behind, making sure the petals are distributed evenly. The rows stretch further and further down the road that, eventually, leads all the way to the Pacific Ocean. More and more baskets are brought out. The men work fast, and yet they still seem to be racing the sun as they disappear closer to the horizon.

The pink petals run out first. Omar's color. Baskets of white and yellow petals continue to be spread, further and further. He promised to be loyal to the new queen. Ivy won't have any problems.

"Paxostasis," I say.

They both turn to me.

I taste the word.

"I'm not sure where this one comes from. It could be very old." I tap my lips. "Or it could be new."

"What does it mean?" Ivy says.

I spread my arms out wide. "It's got the energy of the expansion of the universe. Holding balance means spreading evenly in every direction, like rolling out a pie crust. We need friction to expand."

In the distance, men are stacking up empty baskets. There

are still more votes. But they're only adding to the row on the right.

The white petals.

I stand up. "Did they lose a basket? Where are the votes from South Caleaf?"

Ivy laughs. "Stop with the false humility, Deer. You're winning. They want you. Is that so hard for you to see?"

"I can't!"

I sit down and drop my head to my knees.

Ivy rubs my shoulder. "I even voted for you. We've got kids stranded on a war planet and negotiations with the Oxalis. We need someone who's not afraid."

My vision blurs. "I am afraid. I have been this whole time."

"But you did it anyway," Ivy says.

Next to me, Marigold's daughter strikes the gong. She places a single note. The street is quiet. In their homes, women are waiting to hear if it's a single strike for Ivy. The woman strikes the gong again. If she stops now, that tells everyone I win. It would be three times for Omar.

After a pregnant pause, the hesitant cheers erupt from the windows. Their voices chant together, and the sound carries from town, to the outer residences, and beyond.

Queen Deer!

Queen Deer!

Omar hands me the amplifier.

"Congratulations," he says.

I stand up. The government workers walk towards me. Women who were walking the gardens come to the front steps of the tower.

I address them.

"I never set out to be queen. Sometimes I'm not sure I should even be a poet," I say.

"But I believe in rising to the role you are given. What I can promise you is what my now-transitioned mentor taught me every poet must do."

I pause.

"I will tell the truth."

THIRTY-TWO

On my first day as queen, Omar meets me at the government gates. "Let me show you the Queen's residence," he says.

We turn left past the government tower to the more ornate building where the former Queen lived—where I'll now live. Omar leads me through the geometric steel doors of the laser-cut stone structure. I thought his work was mainly in the government building. To my surprise, he has been inside her home, too. I'm jealous.

I imagine him inside her personal space and wonder how close they were. His fluffy hair. His soft hands. What drove his unending loyalty.

He points to the door to the Queen's bedroom, where the linens have already been replaced and a wardrobe is on order from the top-rated designers.

He takes me to the library on the second floor—the only space on the island with printed books. The Queen's cats rush by us in the hallway, as if anticipating our next move.

I've never seen a physical manifestation that looks so much like the Records. Spines of books line up in a speckled mirage of color, stretching floor to ceiling, corner to corner, on all four walls of a massive room. Rope ladders hang on hooks so you can reach the upper shelves.

In the middle of the room, a 360-degree fireplace is circled by lounge chairs, its chimney extending up through the high ceiling.

Omar points to a crushed velvet chaise lounge. "You would like to know more about the Oxalis?" He speaks the question affirmatively, as if it is a statement. "I can lead you into their Records. I have done it for the Queen many times."

"They have their own Records?" I say with awe.

"You'll see," he says. "Lie comfortably, and follow my voice."

I sit on the chaise lounge and prop my feet up, leaning back, and bring my hands to rest on my heart.

Omar sits in the armchair near my head. He cues breaths. Inhale for four counts, exhale for four counts. I feel my mental activity dissipate. He hums to open the Records. I see my Record Keeper. I see the library.

"Now, turn to the left, and look for a red door," Omar says. "Tell me when you see it."

"I see it," I say. The Records are vast. I've been in many rooms. This door was never there before. But, I didn't know to look for it."

"Open the door," Omar says.

Inside this room, there is a huge bird. It has speckled markings on its white chest, and brown wings. "I am your Record Keeper here," the bird says.

If Omar continues to speak, I don't hear him consciously. I only follow the bird along the shelves, my feet lightly touching the floor. The bird pulls a book from the shelf between its feathers. The title reads, *Best of Oxalis*.

The library room fades. I'm floating above steep canyons. Between them, a blue line traces the center. A river. But there are floating residences seemingly unattached to the canyon walls. I can't imagine the shiny materials are stone or metal, which would surely be too heavy to support, even with the free energy transistors that power our self-fueling carts.

And more importantly: How do people get around?

The scene fades. My beaked Records keeper guides me to another section and hands me a thick red book with no discernable title.

I'm whisked back to the canyons, but this time, horses run along the canyon walls, ridden by figures in full body armor, feathers in their hats. The group comes across a settlement, and a bloody battle ensues. I look away. Pages flip forward. Now, I'm on a desert plain. There's more fighting. An explosion. More pages flip. I'm shown battle after battle. I recognize some weapons from the history books, and each time a heavy object is slammed down onto a human form, I feel the rabbit under my construction tool. A little of my own life seemed to die with it.

"Thank you," I say to the feathered Record Keeper. I find my way back to the red door, back to the familiar shelves. As I do, the texture of crushed velvet underneath me returns and I blink my eyes open to the Queen's library.

"There was a lot of fighting," I say to Omar.

"They do that," he says. "They haven't spent hundreds of years rewarding their subjects for peaceful behavior."

ON MY SECOND day as queen, I call in my trusted advisors for a meeting.

The long oak table, also used for dinner parties, is cleared of the usual dishware. To my delight, Grandma El's famous set remains in the residence—a poignant perk in light of my new responsibility.

I take the seat closest to the hearth. Omar and his team sit to my right, while Sequoia, Edgar, and Marigold take the seats to my left.

"We've got a health crisis without the Sages and their tinctures," I say. "It is unclear if we can navigate a voyage without them. I'd like to propose some changes to the red flag system. But first, let's talk about the answer the people want. About the Poon. Omar, what do the historical documents say?"

I adjust the sleeves on my new smocked linen dress. It's made to my measurements, but it's still more snug than my sundresses ever were.

Omar motions back to his team. "We've been reviewing the queen's meeting notes over the past 800 years. Some 500 years ago, a Queen named Iris created an initiative to get rid of the Poon. It was on the weekly agenda for 20 years."

He flips to a new page in his notes. I'm continually impressed by how good Omar is at his job. He's direct. He's detailed. He clarifies, but doesn't question. And while his hair is groomed short, there's still enough of it for that distinguishable fluff from Sister Earth.

"The Sages debated the most compassionate way to kill a snake," Omar says, "and invented many creative tools, but none was ever approved unanimously. The objection was always that introducing a weapon onto Sister Earth would have permanent consequences to the quality of life there."

Omar opens a second folder of notes.

"In fact, early in her reign, Queen Ande brought it up again, and the same reason was given. This time, on the Homecoming Voyages, several attempts to communicate with the Poon were made. All unsuccessful."

I nod. "Thank you, Omar and team. And Sequoia, you're here to fill us in on how the Code might be interpreted ... based on new knowledge."

"That's right," Sequoia says. "In defense of the Poon, the

Sages have cited the Law of Mutualism. According to the Code, this means that as a natural predator, the Poon is filtering blood-lines in our favor."

"But to put it more colloquially," Sequoia continues, "the theory is that the Poon picks off the kids that fight back." She reaches for Edgar's shoulder. "We've made a map of the beach, based on my own memory as well as interviews with mothers from various voyages, especially those who have a memory of the Poon. The mothers most affected, including your mother and Ivy's mother, had laid their eggs on the north end of the beach near the rocks. Since we lay where we're hatched, the affliction becomes a family trait."

I lean forward with intrigue. "So those of us who lost a sibling are just unlucky due to proximity? Not genetically prone to fighting?"

Sequoia pauses, then speaks carefully. "It is more likely that the sudden and morbid loss of a sibling, never properly processed, may make a child more prone to conflict."

I consider it. My instinct towards avoidance and rebellion, contrasted with Ivy's eagerness to be liked, but quickness to demand punishment of others who cross a line. We're not exactly the same, but not so different.

Edgar holds out a palm as if to make an offer. "There's something else that indicates the Sages were right about the way the Poon picks kids, just not exactly the way they describe.

Omar interrupts. "According to the Terminal, the Poon is blind. It is attracted to human fluids—"

Edgar holds his hand up again, this time as a stop signal. Omar yields.

"We came across a familiar word in the code," Edgar says. "Piezoelectric." He looks at me. "We know Deer is familiar with this one. In context, the foremothers use it to describe human flesh, particularly when the hatchlings break out of their eggs. The mechanical pressure charges up their energetic system."

When I was first exploring *piezoelectric*, my Records Keeper showed me that treatment room. The human body is piezoelectric.

"So yes, the Poon's digestive system does biologically break down its—meals," Edgar says, his discomfort clear. But he continues. "What the Poon is attracted to are the flashes of light, the energetic release from the broken eggs. The initial electric charge is what sustains life. So it's going after the brightest flashes."

"So the Poon is eating the most powerful kids," Sequoia says. "And that does maintain peace. At least, homogeneity."

I look at the rock on the mantel. The gift from the Sage, which I've kept, but I am still not ready to view its memory..

I address both sides of the table. "So how do we destroy it?"

Sequoia answers. "What we know about Sister Earth is, there's already weapons, and that's a situation we hope to reverse. We don't want to bring more. No one's ever tried to eliminate the Poon. It could be a never-ending mission. Remember, it's not just one snake. There are hundreds." She pauses to catch a breath. "The other way we kill it is to stop feeding it."

I stand up to pace. "We would have to stop laying eggs there. Starve it. How long will that take?"

"We estimate at least 20 years," Edgar says.

Omar sighs. "This will mean a much bigger negotiation with the Oxalis than the one we're already preparing."

I rub my neck, feeling stifled in the thick fabric and closed doors. "And what do we do about the kids on Sister Earth?"

"We need to know what state they're in," Omar says. "I volunteer to lead a voyage." He looks around the room, as if to intercept any early doubts. "I'm familiar with the sensors on the Terminal, the space maps, and I believe I can guide a voyage successfully, even without a Sage. And, I will be unbiased when I evaluate the health of the kids."

At that, Sequoia looks down.

"Marigold—your thoughts?" I ask.

She clucks her tongue. "I would consider how many voyages you are willing to lose before you invite the Sages back home."

I bring my elbow to the mantel and lean. My first meeting has exposed conflicting personalities, and with it, a willingness for each advisor to stand up for what they think is right. I'll take that as a win.

And now I can move on to the real work, which won't happen while breathing indoor air behind closed doors.

"Thank you for your input," I say. "I'll be deliberating in my maze until further notice."

DAMP SOIL SHOWS the bushes have been recently transplanted. Raised planters of roses mark the entrance to the maze.

"Which way?" I murmur to myself. Last time I was here, Walt was holding my hand.

I take the path on the far left. After a few yards, I reach a corner. It turns into a switchback, with tall hedges blocking view of the queen's residence or the hillside horizon. I run my fingers along the leaves, taking in their aroma.

The fall Homecoming Voyage promises hope—or new crisis. The Oxalis have not responded to our messages. Calefeans are increasingly ill. Volatile. Territorial. They shun both the first years, and the women with red flags. No matter their queen has a red flag herself! Had the wool showed up, I suppose I could hang it over my official residence.

As I walk, I let my eyes shut, using my fingertips on both

hedge walls as guide. My foot crushes a leaf. I turn a corner. The smell of eucalyptus wafts around me. A breeze picks up. Behind the lids of my eyes, I see beyond the maze and into the wilderness. It's a forest path with trees thicker than a papasan chair.

A familiar face turns back at me, as if I'm following him down the tree-covered trail. It's Walt. He's smiling.

My entire body fills with effervescence like relief. I know he's okay. And he might be my solution to healing my people— without the Sages.

Knowing the right flower tincture for the right ailment requires talking to the plants. Not just sensing, like when I feel the ocean's next swell. The dialogue with the plants establishes ideal growing conditions, proper preparations, and dosage. Only the Sages produce flower tinctures to ensure quality. They don't even use workmen to transport the glass bottles down to South Caleaf for fear of diluting their purity.

I open my eyes. I'm still alone in the maze. I turn and circle back to the beginning, this time taking the middle path. How am I supposed to find Walt if even his brother doesn't know where he is?

The middle route takes me to the eucalyptus tree I smelled. Beyond, I reach a terrace with a hanging bench, encircled by jasmine bushes. I resist the temptation to rest in the swing.

The intelligence of the maze requires clear intent. The queen must want to solve its riddle, and when she does, she knows the other decision she's reached is sound.

I press on along a brick wall covered in ivy and a line of emerald arborvitae trees.

My bare feet sink into the grassy earth, still soft from the morning dew. My toe hits a rock, and my ankle twists. "Ow!" I yelp, falling to my knees.

I look back, considering the bench swing. The pain only galvanizes me to keep going.

As I limp forward, my mind sparks. A phrase lands inside me.

"Friction creates polarity which is power," I say.

The survival instinct of a hatchling to use all its strength to break its shell—which converts to electrical charge. The disagreements in my circle of advisors that require us to produce even better solutions. I don't have multiple decisions. It's all one question.

Everything comes down to asking the right question.

I turn the corner, and cross under the climbing pink rose arch trellis marking the maze's exit.

"WHERE DOES IT HURT?" I speak into a glass vocal amplifier in my first public address. "Through the Sages, we have learned to treat by centering on the most painful symptom first."

My pleated cotton midi skirt gives my legs space to breathe. Underneath, my sore ankle is wrapped with arnica for the pain. My knees are shaking. The sweat that drips down the sides of my torso cannot be attributed to heat, in the crisp fall air.

With my heart pounding, I continue. "If someone is on a different path, there is something to be learned. Women who have gotten red flags have sensed a crack in the system and we need to know about that crack."

The crowd is silent. My fingers graze the tail of my long braid.

"I will personally meet with all of the first years, and all women who have red flags. Including my own mother."

A few women chuckle.

"Everyone will be heard," I say.

A few women snap in approval, but the sentiment is far from universal.

"And, there will be changes on the Homecoming Voyage. I have asked Sequoia and Edgar to lead. Sequoia has a gift for memory, and she's been through the Womb Tunnel before."

I pace up the stage, then turn back to the crowd.

"This is not the usual voyage. It may require her to search Sister Earth's topography for survivors, mediate conflict, and make flash decisions. That's why she'll have Edgar with her. We need his blend of intuition and strength. They are a dream duo."

No snaps this time.

"Some may say their involvement in the seed of the crisis would disqualify them, but something I've learned from many forays into the Records is that every great leap in civilization is preceded by crisis, and the crisis itself contains the key to evolution. They may not know it yet—" I look to where Sequoia and Edgar are standing in the front row. "But the knowledge we need to bring Sister Earth back to harmony, and safe from the Poon, is already within them."

EPILOGUE

Three months later, I'm reviewing my red flag meeting notes in my library when Omar runs in, unannounced.

"Deer!" he says breathlessly. "There's a ship on the launch lawn. But it's not ours."

Our Mothership is safely stored in the cave, and the Homecoming Voyage ship is in space, with Sequoia, Edgar, and a team of crew members aboard, after Ivy successfully led the women in powering it up.

I grab the hem of my long skirt in my fist and follow Omar down the front steps. We break into a jog, down the sea glass paved road, past the eucalyptus trees, and out to the cliffs, following the trail up to the clearing.

The ship looks like ours. Its pointed base is cutting a divot into the grass, but the earth here is more dense than the sand we landed on on the alternate Sister Earth. Without landing the pointed base against the face of the cliff, the door is the equivalent of three flights up. The ship continues to spin.

We slow to a walk. The door on the ship opens. I wait for a rope ladder to drop down, or the ship to tilt so the door comes to a pause closer to the ground.

Instead, a figure appears. He steps out, into thin air—and for a moment, is suspended. Then he steps left, then right, almost as if making switchbacks through the air, until he is a few feet from the ground. His bare feet drop to the grass.

He approaches us. His mouth forms a series of intelligible sounds. He waves an arm out in a flourish, and bows.

Omar turns to me. "He says he is an xx from the Oxalis. He has come to deliver a message."

Omar's language studies have proven useful.

"Why haven't they been responding on the Terminal?" I ask.

Omar's voice sounds deeper and guttural as he makes the unfamiliar sounds of the Oxalis language. Not like himself.

The man tilts his head, nods, and responds.

"He says, he's here as a warning." Omar and the man continue to go back and forth, Omar pausing to translate for me.

"They see our eggs as an act of aggression," Omar says.

I gasp.

"They're a nation of warriors," Omar adds under his breath. "To them, everything is an act of aggression." He continues translating. "They don't actively use the Terminal anymore because their technologies have rapidly advanced in the past two centuries."

Again, Omar adds color for me. "This was what Queen Ande wanted from them. The new technology."

"And," Omar says, "The response you—we—got from them, that the Terminal translated to us as 'affirmative,' that was actually an automatic reply."

Omar leans in and brings a hand to my shoulder. "The words for 'hello' and 'yes' are the same in their language. It's an acknowledgement. There is a different word that would be used for a decisive agreement."

I take it all in.

The man bends a knee to the side, and as he does, his other foot lifts off the ground. He hovers, then drops back down.

I point. "Ask him about that. Is that some kind of biohacking technology?"

Omar gestures as he speaks, lifting his own foot as the man had.

The man responds with a laugh, shaking his head.

Omar translates. "All humans have the capability to fly. If your landscape required it, you would remember this skill, too." He looks at me with wonder.

"Their canyon homes," I say. "Their Sister Earth had tall cliffs and we laid the eggs by a lake. When the kids hatch, they won't be able to run up the hill like we did. I had wondered if there was a route around the cliff, or—" I picture hatchlings facing the red rock cliffs, sparked with their full lifeforce of power, and instinct taking the lead.

"My kids are going to fly," I say, the words tasting like pungent cheese in my mouth.

The man interrupts my astonished thoughts, speaking a few lines with a shrug.

"He says we're a few centuries behind other human civilizations on Earth, due to our choice of isolation."

I grip Omar's shoulder. "What are we going to do? What do they want from us?" Omar's warm brown eyes calm my pounding heart.

"They dominate us in weapons, in grit, in innovation, in numbers," Omar says. "The only category we have an advantage ... is our art. Somehow, it must be the cornerstone of our negotiations."

I flip my braid over my shoulder. "Well, I'm no poet if I can't come up with a meaningful overture," I say.

ACKNOWLEDGMENTS

When I woke up from a dream about my friends and I traveling to another planet to lay our eggs in March of 2020, I knew it had to become a fictional universe.

The writing process for this book required me to develop my intuition, which in turn, has completely shifted my perspective of reality. I'm thrilled to finally be able to invite you into the world in my imagination, a place where humans live in harmony with nature, and my hope is that it both entertains and inspires you to bring these values into our current collective situation.

Thank you to my amazing and talented developmental editor, Nadine Shaw—you gave me new confidence and killer recommendations that elevated this story to what it is.

To my book club, Martha and Angie, thank you for being my first readers and cheering me on through this long long journey.

My writing students: Your craft ingenuity, vulnerability, and commitment to your writing continues to inspire me as I develop my own work.

Thank you to my writing groups who gave feedback on the earliest versions of this story, and helped me honor my identity as a writer. WORD: Eva, Kalila, Liana, Mikki, Katie, Meredith, Suzanne, Natalia, Nayomi, Jamie, Irina, and Christine; Dreamers & Doers: Jessica, Allison, and Liz.

Thank you to my many coaches and intuitive guides for helping me believe in myself long enough to bring this book to life: Aleen Apanian, Jamie Wozny, Josie Coleman, Jeroen de

Wit, Krissy Colasonno, Morgan Balavage, Bree Melanson, Amber Lilyestrom, KJ Song, Jess Geist, and Becca Syme.

My 6th grade teacher Ms. Davis, who shares my Oct. 5 birthday: I've never forgotten the compliment you gave me on the story about taking my stuffed pig to Olive Garden.

Thank you to my parents, for loaning me cash so I could complete the first draft of this thing, uninterrupted.

To the women in my lineage, thank you for pushing our healing forward. Mom, thank you for driving me to 6th grade writing club an hour early on Fridays, and that time you taught me to not give up when I wanted to skip softball practice. Katie, thank you for protecting me when I couldn't speak up for myself.

And finally, thank you to my soul dogs, Buttercup and the now-transitioned Bambi, for grounding me through drafts and reminding me to go for walks.

To readers: Thank you for supporting independent art through reading this book. I am most grateful!

ABOUT THE AUTHOR

Dani Fankhauser is a writer and energy healer based in Laguna Beach. Her fiction has been published by NonBinary Review, HAD, Sheepshead Review, and Nightshade Publishing. *Sister Earth* is her first novel.

Instagram: @danifankhauser